Joseph Howe

Poems and Essays

Joseph Howe

Poems and Essays

ISBN/EAN: 9783744766609

Printed in Europe, USA, Canada, Australia, Japan

Cover: Foto ©Andreas Hilbeck / pixelio.de

More available books at **www.hansebooks.com**

POEMS AND ESSAYS,

BY

THE HON. JOSEPH HOWE.

MONTREAL:

JOHN LOVELL, 23 AND 25 ST. NICHOLAS STREET.

1874.

INTRODUCTION.

For a long time Mr. Howe looked forward to having a few years of leisure during which he might be able to complete, and present to the Public in two or three volumes, several unfinished literary efforts, together with a number of his smaller poems written in moments of leisure snatched at intervals from the engrossing occupation of a very active political life. His sudden and untimely death unhappily prevented the realization of this idea, but his family, desiring to carry out, as far as it is in their power, what he wished to accomplish, have determined to publish one volume of selections from his works, that under happier circumstances would have appeared in a larger and more complete form. These selections embrace a number of short poems on various subjects, many of which were written in early life, some portions of an unfinished poem entitled "Acadia," together with the essay read on the tercentenary of Shakspeare in Halifax in 1864, and now out

of print, and several other essays ; the whole forming
a volume that will fairly illustrate the varied phases
of Mr. Howe's literary genius, and that it is hoped
and believed will be prized by his many friends
throughout the Dominion.

ACADIA.

PART FIRST.

Where does the Sun its richest radiance shed?
Where are the choicest gifts of Nature spread?
On what blest spot does ev'ry simple flower
Bear to the sense a charm of magic power,
While Fancy clothes with beauty every hill
And music murmurs o'er each crystal rill?
Where all the eye surveys can charms impart
That twine, unbroken, round the generous heart?
'Tis where our household Gods securely stand
In the calm bosom of our native land,
Where rest the honor'd ashes of our Sires,
Where burn, undimm'd, our bright domestic fires,
Where we first heard a Mother's silvery tone,
And felt her lips, enraptured, meet our own,
Where we first climb'd a doting Father's knee
And cheer'd his spirit with our childish glee.

Yes, there's a feeling, that, from pole to pole,
To one dear spot still fondly links the soul,
Exiled from Home Foscari pined and died,
And as the Hebrew, by Euphrates side,
Thought of the scenes that blest his childish hours,
Canaan's verdant groves and rosy bowers,
The founts of feeling, fill'd in other years,
Pour'd o'er his wasted cheek a flood of tears.

The wand'ring Swiss, as through the world he roves
Sighs to behold the Alpine land he loves ;
And ev'n Lapland's rude, untutored child,
With icy pinnacles around him piled,
Slumbers in peace upon his lichens grey,
Though the gaunt wolf howls round him for his prey.

And bless the feeling, for it ever leads
To sacred thoughts and high and daring deeds ;
'Twas that illumed his eye when Nelson fell,
'Twas that which urged the unerring shaft of Tell,
Inspired the plaintive and the patriot strains
That Burns pour'd freely o'er his native plains,
And breathes the influence of its sacred fire
O'er many a chord of Moore's seraphic lyre.
With daring hand that feeling bids me now
Twine a rude wreath around my Country's brow,
And tho' the flowers wild and simple be,
Take, my Acadia, those I twine for thee.

Pearl of the West—since first my soul awoke
And on my eyes thy sylvan beauties broke,
Since the warm current of my youthful blood
Flow'd on, thy charms, of mountain, mead, and flood
Have been to me most dear.   Each winning grace
E'en in my childish hours I loved to trace,
And, as in Boyhood o'er thy hills I strode,
Or on thy foaming billows proudly rode,
At ev'ry varied scene my heart would thrill,
For, storm or sunshine, 'twas my Country still.
And now, in riper years, as I behold
Each passing hour some fairer charm unfold,

In ev'ry thought, in ev'ry wish I own,
In ev'ry prayer I breathe to Heaven's high throne
My Country's welfare blends—and could my hand
Bestow one flower't on my native land,
Could I but light one Beacon fire, to guide
The steps of those who yet may be her pride,
Could I but wake one never dying strain
Which Patriot hearts might echo back again,
I'd ask no meed—no wreath of glory crave
·If her approving smile my own Acadia gave.

What though the Northern winds that o'er thee
    blow
Borrow fresh coolness from thy hills of snow,
And icy Winter, in his rudest form,
Breathes through thy vallies many a chilling storm
Still there is health and vigor in the breeze
Which bears upon its wing no fell disease
To taint the balmy freshness of the air
And steal the bloom thy hardy children wear.
No with'ring plague spreads o'er thy smiling plains
Its sickening horrors and soul sickening pains ;
No wild tornado, with its voice of wrath,
Spreads desolation in its fearful path ;
No parching Simoom's warm and sickly breath
Casts o'er thy hills the pallid hues of death ;
But Health thy rosy youth to labour cheers
And teaches age to brave the blight of years.

And when mild Spring, with all her magic powers,
Spreads o'er the land her simple robe of flowers,

And fairy zephyrs softly steal along
Sweet as the mingled melody of song,
And Heaven's unclouded and inspiring ray
O'er wave and mountain lingering, loves to play,
And gentle streamlets through the valley rove,
And Birds repeat their tender notes of love,
And clad in green thy teeming vales appear,
Oh! then, Acadia, thou art doubly dear.

'Tis Spring! 'tis Spring! stern Winter's reign is
        o'er,
And North winds bend our forest groves no more.
Now life and beauty breathe on ev'ry hill,
Bidding each heart with hope and gladness thrill.
In flowery valley, and in leafy grove,
Man reads in glowing lines his Maker's love ;
Hears the bright stream its joyous anthem raise,
While gently swelling ocean hymns His praise.

The Mayflower buds in simple beauty bring
Home to the heart the first glad thoughts of Spring ;
A herald more attractive never bore
Tidings to man of pleasure yet in store,
Gently reposing on its mossy bed,
In modest loveliness it rears its head,
And yields its fragrance to the wanton air
That lifts its leaves to rest and revel there.
Long may we greet its charms at early morn ;
Long may its buds Acadia's wilds adorn ;
Long may its tints, so delicately rare,
Rival the bloom her lovely daughters wear.

Fancy ne'er painted to the son of song
Scenes to which more of Nature's charms belong,
The towering Pines a brighter dress assume—
The dark green Fir puts on a richer bloom ;
The Maple's purple blossoms now appear,
And the Birch spreads its verdant leaflets near—
The Spruce throws off its dark hued Winter dress—
The Poplar blooms in passing loveliness—
The stately Hemlock and the spreading Beech,
Their branches o'er the gentle waters reach,
While the Oak boughs, which many a storm have braved,
In graceful majesty are proudly waved ;
The bending Sumach and the downy Palm,
The stately Ash, lend every grove a charm ;
The Alder's tassels wave with every breath—
The Laurel spreads seductive flowers of death—
The leafy Withe and Juniper are seen
Waving above the fadeless evergreen,
While the sweet Fern and aromatic Bay
Shed perfume for the breeze to bear away.

Wild flowers and bursting buds are gaily spread
In rich luxuriance whereso'er we tread,
The milk-white Stars are sprinkled o'er the ground—
The rosy Clover spreads its fragrance round,
While here and there the Buttercup displays
Its golden bosom to the Sun's bright rays,
And azure Violets, whose cerulean dye
Boasts of a deeper blue than Beauty's eye.
Each lovely flower, and tall majestic tree
Speak to the Spirit, gentle Spring, of thee.

There the smooth lake its glassy bosom shows,
Calm as the wearied spirit's last repose ;
Here frowns the beetling rock high o'er the tide,
Fanned by the branches of the forest's pride ;
Here gently sloping banks of emerald dye
Kiss the pure waves that on them softly lie,
While buoyant flowers, the lakes' unsullied daughters,
Lift their bright leaves above the sparkling waters.
There foams the torrent down the rocky steep,
Rushing away to mingle with the deep,
Shaded by leaves and flowers of various hues ;
Here the small rill its noiseless path pursues,
While in its waves wild buds as gently dip
As kisses fall on sleeping Beauty's lip.

So blooms our country—and in ages past,
Such the bright robe that Nature round her cast,
Ere the soft impress of Improvement's hand,
By science guided, had adorned the land ;
Ere her wild beauties were by culture graced,
Or art had touched what Nature's pencil traced ;
When on her soil the dusky Savage stray'd,
Lord of the loveliness his eye survey'd ;
When through the leafy grove and sylvan dell,
His fearful shout or funeral chant would swell,
While death notes breathed on every passing gale,
And blood bedew'd the flowers that sprung along the vale.

But let us pause, nor deem the labor vain,
O'er scenes which never can return again.
From shore to shore see stately woods extend,
And to the wave their verdant shadows lend,

No treacherous steel assails their stems of pride,
To God they bow, but stoop to none beside,
And 'neath the shelter of these ancient groves,
The Cariboo with fearless footstep roves,
Or the gay Moose in jocund gambol springs,
Cropping the foliage Nature round him flings.
No gallant sails o'er ocean's bosom sweep,
No keel divides the billows of the deep
That fling o'er rock and shoal their dizzy spray,
Or, softly murmuring, seek some lonely bay.

But see, where breaking through the leafy wood,
The Micmac bends beside the tranquil flood,
Launches his light canoe from off the strand,
And plies his paddle with a dexterous hand ;
Or, as his bark along the water glides,.
With slender spear his simple meal provides ;
Or mark his agile figure, as he leaps
From crag to crag, and still his footing keeps,
For fast before him flies the desp'rate Deer,
For life is sweet, and death she knows is near.
No hound or horse assist him in the chase,
His hardy limbs are equal to the race,
For, since he left, unswathed, his mother's back
They've been familiar with each sylvan track ;
They've borne him daily, as they bear him now,
Swift through the wood, and o'er the mountain's brow—
But mark—his bow is bent, his arrow flies,
And at his feet the bleeding victim dies.

While o'er the fallen tenant of the wild
A moment stands the forest's dusky child

From his dark brow his long and glossy hair
Is softly parted by the gentle air.
The glow of pride has flush'd his manly cheek,
And in his eye his kindled feelings speak.
For, as he casts his proud and fearless glance,
O'er each fair feature of the wide expanse,
The blushing flowers—the groves of stately pine—
The glassy lakes that in the sunbeams shine—
The swelling sea—the hills that heavenward soar—
The mountain stream, meandering to the shore—
Or hears the birds' blythe song, the woods' deep tone—
He feels, yes proudly feels, 'tis all his own.

Thus, as the am'rous Moor with joy survey'd
The budding beauties of Venetia's maid,
Drank in the beamings of her love lit eye,
Her bosom's swell, the music of her sigh
He felt, and who can tell that feeling's bliss,
Moor though he was, her beauties all were his.

With practised skill he soon divides his prey,
Then to his home pursues his devious way
Through many an Alder copse, and leafy shade,
And well known path by former ramble made,
To where a little cove, that strays between
Opposing hills, adds beauty to the scene
Which natures hand has negligently dressed
With charms well suited to the Indian's breast.

The Camp extends along the pebbly shore,
A sylvan city, rude as those of yore,
By Patriarch hands within the desert built,

When fresh from Eden's joys and Eden's guilt.
Like those, 'tis man's abode where round him twine
Those ties that make a wilderness divine.
No architectural piles salute the sky,
No marble column strikes the gazer's eye,
The solemn grandeur of the spacious hall,
The stuccoed ceiling and the pictured wall,
Art's skilful hand may sedulously rear,
The simple homes of Nature's sons are here.

Some slender poles, with tops together bound,
And butts inserted firmly in the ground,
Form the rude frames—o'er which are closely laid
Birch bark and fir boughs, forming grateful shade,
And shelter from the storm, and sunny ray
Of summer noon, or winter's darker day.
A narrow opening, on the leeward side,
O'er which a skin is negligently tied,
Forms the rude entrance to the Indian's home—
Befitting portal for so proud a dome.
A fire is blazing brightly on the ground—
The motley inmates scatter'd careless round.
Some strip the maple, some the dye prepare,
Or weave the basket with assiduous care ;
Others, around the box of bark entwine
Quills, pluck'd from off the "fretful porcupine,"
And which may form, when curiously inlaid,
A bridal offering to some dark-eyed maid.
Some shape the bow, some form the feather'd dart,
Which soon may quiver in a foeman's heart.
The Squaws proceed, upon the coals to broil,

Steals out from off the newly furnished spoil,
And these with lobsters, roasted in the shell,
And eels, by Indian palates loved so well,
Complete their frugal feast, for sweet content,
Which thrones have not, makes rich the Indian's tent.

As to the West the glorious Sun retires,
The Mic-macs kindle up their smouldering fires,
The aged Chiefs around the tents repose,
The dark Papoose to laugh and gambol goes;
While youths and maidens to the green advance,
And clustering round, prepare them for the dance.
Nor smile ye modern fair, who float along,
The dazzling spirits of the nightly throng,
Wafted by mingled music's softest tone,
With fashion's every grace around ye thrown,
Smile not at those, who, ere your sires were born,
Danced on the very spot you now adorn,
Kindling, with laughing eyes, love's hallow'd fire,
And swelling gallant hearts with fond desire.

Crossing his legs upon a mossy seat,
With maple wand a youth begins to beat
On some dried bark, with measured time and slow,
A soft low tune—his voice's solemn flow
Mingling with every stroke. The dance begins,
Not such as now the modern fair one wins
To mazy evolutions, wild and free,
Where forms of radiant beauty seem to be
Like heavenly planets, whirling round at will,
Yet by fixed laws controll'd and govern'd still,

But slow and measured as the music's tone,
To which the dancers first beat time alone,
Murm'ring a low response.   A broken shout,
To mark the changing time, at times rings out,
When all is soft, and faint, and slow again,
Till, by degrees, the music's swelling strain,
Sweeps through the Warriors' souls with rushing tide,
Rousing each thought of glory and of pride ;
Then, while the deeds of other days return,
By music's power clothed in words that burn,
When ev'n the Dead, evoked by mem'ry's spell,
Burst into life, to fight where once they fell,
A savage joy the dancers' eyes bespeak,
A deeper tinge pervades each maiden's cheek,
The glossy clusters of their long dark hair
Are floating wildly on the ev'ning air,
As from the earth, with frantic bounds they spring,
And rock and grove with shouts of triumph ring.
Thus we may see the River steal along
Noiseless and slow, till growing deep and strong,
Its turbid waters foam, and curve, and leap,
Dashing with startling echo down the steep.

For ages thus, the Micmac trod our soil,
The chase his pastime, war his only toil,
'Till o'er the main, the adventurous Briton steer'd,
And in the wild, his sylvan dwelling rear'd,
With heart of steel, a thousand perils met,
And won the land his chidren tread on yet.

When first the Micmac's eye discerned the sail

Expanding to the gentle southern gale,
He started wildly up the mountain side,
And look'd with doubting gaze along the tide,
Deeming he saw some giant sea bird's wing
Cleave the light air, and o'er the waters fling
Its feathery shadow.   As the Bark drew nigh,
He thought some spirit of the deep blue sky
Had, for a time, forsook its peerless home
With the red Hunter o'er the wilds to roam ;
Or that a God had left his coral cave,
To breathe the air, and skim along the wave.
Lost in amaze the lordly savage stood
Conceal'd within the foliage of the wood,
And watch'd the proud Ship, as she wing'd her way,
Till she cast anchor in the shelter'd bay.
But, when the white man landed on the shore,
His dream of Gods and Spirits soon was o'er,
He saw them rear their dwellings on the sod
Where his free fathers had for ages trod ;
He saw them thoughtlessly remove the stones
His hands had gather'd o'er his parents' bones ;
He saw them fell the trees which they had spared,
And war, eternal war, his soul declared.

PART SECOND.

As Britain's Son hangs o'er the Historic page,
Fraught with the records of a darker age,
When o'er his feeble land each wand'ring horde
Of rude Barbarians roved, with fire and sword,

When freedom's shrine, by lawless power profaned,
With many a gory sacrifice was stain'd,
While foul oppression o'er the spirit threw
The gloomy influence of its sombre hue.
He lifts his eye, and sees his flag unfurl'd,
The hope—the guide—the glory of a world,
Surveys the fabric, splendid and sublime,
Whose arch, like Heaven's, extends from clime to clime—
Whose pillars, like the dreadful angel, stand
On the deep sea, as firm as on the land,
While 'neath the dome the sun of Science gleams.
Religion cheers—Imagination dreams,
The Muse's Lyre ennobling thoughts recalls,
And Art his treasures hangs around the walls.
Struck with the change, his tears embalm the dead
Whose patriot blood on many a field was shed,
Whose fervid eloquence the land awoke,
Whose gifted minds oppression's fetters broke,
Who, like the fire by night, the cloud by day,
Out from the realms of bondage led the way ;
Who reared, by ceaseless toil, the glorious pile
Beneath whose shade reposing millions smile.

    Thus, while Acadia's charms my eye surveys,
My soul, unbidden, turns to other days,
When the stout-hearted rear'd amidst the wood,
Their sylvan Homes, and by their thresholds stood
With stern resolve the savage tribes to brave,
And win a peaceful dwelling, or a grave.
Gone are the Patriarchs—but we still may weep
Where " the forefathers of our Hamlets sleep."

For us they freely pour'd life's crimson tide,—
For us they labor'd, and for us they died.
And though they rest in no time honor'd tomb,
Acadia's wild flowers o'er their ashes bloom.
Oh ! could they now her smiling fields behold,
While in the breezes wave their crops of gold,
While on her thousand hills, her children stand,
And **Peace** and **Plenty** crown the happy land,
'Twould glad their Spirits, like some Seraph's strain
To know they had not toiled, and died in vain.

They felled the forest trees with sturdy stroke,
The virgin soil, with gentle culture broke,
Scatter'd the fruitful seeds the stumps between,
And **Ceres** lured to many a sylvan scene.
Then rose the Log House by the water side,
Its seams by moss and sea weed well supplied,
Its roof with bark o'erspread—its humble door
Hung on a twisted withe—the earth its floor,
With stones and harden'd clay its chimney form'd,
Its spacious hearth by hissing green wood warmed,
Round which, as night her deep'ning shadows throws,
The Hamlet's wearied inmates circling close.
The sturdy settler lays his axe aside,
Which all day long has quell'd the forest's pride.
The wooden cleats that from the walls extend,
Receive his gun, his oft tried faithful friend,
Which crowns his frugal board with plenteous meals,
And guards his rest when sleep his eye-lids seals.

As cautiously the miser locks his store,

The anxious parent barricades the door,
Then, having cleansed the balsam from his palm,
He bends him down, to where with cheek as calm
As summer ev'nings close, his Infant lies
Breathing as softly as a floweret sighs,
And while a father's transports swell his breast,
A kiss upon its coral lips is press'd.
A look of earnest rapture fondly given,
A prayer, in silent gladness, breathed to Heaven.
Meanwhile his wife, the mother of his child,
His dear companion in the dreary wild,
Spreads o'er his humble board their ev'ning fare,
And soothes his spirit with assiduous care,
Returns with grateful lips and fond embrace,
The kiss imprinted on her Babe's sweet face.
And while her eye betrays a mother's pride,
Points to her first-born, standing by her side,
Who waits the signal to his arms to spring,
And round his neck with filial transport cling.

Their supper o'er, the grace with fervor said ;
Another log upon the fire is laid,
And, as the blaze its cheering light bestows, .
The happy pair their seats together close,
The Father's arm, the Mother's waist entwines,
While on their knees the fair-haired Boy reclines,
A prattling go-between, whose heart o'erflows,
Exchanging kisses each in turn bestows,
And oft he begs the story nightly told,
Of monstrous giants slain by Jack the bold ;
Or begs his mother to repeat, once more,

Some thrilling ballad from her fruitful store ;
And as the simple notes melodious rise,
The tears, uncall'd, bedew the parents' eyes,
Whose thoughts are borne to scenes, now far away,
Where first their ears drank in that simple lay ;
While " absent friends," like spirits round them throng,
By Mem'ry painted with a tint as strong
As though but yesterday the joyous smile
Beam'd from those eyes, that, once in Albion's isle,
Their rays of gladness scatter'd o'er the flowers
Of hope and joy, in childhood's sportive hours.

    Then, half forgetful of their present lot,
They rove o'er scenes that ne'er can be forgot,
The joys and griefs of life—the light and shade
Of early thought, that ne'er from memory fade
Transport their spirits o'er the Atlantic's foam,
And bid them welcome to their island home.
As now their loved boy rests upon their knee,
They nestled once, as light of heart as he ;
Anon they stand beside the narrow bed,
And hear cold earth on aged temples spread,
And mark the bursting sob and tearful eye,
That send to their lone hearts a sad reply.

    The scene is changed—upon a verdant seat,
A glassy streamlet smiling at their feet,
Fast by a crumbling castle, where decay
With silent tooth gnaws stone by stone away,
A gallant oak, extending overhead,
To guard the simple flowers around them spread ;

Clasp'd to each other's bosom they recline,
While, from each heart's unfathomable mine,
The wealth of mutual love, so long concealed,
By Passion's magic power is all revealed ;
And while their hearts with rapturous feelings swell,
Vows are exchanged they long had burned to tell.

And then on Albion's distant shore they stand,
And feel the parting grasp of many a hand,
And see kind eyes bedew'd with many a tear,
While fond farewells fall heavy on the ear,
And scenes they never shall behold again,
And thoughts that burn are thronging on the brain.
" Why do you weep ?" exclaims their gentle Boy,
Who knows not what obscures the general joy,
Who understands not how the shadowy past
O'er present bliss a sombre cloud may cast ;
The fond enquiry, and the anxious glance,
Arouse their spirits from their waking trance,
And absent friends, and Albion's polish'd isle,
Are banish'd by their prattling playmate's smile.
Then other thoughts succeed—while Hope displays
The gifts prepared to gild their future days ;
And thus they muse, and plan—now sad, now blest,
Till Nature warns them to their wonted rest.

For them no stately canopy is spread :
Dried fern and withered leaves compose their bed—
Rough couch—but still their waning strength it cheers,
For Labour sweetens it, and Love endears.
How oft Ambition, on his softest down,

Implores the God of Sleep his cares to drown :
How oft the anxious child of Commerce tries
To calm his thoughts and close his sleepless eyes,
While Slumber mocks his unavailing prayer,
And seeks the hut to strew its poppies there.

Why starts the mother from that soft repose ?
What means the horror that her looks disclose ?
Why are her children clasped with eager care,
While Hope seems wildly struggling with Despair ?
Why has the father seized the axe and knife,
Like one resolved to combat Death for Life,
And yield no vantage that his arm can hold
Though hungry wolves assail his gentle fold ?
Hark to that horrid and soul-piercing yell
That seems the war-cry of a fiend from Hell ;
That starts the raven from the lofty pine
On which he closed his wing at day's decline,
And echoing back from the surrounding hills,
The beating hearts in that lone cottage chills ;
For Hate, Revenge, and Murder's deepest tone,
Tell them the Micmac's toils are round them thrown.

From the wild covert of the forest shade,
By stealthy march their slow approach was made,
Now, by the spreading foliage concealed,
Now, by some sudden op'ning half revealed, .
As to the settler's dwelling they drew nigh,
And gazed upon it with malignant eye.
'Twas yet high noon when it appeared in sight,
But for his work the Indian loves the night.

In patient ambush scattered round they lay,
Content to linger ere they seized their prey.
They marked the settler at his weary moil,
And smiled to think how they'd repay his toil ;
Saw him partake the draught his boy would bring
To cheer his labor, from the crystal spring,
And vow'd, e'er morning's dawn, their souls should
    laugh,
While the parch'd earth his blood should freely quaff ;
And when he sought his home at eventide,
To taste the pleasures of his dear fireside,
With ears attentive—footsteps light and true,
And treacherous hearts, around the eaves they drew,
Listen'd the song the mother sung her child,
Heard the light converse that the hours beguiled,
And joyed to think the time would not be long
Ere midnight's cries would follow evening's song.

    When sleep had closed the weary cottar's eyes,
They sought to take the slumberers by surprise—
Essay'd the door, and then the window tried
With gentle pressure, studiously applied,
Nor knew how light a doting mother sleeps,
When near her babes its watch the spirit keeps.
The first faint whisper of alarm within,
Convinced them force, not fraud, their prey must win.
'Twas then their shout of fierce defiance rose,
While fast and vehement their heavy blows
On door and shutter diligently fell,
Each followed by a wild tumultuous yell ;
Nor are the inmates idle—logs of wood,

Trunks, cribs, whate'er can make defences good,
Are piled against the bars that still are true,
Despite the efforts of the howling crew.
This done, the gun is seized—the Father fires,
Chance guides—a groan—one bleeding wretch ex-
     pires.
Again he loads, again a savage dies—
Again the yells upon the welkin rise,
Hope half persuades that till the dawn of day
The fierce besiegers may be kept at bay.
What scene so dark, what stroke of fate so rude,
That Hope cannot a moment's space intrude?
But soon he flies, for now an Indian flings
Himself upon the roof, which loudly rings
To every stroke the polished hatchet lends;
The bark which bears him, to the pressure bends,
It yields—it breaks—he falls upon the floor—
One blow—his fleeting term of life is o'er,
The settler's axe has dashed his reeking brain
Upon the hearth his soul had sworn to stain.
Fast through the breach two others downward leap,
But, ere they rise, a knife is planted deep
In one dark breast, by gentle Woman's hand,
Who, for her household, wields a household brand;
The axe has clove the other to the chin.
But now, *en masse*, the shrieking fiends leap in,
Till wounded, faint, o'erpowered, the Father falls
And hears the shout of triumph shake his walls.
The wretched Mother from her babe is torn,
Which on a red right hand aloft is borne,
Then dashed to earth before its Parent's eyes,

And, as its form, deform'd and quivering lies,
Life from its fragile tenement is trod,
And the bruised, senseless, and unsightly clod,
Is flung into the soft but bleeding breast
To which so late in smiling peace 'twas press'd.

Nor does the boy escape—the smouldering fire
Is stirred,—and, as its feeble flames aspire
In wanton cruelty they thrust his hands
Into the blaze, and on the reddening brands,
Like Montezuma bid him seek repose
As though his couch were but a perfumed rose.
Sated with blood, at length the scalps they tear
Ere life be yet extinct—for these, with care,
The Indian tribes, like precious coins, retain
To count their victories, and the victims slain.

Now plunder follows death—then one applies
Fire to the bed, from which the flames arise
Fiercely and fast, as anxious to efface
All record of so sad, so foul a place.
Around the cot the Indians form a ring,
And songs of joy and triumph wildly sing
With horrid gesture and demoniac strain,
Then plunge into the forest depths again.

Such are the scenes Acadia once display'd ;
Such was the price our gallant Fathers paid
For this fair land, where now our footsteps rove
From lake to sea, from cliff to shady grove,
Uncheck'd by peril, unrestrained by fear
Of more unfriendly ambush lingering near

Than timid rabbits lurking in the fern
And peeping forth your worst intent to learn ;
Or mottled squirrel, frisking round the pines
To seek the buds on which he lightly dines ;
Or feather'd fav'rites, who, on ev'ry spray
Cheer and enchant with many a simple lay,
And though their plumage cannot boast the dyes
That deck the feather'd tribe 'neath milder skies,
Their ev'ning songs can sweeter strains impart
To charm the list'ning ear, or touch the heart.

While in her backward flight, the Muse essays
To paint the gloomy scenes of darker days,
The bloody strife, the discord, and the fears,
That soiled Acadia's infant face with tears—
That checked improvement, kept repose at bay,
And frighten'd bright eyed science far away ;
Her vision rests with retrospective glance
Upon the stately Oriflamme of France,
As on the fresh'ning breeze each lilied fold,
Gleam'd in the ray of morning's dazzling gold,
And from Port Royal's rude but massy wall
Proud warning gave, that here the valiant Gaul
With England's Sovereign claim'd divided sway,
And strove from England's crown to tear away
This western gem—then rayless and obscure,—
Now, wrought by time, so precious and so pure.

In vain he strove—in vain his thunder peal'd
O'er many a startled wave and gory field,—
In vain his warriors trod Acadia's hills—

In vain their blood ran down the mountain rills
To lose its tint in Ocean's boundless wave,
As fades the purple cloud diffused o'er Heaven's blue
    nave.

    The alternate conquest, stratagem, and toil,
The leaguer'd fortress and the cruel spoil,
The patient ambush and the dire surprise,
The warrior's groan, the maiden's streaming eyes,
The Muse might paint—of fair La Tour might tell,
Who bravely stood where sturdy warriors fell.
True to her faith, her country and her lord,
With high soul'd valor waved her husband's sword,
Spurn'd at the foe—their worst revenge defied,
And check'd their power with all a woman's pride,
Till sold, betrayed, a cruel victor's hand
Tore from her gentle grasp the purple brand,—
Forced her to view her faithful followers fall
Unarm'd, beside their long defended wall—
Forced her the ignominous cord to wear,
Unseemly ornament of neck so fair.

    O'er gallant d'Anville's fate the Muse might bend,
And freshening tints to fading memory lend—
Might paint the fleet, as o'er the western waves
It bore the warriors to ignoble graves,
While hope, and joy, anticipations proud,
Swell'd the warm bosoms of the active crowd,
Who in their dreams, Acadia's bosom press'd,
And called it theirs. Within that bosom rest
Their mouldering bones—their shatter'd ships repose

Where Bedford's placid wave above them flows—
Their disappointment, sufferings and despair,
The Muse reluctant leaves to dark Tradition's care.

For, ere a moment rests her wearied wing,
E'en sadder scenes across her spirit fling
Their sick'ning shades of anguish and of woe,
And bid her tears in sorrowing gushes flow.
Oh! for the Bard of Auburn's melting strain !
Oh! for a Harp whose strings are tuned to pain,
To sing the horrors of that fatal day
When from their homes and country torn away,
The sons of Minas left Acadia's shore
To weep and wander, but return no more,—
To rove o'er hills, and hear in every tone
Of whisp'ring winds—" Oh ! these are not mine own ;"
To pluck from southern vales the fairest flowers,
And fling them by with thoughts of childhoods hours—
To mark strange forms—to seek in vain to trace
Some sign of kindrèd in each unknown face,—
To hear, where all are calm and joyous round,
A general discord in each social sound,—
To feel—what Exiles feel—that earth's wide breast
Contains but one dear spot where they would rest,
A grave of native mould—whose flow'ry sod
The buoyant steps of childhood lightly trod.

Methinks I see the sad and mournful throng,
With slow and measured footsteps move along—
Now looking back, and, through the starting tear,
Gazing their last on all their hearts hold dear,—

The joyous streamlet, whose refreshing wave
Strength to their fainting spirits freely gave,—
The budding corn they fondly hoped to reap,
The sportive flocks that round the pastures leap,
The verdant fields their toils had taught to bloom,
The stately woods, whose reverential gloom
A holy fervor to their prayers supplied,
As bow'd their knee at placid eventide.
Oh ! power divine ! that by a thousand ties
Can bind the heart to all that round it lies,
How many tender thoughts the bosom swell
When e'en to woods and wilds we say farewell.

Methinks as on the sorrowing Exiles move,
I see their pathway strewed by those they love,
Mark the pale cheek, the swoll'n and streaming eye,
And hear the bursting sob and thrilling cry ;
While aged temples to the dust are bow'd,
And wailing infants swell the mournful crowd ;
To Boyhood's breast the form of Beauty springs,
And round his neck with frantic fondness clings,
While looks that waft the eloquence of years,
From soul to soul, are beaming through their tears.
The Father stoops, while yet he may, to trace
His manly features in his infant's face,
To soothe the anguish of the heaving breast,
That form'd the pillow of his nightly rest,
And knows that ere a few short hours expire
His Wife will want a mate, his child a sire.

Methinks I hear the solemn hymn they sung,

To calm the cries that through the welkin rung,
To raise their thoughts to Him whose willing ear
The Widow's moan and Orphan's sigh will hear.
Methinks I see the shining sails unfurl'd,
The azure waters by the zephyrs curl'd,
While far and wide the flickering flames arise
From burning cots, whose blaze the night defies,
While round their light the frighted watch dogs bay,
And seek the hearth where erst they loved to play.

     *   *   *   *   *   *   *   *

    But when the flowers shall o'er his ashes spring
Who now his country's charms essays to sing ;
When on the sod that decks his lowly rest
The wanderer's foot unconsciously is pressed ;
And when his spirit's dim and fading fire
Returns to Him who breathed it o'er the lyre ;
When his untutored verse and humble name
Not e'en a sigh from dreaming mem'ry claim ;
Still my Acadia, may the gentle gales
Fan into loveliness thy peaceful vales ;
Still may thy thousand streamlets raise their song
Of joyous music as they steal along ;
Still may the brilliant beams of science shine,
And learning's boundless stores of wealth be thine ;
Still may the muse, to simple nature true,
Her wreaths of fadeless verdure twine for you ;
Still may thy Fair—neglecting flimsy art,
Charm by the holy magic of the heart ;
May manly breasts with noble feelings thrill
And freemen proudly roam o'er every hill ;

And may the storms that rush o'er rock and wave
In their free passage never meet a slave.

   *   *   *   *   *   *   *   *   *

Who has not marked with an admiring eye,
As storms and clouds obscured the arching sky,
The hostile elements their warfare cease
Assuming lovely forms and moods of peace?
No longer harass'd by unsparing foes,
Thus has Acadia found a sweet repose :
War, and its scenes of hardship and of strife,
The ambush'd savage, and the bloody knife—
The siege,—repulse,—the rescue and surprise,
The mothers' shriek,—the maidens' piercing cries ;
The manly struggle, and the midnight fray,
With all their horrors, where, Oh! where are they?
Go seek the records of a fearful age
In dark Tradition's stores, or History's page,
Of scenes like these you now shall find no trace
On fair Acadia's calm and smiling face.

O'er the stout hearts that death and danger braved,
The flag of Britain soon victorious waved,
And races, hostile once, now freely blend
In happy union, each the others friend ;
Striving as nobly for the general good
As once their fathers strove in fields of blood.
Here England's sons, by fortune led to roam,
Now find a peaceful and a happy home ;
The Scotchman rears his dwelling by some stream,
So like to that which blends with boyhood's dream,
That present joys with old world thoughts combined

Repress the sigh for those he left behind ;
And here the wanderer from green Erin's shore
Tastes of delights he seldom knew before.
He toils beneath no law's unequal weight,
No rival parties tempt his soul to hate ;
No lordly Churchman passes o'er his field,
To share the fruits the generous seasons yield.
With joy, Acadia welcomes to her strand
These venturous wanderers from their Fatherland—
A Mother's love bestows—with pride, beholds
Them mark the charms her simple form unfolds—
Then to her breast with filial rapture cling,
And cast their lot beneath her pleasant wing.

With equal pride a numerous race she rears,
Sons of those sire's who braved the Indian spears ;
And those who've sprung from that devoted band,
Who, when rebellion reared its impious hand,
Spite of her faults, to Albion's standard true,
Fought 'neath its folds, till fate her power o'erthrew ;
Then sought amidst Acadia's wilds to claim
A Briton's feelings, and a Briton's name.
But see, extending upon every side,
Her Cottage Homes ! Acadia's noblest pride ;
There honest Industry, by daily toil,
Covers with fruits and flowers his native soil ;
And calm contentment, with an Angel's air,
And humble hopes, and smiling joys, are there.

But has not time—that drowned the dim of arms,
Defaced Acadia's wild and simple charms,

Broke the deep spells of woodland solitude,
And banished nature with a hand too rude ?
Oh ! no, together Art and Nature reign,
Smile on the mountain top and deck the plain ;
Though Labor's hand full many a scene has cleared,
Of all that erst upon its face appeared;
Yet there are spots by Art still unprofaned
Where Nature reigns as ages since she reigned.

Such sweet Lochaber * Sydney's sylvan pride,
Lake of the woods, the forests gentle bride—
It is thy lot to be ; Lifes bubbling stream
Must cease ere I forget the vivid dream
Of olden time, that tranced me as I stood,
Beneath the shadows of thine ancient wood.
Fresh is the vision, yes I see thee yet,
A sparkling Diamond in an Emerald set.
The morning's sun illumes thy placid wave
Where chaste Diana might her beauties lave,
Nor fear to be observed—so deep—profound
The lulling stillness that prevails around.
Winding, in graceful folds, 'twixt hills that rise
On either side, the fair Lochaber lies.
Now to the eye its glowing charms revealed,
Now, like a bashful Beauty, half concealed
Beneath the robe of spotless green she wears,
The rich profusion of a thousand years.
No axe profane has touched a single bough,
No sod has yet been broken by the plough ;
Far down the ancient trees reflected lie
Stem, branch, and leaf, like fairy tracery

Wove round the homes of some enchanting race,
The guardian nymphs of this delightful place.

Such is the scene, beneath Canaan's height,
Where Nature seems to shrink from human sight;
And shun the intruding step, and curious eye,
That seek to know where her deep mysteries lie.
There might you stand, beside that falling stream,
Nor ought of man or of his doings dream;
While high above you towers the rifted rock,
Crowned by old groves, unscathed by tempest's shock
As from the steep its falling waters spring
And at your feet their broken foam wreaths fling.

'Tis evening, and the suns retiring ray
From rock and hill is fading fast away;
Yet, like a friend who parts but for a while,
Wears, as he bids farewell, his sweetest smile.
The gentle breeze that blows from off the shore
Scarce curls the blue wave as it dances o'er.
With loaded bill the sea bird seeks its nest
To feed its young, or taste the sweets of rest.
Acadia's hardy son, with ready hand,
His frail bark launches from her rocky strand,
Hoists his white sail before the gentle wind
And leaves his humble home, far, far behind.
Born on the wave, accustomed to its swell,
His manly bosom loves its motion well.
His reckless spirit toil nor danger fears,
While for the sea his dauntless course he steers;
Ocean and Ocean's storms he nightly braves,
For God has cast his bread upon the waves.

As twilight fades, and all around is dark,
He furls his sail and·moors his little bark ;
And as his line to ocean's depths descends
In patient hope he o'er the gunwale bends,
And if with plenty Heaven his prayers shall bless,
Heeds not the toil that's followed by success.
But if kind fortune should refuse to smile,
Thought, busy thought, will many an hour beguile ;
The swelling billow rarely breaks his rest,
But seems the heaving of a mother's breast,
For now the moon is up, and all her pride
Of pomp and splendor rests upon the tide ;
Dear to the Lover is her silver gleam,
Dear, doubly dear, the Poet loves her beam ;
But, holier far, the charms her smiles impart,
To cheer the lonely Fisher's drooping heart.

But see, yon little cloud, slow rising o'er
The horizon's edge, is spreading more and more ;
Though but a speck, when first it met the eye,
'Tis stealing fast o'er all the bright blue sky,
Till like the conq'rers path, although we find
Beauty before, there's nought but gloom behind.
The winds are up, and o'er the arch of Heaven
With many a crash the fiery bolts are driven,
While waves o'er waves in Alpine grandeur rise,
As though they spurned the threatenings of the skies.
The Fisher's mooring parts, and high in air
His Bark is tost, but God he feels is there ;
Down in some frightful gulf it next descends,
But still on skill and coolness he depends.

Back to the shore his prudent course he steers
And his heart gladdens as a light appears ;
But see, yon mighty wave comes rolling on,
Where is his Bark ? to ocean caves she's gone ;
And where is he ? wrapt in the billow's foam
While maddening thoughts of children and of home
Nerve his strong arm, and animate his soul—
Life the rich prize,—the shore the longed for goal—
For oh ! tis hard upon the wave to die
With our own firelight gleaming in the eye.

But vain his struggles, for his shortening breath
And wearied limbs speak fearfully of death.
Ere light winged Hope deserts him, with a sigh,
He casts one earnest lingering look on high,
And that omniscient Eye which looks o'er all,
And even notes the tiny sparrow's fall,
Beholds and pities, and while life remains,
A billow wafts him and the beach he gains.

Lull'd on the lap of luxury and ease,
With cheeks unfann'd but by the mildest breeze,
The listless sons of wealth and pride repose
Nor heed the poor man's toil—the poor man's woes.
Oh ! little think they, when the snows of Heaven
Around their sheltered homes are wildly driven ;
While round their warm and brightly burning fires
Wit lends its mirth, and Beauty's smile inspires ;
Oh ! little dream they then, how many poor
Industrious, active, children of the oar
Toil on the waste of waters—while the hail,

And sleet, and snow, their manly limbs assail;
How many weeping wives, and children mourn,
The loss of those who never can return.

Inured to toil, familiar with the storm,
Around our coast these hardy boatmen swarm,
With nerves well strung to battle with the wave,
And souls as free as are the winds they brave.
Acadia loves to hear her rocky shores
Echo the music of their dashing oars;
And hails the offspring of her sea girt strand
The strength, the pride, and sinews of her land.

But let the Muse the willing fancy bear
Home with the Boatman, and behold him there
Safe from the stormy peril of the deep,
With grateful heart he climbs the rocky steep,
To where, just clinging to the mountain side
His humble cot o'erlooks the troubled tide.
Through the clear pane he fondly stops to gaze,
And sees, around the cheerful fagot's blaze
His little happy flock, his hope and pride,
Whose laughing eyes adorn his fireside,—
Two mend the net, a third, with wonder, reads
Of Crusoe's hairbreadth 'scapes and daring deeds,
And as strange scenes his infant thoughts beguile,
Half wishes he were cast on Crusoe's Isle.

With anxious brow that ill her care conceals,
The watchful mother to the casement steals,
And tries to pierce, with an enquiring eye,
The frightful gloom that darkens earth and sky,

Trembles at every gust that wildly raves,
While her thoughts fly to him upon the waves ;
As the wind rises, still her fears increase,—
A step,—a voice—'tis his, and all is peace.

Oh ! Love, in stately dome, or princely bower,
Man owns thy holy soul-subduing power,
Feels that the sweetest charm his spirit knows
From thy unsullied, sacred fountain, flows ;
For splendor sheds a cold and cheerless glare,
If Love diffuse no ray of gladness there ;
But, if you have a still more precious charm,
A smile more lovely, or a ray more warm,
Oh ! it is that which fondly lingers o'er
The rude and lowly cabins of the poor.

Their humble meal the mother now prepares,
O'er which they soon forget their former cares ;
The children's prattle crowns the parents' joy,
Who often dwell upon their wandering boy—
For 'twas but yesternight that they received
News too delightful to be disbelieved.
Fraught with glad tidings from a distant land,
The letter trembled in the father's hand ;—
The seal was broke, while all the little crowd
Around him press'd, to hear it read aloud,
For he, the cause of all their anxious fear,
In foreign lands had wander'd many a year,
Led by that ceaseless restlessness of soul,
Which still points onwards to some brighter goal.
O'er many lands his wayward steps had roved,

Since last he bade farewell to all he loved.
They deemed him dead, and long had ceased to mourn,
Or look, or pray, or hope, for his return ;
And all they dared to think the scroll could tell,
Was where, and how, and when, the wand'rer fell.
But when the father's eye, undimmed by age
Had cast one hasty glance upon the page,
And read " Dear Parents," with a burst of joy,
He cried, " 'tis from my Boy, my long lost Boy !"
While to each heart a throb of gladness sprung,
And prayers and praises faltered from each tongue.
But from the mother's lips no accents fell,
Though her eye beamed with more than words could tell ;
Had she not looked more earthly than the dead,
One might have thought her joyous soul had fled—
And it had fled, on memory's airy wing,
Back to the past, round sacred hours to cling,
While many a feeling which despair had dried,
Rushed to her heart in one impetuous tide,—
In thought, she saw her first born on her breast,
And softly lull'd him to his evening rest,—
In thought, descended on her raptured ear
Those faint, first words, to mother's heart so dear,
While every smile he wore in boyhood's days,
Like magic sprung 'neath mem'ry's backward gaze,
'Till her tranced soul, recall'd from former years,
Was soothed and calm'd by one long burst of tears.
The letter told of much that he had viewed,
In busy crowd, or trackless solitude—
Of joys and perils, hours of bliss and pain,
But still his spirit sighed for home again.

For, though Acadia's sons may stray at times
To lands more fruitful, and to milder climes,
Still, though the flowers may richer odour breathe,
And, overhead, the vines their tendrils wreathe,
Though the sun's constant and serenest ray
O'er scenes of beauty fondly loves to stray—
Though all that's fairest falls from Nature's hand,
The exile pines to tread his native land ;
Her rocky mountains, and her wintry storms,
Her fertile valleys, and her lovely forms,
Crowd on the mind with dreams of mighty power,
And cheer his heart in many a lonely hour.

*   *   *   *   *   *   *   *

SABLE ISLAND.

Dark Isle of Mourning—aptly art thou named,
  For thou hast been the cause of many a tear ;
For deeds of treacherous strife too justly famed,
  The Atlantic's charnel—desolate and drear ;
A thing none love—though wand'ring thousands fear—
  If for a moment rests the Muse's wing
Where through the waves thy sandy wastes appear,
  'Tis that she may one strain of horror sing,
Wild as the dashing waves that tempests o'er thee fling.

The winds have been thy minstrels—the rent shrouds
  Of hapless barks, twanging at dead of night,
Thy fav'rite harp strings—the shriek of crowds
  Clinging around them feebly in their fright,

The song in which thou long hast had delight,
　　Dark child of ocean, at thy feasts of blood ;
When mangled forms, shown by Heaven's lurid light,
　　Rose to thy lip upon the swelling flood,
While Death, with horrid front, beside thee gloating
　　　　stood.

As lurks the hungry tiger for his prey,
　　Low crouch'd to earth with well dissembled mien,
Peace in his eye—the savage wish to slay
　　Rankling around his heart—so thou art seen
Stretch'd harmlessly on ocean's breast of green,
　　When winds are hush'd, and sleeps the placid wave
Beneath the evening ray—whose glittering sheen
　　Gilds the soft swells thy arid folds that lave,
Unconscious that they cling around a yawning grave.

The fascination of the Siren's song,
　　The shadow of the fatal Upas tree ; ·
The Serpent's eye that lures the bird along
　　To certain doom—less deadly are than thee
Even in thy hours of calm serenity,
　　When on thy sands the lazy seals repose,
And steeds, unbridled, sporting carelessly,
　　· Crop the rank grass that on thy bosom grows,
While round the timid hare his glance of caution
　　　　throws.

But when thy aspect changes—when the storm
　　Sweeps o'er the wide Atlantic's heaving breast ;
When, hurrying on in many a giant form,
　　The broken waters by the winds are prest—

Roaring like fiends of hell which know no rest,
  And guided by the lightning's fitful flash ;
Who dares look on thee then—in terror drest,
  As on thy length'ning beach the billows dash,
Shaking the heavens themselves with one long deaf'ning
      crash.*

The winds are but thy blood-hounds, that do force
  The prey into thy toils ; th' insidious stream †
That steadily pursues its noiseless course,
  Warmed by the glow of many a tropic beam,
To seas where northern blasts more rudely scream
  Is thy perpetual Almoner, and brings
All that to man doth rich and lovely seem,
  Earth's glorious gifts,—its fair and holy things,
And round thy dreary shores its spoils profusely flings.

The stateliest stems the Northern forest yields,
  The richest produce of each Southern shore,

---

* Those who have not personally witnessed the effects of a
storm upon this place, can form no adequate idea of its horrors.
The reverberated thunder of the sea, when it strikes this attenua-
ted line of sand, on a front of thirty miles, is truly appalling, and
the vibration of the Island under its mighty pressure, seems to
indicate that it will separate and be borne away by the ocean.
Haliburton.

† There is sufficient reason to believe that the Gulf Stream at
42° 30′, running E. N. E. occasions the waters of the St. Lawrence,
running S. S. W., to glide to the westward. The strength of this
current has never been noticed, and three-fourths of the vessels
lost have been supposed to be to the eastward of the Island, when
in fact, they were in the longitude of it. *Ibid.*

The gathered harvests of a thousand fields,
    Earn'd by man's sweat—or paid for by his gore.
The splendid robes the cavern'd Monsters wore,
    The gold that sparkled in Potosi's mine,
The perfumed spice the Eastern islands bore,
    The gems whose rays like morning's sunbeams shine,
All—all—insatiate Isle—these treasures all are thine.

But what are these, compared with the rich spoils
    Of human hearts, with fond affections stored :
Of manly forms, o'ertaken by thy toils—
    Of glorious spirits, 'mid thy sands outpoured.
Thousands who've braved War's desolating sword,
    Who've walk'd through earth's worst perils undismayed,
Now swell the treasures of thy ample hoard ;
    Deep in thy vaults their whitening bones are laid,
While many a burning tear is to their mem'ries paid.

And oft—as though you sought to mock man's eye—
    Thy shifting sands their treasured spoils disclose : ‡
There may we some long-missing wreck descry,
    Some broken mast, that once so proudly rose
Above the peopled deck ; some toy, that shows
    The fate of her upon whose breast it hung,
But who now sleeps in undisturbed repose,
    Where by the waves her beauteous form was flung,
May peace be with her manes—the lovely and the
      young.

---

‡ After a gale of wind human skeletons are sometimes exposed
to view, and timber, and pieces of wood, are disinterred which
have been buried for years. *Haliburton.*

Why does the Father, at the dawn of day,
  Fly from his feverish couch and horrid dreams,
And up the mountain side pursue his way,
  And turn to gaze upon the sea, which seems
Blent with the heavens—until the gorgeous beams
  Of the bright sun each cloud and wave reveal?
Whence comes the tear that o'er that pale cheek
      streams—
  As, tired with gazing, on the earth he kneels,
And pours in prayer to God the anguish that he feels?

Why does the matron heave that constant sigh?
  Why does she start at every distant sound?
Her cheerful fire is blazing 'neath her eye,
  Her fair and happy children sporting round,
Appealing to her heart at every bound,
  While on her lap one rose-lipped babe reclines,
And looks into her face with joy profound.
  But yet the mother secretly repines,
And through a tearful eye her spirit dimly shines.

Why does the maiden shun the giddy throng,
  And find no pleasure in the festive hour?
Strange that the mazy dance, and choral song,
  O'er one so young should hold no spell of power.
Why droops her head, as in her fairy bower
  Her lute is only tuned to sorrow's strain?
Is there no magic in the perfumed flower,
  To lure her thoughts from off the bounding main?
Oh! when shall joy return to that pure breast again?

Canst thou not read this riddle, gloomy isle?
Say—when shall that old man behold his boy?
When shall a son's glad voice—a son's bright smile
Wake in that mother's heart the throb of joy?
When shall glad thoughts that maiden's hours employ?
When shall her lover spring to her embrace?
Ask of the winds accustomed to destroy—
Ask of the waves which know their resting-place—
And they in thy deep caves their early graves may
trace.

Farewell! dark Isle—the Muse must spread her wing,
To seek for brighter themes in scenes more fair,
Too happy if the strain she strove to sing,
Shall warn the sailor of thy deadly snare;
Oh! would the gods but hear her fervent prayer,
The fate of famed Atlantis should be thine—
No longer crouching in thy dangerous lair,
But sunk far down beneath the 'whelming brine,
Known but to History's page—or in the poet's line.

THE STEWIACKE.

[The River Stewiacke takes its rise in the high lands to the south-
ward of Mount Tom, and flowing for a distance of 40 miles through
one of our finest Agricultural settlements, empties into the Shu-
benacadie at Fort Ellis.   The Inhabitants like those of Musquodoboit, whom they nearly resemble, are off-shoots from the Truro and
Onslow stock—but preserve greater simplicity in dress, and manners, than the present Inhabitants of those older Townships.   The
writer of these lines has done but very imperfect justice to the
beauty of the Vale, or the sterling qualities of its Inhabitants ; but,
believing that there are not wanting in this Country, the materials
for poetry, he would fain stimulate others by a few rude illustrations
of that opinion.]

Flow on bright spirit of a pleasant vale—
Type of the social life its fruits sustain :
With steady strength thy noiseless waves prevail
O'er links that check, and fret, but ne'er restrain
Thy gentle passage through the smiling plain ;
Till, blent with other streams, thy beauties fade,
Thy folds are lost within the boundless main :
As they who tread thy banks, in smiles arrayed,
Shall, mingling with their God, forget the forms he made.

Sweet River—'tis not that the sunbeams rest
Like Lovers' thoughts upon thy swelling tide,
Catching and shedding beauty—nor that blest
By gushing streamlets from the mountain side,
Thou roll'st along in loveliness and pride,
That I, with such delight am ling'ring here ;
Not e'en the Elms that gracefully preside
Thy banks above, could start the grateful tear,
Nor all the emotions prompt that render thee so dear.

The fruitful fields that spread on either hand,
Won from the forest, by a hardy race ;
The Cottage Homes that near them meekly stand,
Where all my Country's features I can trace—
Where life's best feelings have their dwelling place,.
Its sterner virtues and endearments sweet,
Where health sits blooming upon every face,
And hearts with conscious independence beat,
These make me love, fair stream, thy sparkling wave to
      greet.

Tho' richer harvests crown the slimy Nile,
A race of slaves are there the fruits to reap ;
Tho' clearer skies above the Tagus smile,
Let the degenerate hounds their river keep,
And make it still, with tears of blood to weep ;
Beside thy banks, Stewiacke, let me recline,
And in thy rural charms my senses steep,
For Freedom, Peace, Industry, all are thine,
And here Religion guards her meek and holy shrine.

Here dwell the gray haired Sires, who pleased, survey
Their children scattered o'er the fruitful soil ;
Who, looking back to many a weary day,
Yet feel themselves repaid for all their toil,
They know, when e'er they quit this " mortal coil,"
A numerous progeny their steps shall tread,
Whose birthright, lawless power can ne'er despoil,
But who in peace will earn their daily bread,
And hallow in their lives the memories of the dead.

Here dwell the fruitful mothers, who supply
The tide of life that swells along the vale,
On whose chaste beds no blighting curses lie,
Whose hands ne'er tire—whose spirits rarely fail.
Unlike the wretched beings, worn and pale,
Who, in the crowded city's poor retreats,
Hear with dismay, the newborn infant's wail,
And ill can spare the scanty food it eats,
While luxury's pamper'd steeds go prancing through the
    streets.

Here buoyant youths their hardy nurture speak,
With brows erect, and manners frank and free ;
The well knit frame, and ruddy sunburnt cheek,
Shew that the sons of sloth they scorn to be.
With grateful thoughts thy pleasant fields they see,
And, as their fathers sink into the grave,
Resting, sweet stream, their time worn forms by thee,
They think of all they dared—of all they gave,
And go with cheerful hearts their lighter cares to brave.

And few there are in loneliness that ply
The varied labors that their hands employ ;
There's many a rosy lip and beaming eye,
And many a face all radiant with joy,
To catch the fancy of the sanguine boy,
And lure to love-walks by the River side.
No maidens these with idle fools to toy,
The slaves of fashion, or the dupes of pride,
But form'd true hearts to prize, and poor men's house-
    holds guide.

Oh! mighty Father, whose judicious hand
Taught this sweet Vale to "blossom as the rose,"
Still bless with scenes like this my native land ;
Where'er a sparkling River onward flows,
Foster the habits that ensure repose,
And strike the gen'rous roots of virtue deep ;
O'er Luxury, and all its train of woes.
Let not my Country e'er have cause to weep,
But still its nerves of steel, and graceful vigor keep.

MELVILLE ISLAND.

Record of War, behold yon little Isle,*
Whose brow is crown'd by many a mouldering pile,
Where groups of buildings sinking to decay
Throw their dark shadows o'er the narrow bay,
Which, with a mirror's smoothness, brightly shines,
While the last ray of summer's sun reclines
Upon its placid breast—where the blue sky,
And blended rocks, and groves, reflected lie.
As round the winding path we onward stroll
Beyond the Isle the Arm's clear waters roll,
Along whose eastern margin spots of green
And rural cottages fill up the scene.
No sound disturbs the cove where echo sleeps,
Unless some fish through the calm surface leaps ;
Perchance a gull, while high in air he soars,

---

* Melville Island was used as a prison during the war of 1812–15.

His wild and startling note of discord pours ;
Or the scared partridge, as she upward springs,
Breaks the deep silence with her noisy wings.

    The Guard House there, with fissures well supplied
To point the ready gun on every side—
Where walked the wakeful sentry day and night,
Lest some might strive to make a desperate flight—
Where once the cup, the laugh, the jest, went round,
Is still and drear, unconscious of a sound—
And the small spots which used to glow with flowers,
The soldier's pastime, in his leisure hours,
Redeem'd from rocks, with cultivation smiled,
And look'd the lovelier bosom'd in the wild,
With stubble, briars and brambles overgrown,
Nature may now reclaim them as her own.

    We cross the bridge, where erst the cannon stood,
To guard the narrow passage o'er the flood.
Here Time, as with light wing he onward flew,
Has left his footprint upon all we view.
How changed—how different everything appears—
How all unlike the scenes of other years.
Each door which once was watch'd with jealous care,
Unhing'd, admits the balmy evening air.
The large red building which appeared alive
Some twelve years since, a perfect human hive,
Crowded and busy, where the eye might see
All save the calm contentment of the bee,
Now with its dreariness the heart appals,
So still and lifeless are the silent walls ;

Each narrow window, and each iron bar,
Speak to the soul of all the ills of war.

The bugle note may elevate the soul,
The heart beat high while round the thunders roll,
The shout of triumph and the hard won field,
A glorious rapture to the warrior yield.
This is war's brightest side—and still will charm
The youthful heart, while youthful hearts are warm.
But, the last groan of him who fights and falls,
And on his God to feed his orphans calls—
The widow's anguish and the mother's sigh,
The shrieking maniac's wild and bitter cry,
And the lone prison, on the mind will urge
The truth, that War, in detail, is a scourge.

While o'er the spirit Mem'rys spell is cast,
We leave the present, to recall the past.
To the mind's eye how vividly appear
The busy crowds, which used to mingle here,
Doom'd to one common fate, to be confined,
And teach their manly souls to be resigned.
Although a prison, yet the little Isle
Was not a common gaol for culprits vile—
No felon's foot its genial soil impressed,
No frightful dream here broke the murderer's rest—
Their only crime who round its confines moved,
Was nobly daring in the cause they loved.

Here the grey vet'ran, marked with many a scar,
Deplored the sad vicissitudes of war ;

He loved the cannon's glorious voice to hear,
The cry of " Board !" was music to his ear ;
If on his soul a ray of rapture beam'd,
'Twas when his cutlass o'er his foeman gleamed ;
Shipwreck'd he oft had been, but yet the sea
He fear'd not—on its bosom he was free. ·
Unbending, and impatient of restraint,
How shall the Muse his manly anguish paint ?
When no spectator of his grief was near,
Down his brown cheek oft rolled the burning tear,
And his dark eye, which up to Heaven was turned,
Displayed the spirit that within him burned.
But, if some straggler should, by chance, intrude
Upon his restless, joyless, solitude,
He quickly dashed the tear-drop from his eye,
None saw him weep, or ever heard him sigh.
In the calm hours which Nature claimed for sleep,
E'en then, in dreams, his soul was on the deep,
The deck resounding to his measured tread,
His country's banner floating o'er his head,
His good ship scudding under easy sail,
While all around the laugh, the jest prevail ;
Or, if the God of dreams should strew a train
Of darker, bolder shadows o'er his brain,
His brow is knit—his nervous, powerful, hand,
In fancied triumph grasps a well-known brand,
While locked with his, o'ertaken in the chase,
Some frigate lies, in deadly close embrace ;
Guns roar, swords flash, the dying and the dead,
Mangled and bleeding, o'er the deck are spread—
While the fierce shout, and faint and feeble wail

Together mingled, float upon the gale ;
With nimble foot athwart the yard he runs,
Descends, and drives the foemen from their guns ;
'Midst blood and death their flag he downward tears,
And, in its place, his own loved banner rears.
His shouts of victory through the prison ring,
His startled comrades round his hammock bring,
While drops of sweat his manly temples lave,
His broad chest heaving like the troubled wave,
He starts—he wakes—" Oh ! God, and can it be,
'Am I a captive? am I not at sea?"

Here the fond Father, from his home exiled,
In fancy fondled o'er his darling child,
Folded the little prattler in his arms,
And saw, as fathers do, unnumbered charms,
And made confinement's tedious moments less,
Tasting the bliss of sweet forgetfulness.

Behold yon youth, whose brilliant, speaking, eye,
Is mildly, calmly, fixed on vacancy.
In vain Sol's loveliest beams around him play,
In vain the linnet pours her sweetest lay,
In vain his cheerful comrades, wandering near,
With mirth and gladness strive his soul to cheer,
He sees them not, nor hears their idle jests,
Fix'd as the rock on which his elbow rests,
And, while his head reclines upon his hand,
The boy is thinking of his own bright land ;
In fancy wandering round that happy home
He loved so much, ere honor bade him roam,

Where, while his eye with youthful ardour glowed,
A Father's hand a Father's sword bestowed,
And, as he gave it to the stripling, said:
" Behold, my boy, no spot is on the blade,
" Take it, and use it for thy country's weal,
" This arm, though feeble now, has proved the steel ;
" And when in peace you bring it home again,
" See that the blade wears no unworthy stain."

      And well the youth obeyed the warrior's words.
Where flashed Britannia's best and brightest swords,
There his was wav'd—and when Old England's sons
Drove Gallia's seamen from their silent guns—
When British Tars, whom Valor could not check,
Forc'd ev'ry foeman from the quarter-deck—
E'en when his chief, to stay the deadly strife,
And save an useless waste of human life,
Resigned his ship and sabre to the foes,
The Boy's red arm was dealing desperate blows,
His bright eye flashing with unearthly fire,
He thought of home, and of his gray-hair'd sire,
And when commanded to give up his brand,
He grasped it closer in his bloody hand,
Glanced o'er it once, nor stayed to look again,
But flung it wildly to the watery main,
And proudly uttered "only to the wave,
" Will I resign the sword a Father gave."

      A Prisoner now, while stretched at length he lays,
And ponders o'er the themes of other days,
Perhaps the blessing which his mother gave

Ere he embark'd upon the mountain wave,
Is faintly, fondly, breathed into his ear,
And dims his hazel eye with many a tear ;
While thought on thought, at Mem'ry's bidding, springs,
Around his neck an only sister clings.
Those who have felt, alone can truly trace
A parting sister's lingering, fond, embrace,
While all the joys that guileless childhood knew,
By Mem'rys magic start upon the view ;
And the faint, feverish, tremulous " good bye !"
The heaving bosom, and the broken sigh,
The streaming tear—the blanch'd and bloodless cheek,
Plainer than words a Sister's love bespeak ;
While hurried prayers to God's high throne ascend,
And call on Him to guide, protect, defend ;
While round each neck their youthful arms are cast,
And each fond look is destined for the last :
'Twas thus they parted, and when far from France,
Toss'd on the wave, that Sister's parting glance
Was with him still, and on the little Isle,
Would oft, from all around, his thoughts beguile.

At length the bland and halcyon smile of Peace
Shone forth, and caused the trump of War to cease.
As Spring's mild ray, while Earth's glad breast it warms,
Expels stern Winter, with his robe of storms.
What heartfelt rapture did that beauteous smile
Shed o'er each bosom upon Melville Isle.
"'Tis Peace ! 'tis Peace," around the Island rings,
And blissful visions to each fancy brings.
The thoughts of home, of friends, of children, roll

A tide of heavenly rapture round the soul.
Each trod the earth with firmer, manlier, tread,
No narrow bound before his footsteps spread ;
Each gave the little Isle a blithe good bye,
Joy in his heart, and freedom in his eye,
And, when to home and friends restored again,
Forgot Captivity, and all its pain.

How pure the bliss, how balmy the repose
Which, after all his toils and all his woes,
The weary traveller, doom'd no more to roam,
Tastes in the hallowed precincts of his home.
If of the joys the righteous share in Heaven,
One foretaste sweet to earthly man is given,
'Tis when his Cot—his ark of hopes and fears,
After long absence to his view appears ;
'Tis when that form, the dearest and the best,
Springs to his arms and swoons upon his breast ;
When Woman's lip—warm, passionate, and pure,
Is press'd to his—as if its balm could cure
His wounded soul, if wound should there remain,
And charm it back to joy and peace again.

THE FLAG OF OLD ENGLAND.

[A Centenary Song, written for the one hundredth anniversary of
the landing of Lord Cornwallis at Halifax.]

All hail to the day when the Britons came over,
   And planted their standard, with sea-foam still wet,
Around and above us their spirits will hover,
   Rejoicing to mark how we honor it yet.

Beneath it the emblems they cherished are waving,
  The Rose of Old England the roadside perfumes ;
The Shamrock and Thistle the north winds are braving,
  Securely the Mayflower* blushes and blooms.

CHORUS.

Hail to the day when the Britons came over,
  And planted their standard with sea-foam still wet,
Around and above us their spirits will hover,
  Rejoicing to mark how we honor it yet.
      We'll honor it yet, we'll honor it yet,
      The flag of Old England ! we'll honor it yet.

In the temples they founded, their faith is maintained,
  Every foot of the soil they bequeathed is still ours,
The graves where they moulder, no foe has profaned,
  But we wreathe them with verdure, and strew them
        with flowers !
The blood of no brother, in civil strife pour'd,
  In this hour of rejoicing, encumbers our souls !
The frontier's the field for the Patriot's sword,
  And curs'd be the weapon that Faction controls !
      Chorus—Hail to the day, &c.

Then hail to the day ! 'tis with memories crowded,
  Delightful to trace 'midst the mists of the past,
Like the features of Beauty, bewitchingly shrouded,
  They shine through the shadows Time o'er them has
        cast.
As travellers track to its source in the mountains,

---

* The Mayflower is the emblem of the Province of Nova Scotia.

The stream, which far swelling, expands o'er the plains,
Our hearts, on this day, fondly turn to the fountains
   Whence flow the warm currents that bound in our
      veins.
   Chorus—Hail to the day, &c.

And proudly we trace them : No warrior flying
   From city assaulted, and fanes overthrown,
With the last of his race on the battlements dying,
   And weary with wandering, founded our own.
From the Queen of the Islands, then famous in story,
   A century since, our brave forefathers came,
And our kindred yet fill the wide world with her glory,
   Enlarging her Empire, and spreading her name.
   Chorus—Hail to the day, &c.

Ev'ry flash of her genius our pathway enlightens—
   Ev'ry field she explores we are beckoned to tread,
Each laurel she gathers, our future day brightens—
   We joy with her living, and mourn for her dead.
Then hail to the day when the Britons came over,
   And planted their standard, with sea-foam still wet,
Above and around us their spirits shall hover,
   Rejoicing to mark how we honor it yet.
   Chorus—Hail to the day, &c.

OUR FATHERS.*

Room for the Dead! your living hands may pile
Treasures of Art the stately tents within ;
Beauty may grace them with her richest smile,
And Genius there spontaneous plaudits win.
But yet, amidst the tumult and the din
Of gathering thousands, let me audience crave :—
Place claim I for the Dead—'twere mortal sin
When banners o'er our Country's treasures wave,
Unmark'd to leave the wealth safe garner'd in the Grave.

The Fields may furnish forth their lowing kine,
The Forest spoils in rich abundance lie,
The mellow fruitage of the cluster'd Vine
Mingle with flowers of every varied dye ;
Swart Artizans their rival skill may try,
And, while the Rhetorician wins the ear,
The pencil's graceful shadows charm the eye,
But yet, do not withhold the grateful tear
For those, and for their works, who are not here.

Not here? Oh! yes, our hearts their presence feel,
Viewless, not voiceless, from the deepest shells
On memory's shore harmonious echoes steal,
And names, which, in the days gone by, were spells,
Are blent with that soft music.   If there dwells
The spirit here our Country's fame to spread,

---

* This poem was read at the opening of the first Provincial
Industrial Exhibition of Nova Scotia, October, 1854.

While ev'ry breast with joy and triumph swells,
And earth reverberates to our measured tread,
Banner and wreath will own our reverence for the Dead.

Look up, their walls enclose us.   Look around,
Who won the verdant meadows from the sea ?
Whose sturdy hands the noble highways wound
Through forests dense, o'er mountain, moor and lea ?
Who spanned the streams ?   Tell me whose works
     they be,
The busy marts where commerce ebbs and flows ?
Who quell'd the savage ?   And who spared the tree
That pleasant shelter o'er the pathway throws ?
Who made the land they loved to blossom as the rose ?

Who, in frail barques, the ocean surge defied,
And trained the race that live upon the wave ?
What shore so distant where they have not died ?
In ev'ry sea they found a watery grave.
Honor, forever, to the true and brave,
Who seaward led their sons with spirits high,
Bearing the red-cross flag their fathers gave ;
Long as the billows flout the arching sky,
They'll seaward bear it still—to venture, or to die.

The Roman gather'd in a stately urn
The dust he honor'd—while the sacred fire,
Nourish'd by vestal hands, was made to burn
From age to age.   If fitly you'd aspire,
Honor the Dead ; and let the sounding lyre

Recount their virtues in your festal hours ;
Gather their ashes—higher still, and higher
Nourish the patriot flame that history dowers,
And, o'er the old men's graves, go strew your choicest
flowers.

SONG FOR THE 8TH JUNE.

Hail to the day when the Briton came o'er
And planted his flag where the Mayflower blows,
And gathered the blossoms, unheeded before,
To entwine with the Shamrock, the Thistle, and Rose.

Let us never forget, while our revels we keep
'Neath the shade of the green woods that hang over-
head,
The labors of those in our churchyards who sleep,
But fill up a bumper to honor the Dead.

Oh ! dear to our hearts is the land they bequeathed,
And the standard they reared proudly waves o'er us
yet ;
While we gather and cherish the flowers they wreathed,
Let us never the graves of our fathers forget.

They vanquished the forest to make us a home,
Though the knife of the savage defended each grove ;
And, while ocean's proud waves round our headlands
shall foam,
This day must be honored where'ever we rove.

The valleys their garments of emerald wear,
  The flocks on the mountains unherried repose,
And the songs of our maidens rise mirthful and clear
  By the side of each stream in the starlight that flows.

The Cities are growing with wealth in their train,
  The Hamlet securely expands in the glen ;
And our white sails are glancing far over the main,
  To the islands that nourish'd those stout hearted men.

Then fill up a bumper, uncovered, we'll name,
  And drink to THE DEAD, and the day they've en-
      deared ;
May the spirit they left, like a circle of flame,
  Guard forever the homes and the standard they
      rear'd.

————

THE STREAMS.

In joy and gladness on ye go
  My country's pleasant streams ;
And oft through scenes as fair ye flow
  As bless the Poet's dreams.
From hills, where stately forests rear
  Their heads the breeze to brave—
From dark morass, or fountain clear,
  You roll to ocean's wave.

The noble Lakes your strength supply,
  And now the crystal spring,
Where undisturb'd the wild birds fly,
  Or bathe the weary wing.
Through narrow gorges here you foam,
  There down the valley rove,
Like youths who leave a quiet home,
  The world's delights to prove.

A thousand ceaseless hymns of praise,
  With music in each tone,
In mystic harmony you raise,
  And heard by God alone.
But though to us it is not given,
  The blended song to know,
Sweet sounds, that have the air of Heav'n
  Delight us as ye go.

The granite cliff its shadow flings
  Far down into the tide,
To deck your banks the flow'ret springs,
  And scents ye as ye glide.
As through the spreading intervales
  Your devious course you steer,
The waving grain your passage hails,
  And flocks and herds appear.

And there the graceful Elms are found,
  Your own peculiar tree ;
And there stout hearted men abound—
  The happy and the free.

And childhood's merry laugh is heard
  Along the hills to float,
As, by the gentle breezes stirr'd
  You waft his tiny boat.

Where youthful forms at eve repose.
  And tales of passion tell,
While Beauty's cheek more beauteous grows,
  And snowy bosoms swell—
In joy and gladness *there* ye go,
  My country's pleasant streams ;
And oft through scenes as fair ye flow,
  As bless the Poet's dreams.

THANKSGIVING HYMN.

Almighty Father ! at Thy Throne
  A grateful people kneel.
Father of Mercies, Thou alone
  Canst compass what we feel.

We thank Thee for the pleasant land
  In which our lots are cast ;
The guidance of Thy eydant hand
  Through all its perils past.

We thank Thee for the forms that guard
  The liberties we prize,
For every cherish'd old Church-yard,
  Where rest the good and wise.

We thank Thee for the Altars free,
   The Courts without a stain—
The glowing page of History,
   The Bard's heroic strain;

The Martyr's death—the Prophet's fire,
   The Christian soldier's sword;
But chiefly let our hearts aspire
   To thank Thee for thy Word:

And for the hallow'd life and death
   Of Him to guide us given:
The hopes that hang upon His breath,
   The promised rest in Heaven.

For lesser mercies teach us too
   The grateful song to raise:
Let all we think, and say, and do,
   Be moulded to Thy praise.

We thank Thee for the daily bread,
   That human life sustains;
For flocks and herds profusely spread
   O'er all our hills and plains.

We thank Thee for the wealth we bring
   Up from the pregnant mine,
For ages stored—each precious thing
   Is ours, and yet is Thine.

We thank Thee for the mighty deep,
  To which our sons go down;
For tranquil bays that calmly sleep
  Beyond the tempest's frown.

We thank Thee for the stars above,
  The flow'ry soil we tread,
For friendship's grasp—the smile of love,
  The song bird over head.

In prayer and praise our souls ascend
  To Thy Almighty Throne;
Father of Mercies—guide and friend,
  Our humble tribute own.
Dec. 8. 1868.

——

MY NATIVE PINES.

My native Pines—my native Pines,
  I love beneath your boughs to stray,
While morning's sun upon you shines
  With bright, and warm, and fervid ray;
For oh! 'twas thus in childhood's hours,
  I rov'd beneath them wild and free,
And gathered May's unsullied flowers,
  That sprung around each forest tree.

My native Pines—my native Pines,
  While noon-day breezes steal along,
And 'neath your fringe my head reclines,
  I love to hear your sylvan song.

For oft in youth my form I threw
  Upon that soft and mossy bed,
While every gentle wind that blew,
  Seem'd fairy music round me shed.

My native Pines—my native Pines,
  While Luna's soft and silv'ry beam,
In holy, bright, and dazzling lines,
  Dwells on your boughs,—I love to dream
Of those unclouded moonlight nights,
  When youthful friends around me stood,
And all the blissful, dear delights,
  We tasted in the lonely wood.

My native Pines—my native Pines,
  Your stately tops still proudly rear ;
Than blooming flow'rs—or clustering vines.
  To me your boughs are far more dear.
Your spreading branches still retain
  Their verdant, bright, and emerald hue,—
Oh ! could the feelings thus remain,
  Which first my boyish bosom knew.

FAME.

And what is Fame? Go seek some battle field,
Where the war trumpets deepest tones have pealed ;
Where to the winds proud banners were unfurled ;
Where met the mighty masters of the world,
While noble chargers shook the trembling ground,

And glittering swords a goodly harvest found ;
Where gallant spirits poured their latest breath
Secure of Fame, and smiling upon Death ;
Where Earth's sweet bosom, 'neath her childrens
    wrath,
Seemed like the fell destroying Angel's path.
Here ask what Fame is, but shew no surprise
If Echo's voice alone to yours replies ;
Nor wonder if the winds steal calmly by,
And lovely flow'rets greet the raptured eye ;
While the glad warblers of the peaceful grove
Chaunt undisturbed their mutual songs of love.
Nay, murmur not that Nature hides the stains
Which Man has cast upon her smiling plains,
Leaving no trace to mark where armies stood,
And spreading flowers to cover fields of blood ;
Nor be surprised,—if not a single name
Of warring thousands lives,—*for this is Fame.*
Or breathe the question o'er the mighty deep,
Within whose gloomy caverns millions sleep ;
Where they who startled Nations by their deeds,
Repose on beds of sand or tangled weeds ;—
Where the proud chief, and war's poor menial slave,
Sleep in one vast, unfathomable grave ;—
Where fleet met fleet, and man to battle sprung,
Till death-shouts o'er the placid waters rung ;
While 'mid the stifling clouds of sulphurous smoke,
The Cannon's voice in notes of thunder broke ;
Where the bright sabre, flashing to the sun,
Performed whate'er the bullet left undone,
And warriors, while it reddened with their blood,

Sank to repose beneath the peaceful flood,
And ere their bones had scarcely time to rot,
Their names, their deeds, were by the world forgot.

Then what is Fame? Go ask yon orphan girl,
Whose brow, just breaking through the silky curl,
Is turned to Heaven in meek, imploring prayer,
In hopes to find another Father there ;
Whose little hands which once a parent grasped,
In bitter agony are firmly clasped ;
Whose guileless breast where joy erst built its bower,
Now owns griefs cold and desolating power ;
Whose eyes, on which a Father fondly gazed,
Now dimmed with tears, before her God are raised ;
Whose cheeks, which used the rose's hue to wear,
Now pale and whitened, speak but of despair.
Oh ! she will tell you, it was Fame that wiled
The doting Father from his infant child,
That lured him to the wars beyond the wave,
And plunged him, *nameless,*—in a bloody grave,
And left her desolate, without a home,
O'er life's unsafe and dangerous path to roam.

Or, ask the Mother, who has stolen her Boy,
The cherished source of all her future joy?
Whose step was lightest in the merry dance,
Whose eye beamed joy, whene'er it met her glance,
Who on her breast in childish pastime laid,
While through his flowing hair her fingers strayed ;
O'er whom she watched, prayed, wept, with aching
        heart,

When sickness made her dread lest they might part ;
O'er whom she smiled with mingled joy and pain,
When health, returning, flushed his cheek again.
Yes, she, with all a mother's grief, will tell
How Fame enticed, and how he fought and fell ;
How that bright form a Mother's heart revered,
By blood and dust was blackened and besmeared ;
And how his tombless bones ungathered lie,
And bleach and moulder, 'neath a foreign sky.

    Mark yonder maid, whose vacant, wandering
       gaze,
O'er Earth and all its charms unconscious strays,
As if, for her, it owned no bower of rest,
No spell to calm the tumult of her breast ;
To whose dark eyes unearthly beams are given,
Whose tresses wave before the winds of Heaven.
Oh ! she was lovely once,—yes, far more fair
Than any flower that scents the evening air ;
So pure, so stainless, while bright gleams of soul
Shed light, and life, and beauty, o'er the whole ;
But 'twas her lot to love—the passion twined
Its holiest feelings round her spotless mind ;
And she was loved, as she deserved to be,
With all Youth's fervent, fond, idolatry ;
Hope sweetly smiled upon their future years,
When War's shrill trumpet sounded in their ears ;
He heard, and yielding to the lures of Fame,
Sighed for a laurel wreath, and deathless name ;
While with high hopes his ardent breast would swell
But, brief the tale—he left her, fought, and fell

(As thousands do) unnoticed and unknown,
Remembered, loved, and wept by her alone ;
Though no proud volley echoed o'er his head,
Affection's silent tear for him was shed ;
And if no marble told his place of rest,
He still was shrined in lovely Woman's breast ;
And what can all Fame's empty joys impart
Like the pure homage of one guileless heart?

Oh ! Fame, will man ne'er cease to bow the knee
Before thy bloody shrine, and strive to free
His spirit from thy heavy, galling, chain
Which bows it down to toil, and guilt, and pain?
Can he not see that at thy Altars rise
No incense but of tears, and groans, and sighs ?
That Disappointment, Madness, and Despair,
Are the High Priests that love to linger there?
June 5, 1826.

LA TRIBUNE.

The knell of death is on the blast,
   The seas are wildly driven,
And those who cling around the mast,
   Look up with prayers to Heaven.

While every swelling dark-blue wave
   Strikes terror to the eye
Of men who think they see their grave,
   Yet feel 'tis hard to die.

And who, in such an awful hour,
　Will dare approach the wreck?
When He, who only has the power,
　The waters will not check.

For oh! the deep sea's sullen roar,
　That sounds so fierce and loud,
And mountain waves, that lash the shore,
　Appal the shrinking crowd.

But who his little bark has launch'd,
　And to his oars has sprung?
His cheek by age seems yet unblanch'd,
　His brow is fair and young.

His light, and almost childish, form
　Seems far too weak to brave
The fearful howling of the storm,
　The terror of the wave.

But yet a high and fearless soul
　Is glancing in his eye,
Which tells that he will reach the goal,
　Or on the waters die.

His boat the billow proudly cleaves,
　While bounding from the shore,
And those who on the beach he leaves,
　Ne'er hope to see him more.

But mark the sacred freight he bears
From off the troubled main,
Two human hearts—what bliss is theirs!
Restored to life again.

And oh! what feelings swell the heart
Of that undaunted Boy;
Could Roman triumphs e'er impart
So sweet a throb of joy?

Acadia's child—thy humble name
The Muse will long revere,
The wreath you nobly won from Fame
Shall bloom for many a year.

Long as the thoughts which swell'd thy breast,
The flame that lit thy eye,
Shall in our Country's bosom rest,
Thy name shall never die!

HOME.

A spot there is, from public gaze retired,
Sought but by few, by fewer still admired,
Where Feeling's holy fountains sparkling play,
Illum'd by Reason's calm, yet brilliant ray;
Where the tired spirit, wearied and oppressed
Far from the crowd may find its wished for rest;

Where the heart's purest, best affections spring,
Round which the siren Hope, delights to cling ;
Where Genius loves his valued stores to shed,
And Fancy's rich, yet simple flowers, are spread ;
Where Dissipation, with her frenzied mien,
And sick'ning, tasteless joys, is never seen ;
To which, if sorrow comes, a sacred charm
Pours in its deepest wounds a healing balm ;
Where Disappointment, robbed of half his care,
Forgets to point the pathway to Despair ;
Where, if a tear at times should dim the eye,
It beams the brighter when the tear is dry ;
Where, like the Indian altar's steady flame,
Love's fire burns·on, from youth to age the same ;
So blest a spot, tho' o'er the world we roam,
We ne'er can hope to find, as *Home,* sweet *Home.*

TO THE QUEEN.

[Presented to His Royal Highness the Prince of Wales, at
Windsor, by Lady Laura Phipps, in behalf of the ladies of
Hants county.]

Queen of the thousand Isles ! whose fragile form,
'Midst the proud structures of our Father Land,
Graces the throne, that each subsiding storm
That shakes the earth, assures us yet shall stand
Thy gentle voice, of mild yet firm command,

Is heard in ev'ry clime, on ev'ry wave,
Thy dazzling sceptre, like a fairy wand,
Strikes off the shackles from the struggling slave,
And gathers, 'neath its rule, the great, the wise, the
    brave.

But yet, 'midst all the treasures that surround
Thy Royal Halls, one bliss is still denied,—
To know the true hearts at thy name that bound,
Which ocean from thy presence must divide,
Whose voices never swell the boisterous tide
Of hourly homage that salutes thy ear;
But yet who cherish, with a Briton's pride,
And breathe to infant lips, from year to year,
The name thy budding virtues taught them to revere.

How little deem'st thou of the scenes remote,
In which one word, all other words above,
Of earthly homage seems to gaily float
On every breeze, and sound through every grove—
A spell to cheer, to animate, to move—
To bid old age throw off the weight of years,
To cherish thoughts of loyalty and love,
To garner round the heart those hopes and fears
Which, in our Western Homes, VICTORIA'S name en-
    dears.

'Tis not that, on our soil, the measured tread
Of armed legions speaks thy sovereign sway,
'Tis not the huge leviathans that spread
Thy meteor flag above each noble bay,

That bids the soul a forced obedience pay!
—The despot's tribute from the trembling thrall—
No!   At our altars sturdy freemen pray
That blessings on VICTORIA's head may fall,
And happy household groups each pleasing trait recall.

And gladly, with our Country's choicest flowers,
Thy Son and Heir Acadia's maidens greet,
Who shared thy roof, and deigns to honor ours
For moments rapt'rous, but alas! how fleet!
And if in future times the thoughts be sweet
To him, of humble scenes beyond the sea,
When turning home his mother's smile to meet,
And mingle with the high born and the free—
We'll long remember Him who best reflected Thee!
    1860.

MAKING LAND.

[On viewing England for the first time.]

Land of my Fathers! do I then behold
Thy noble outline rising from the sea?
Is this the Isle of which such tales are told?
Home of the wise, the valiant, and the free,
Dear to her sons,—perchance as dear to me,
Whose tongue is her's—and whose impetuous tide
Of life is of the sap of that great tree,
The trunk of which stands here in all its pride,
For whose majestic limbs the world is scarce too wide.

And is this England? let more sail be spread,
The mother's breast invites her unknown child,
The glorious visions which his youth have fed,
Crowd on the mind and make him almost wild
With ecstacy, as, in the distance piled,
Her verdant cliffs in solemn grandeur rise:—
By mixed emotions every sense beguiled,
The tears are standing in his straining eyes,
While all too slow each cloud the lagging breeze supplies.

And is this England?   Shall I shortly tread
The hallowed soil from which my Fathers came?
Where sleep in honored graves, the mighty dead,
Who built the stately fabric of her fame,
And, in her Temples, still have kept the flame
Of Freedom burning on from age to age?
How, like familiar words, each magic name,
In childhood conned from the historic page
Of Patriot, Warrior, Poet, Saint or Sage,

Comes back upon me now, while drawing near
The soil on which they labored, fought and sung;
And shall I view the scenes they made so dear,
And stroll, entranced, their mouldering tombs among?
Stand where, from craven John reluctant wrung,
The Charter's ample guards were first unroll'd,
Where, 'neath the Lion Banner, old and young,
The hardy Yeoman, Priest, and Baron bold,
A lesson gave their sons more precious far than gold?

And shall I rove beside the very stream
Which Shakspeare loved?   beneath the trees recline,

That broke from his high brow the noonday beam,
Less radiant, aye, and almost less divine
Than were the gems from that exhaustless mine
The brow contained, whose wealth the world supplies,
Whose teeming fancies, like to generous wine,
Ripen with age?   Sweetest of England's ties,
Where'er her children live, there Shakspeare never dies.

On, on, good Bark !—I go where Milton sleeps,
Where Hampden's soul despotic power defied,
Where Nelson's urn a grateful Nation keeps,
Where Dryden wrote, and gallant Russell died,
Where in her ancient Temples, side by side,
The master spirits of my Country strove,
Where Fox and Chatham thundered in their pride,
Where Spencer lines of varied sweetness wove,
Where precious memories haunt each mountain, stream
        and grove.
1838.

THE RHINE.

The Rhine—the Rhine—beneath me now,
    A mighty volume pours,
Its source, the distant mountain's brow,
    Its grave the northern shores.
By nations loved, by poets sung,
    The noble stream goes by
By crumbling fane and tow'r o'erhung,
    And cliffs that charm the eye.

But yet, three thousand miles away,
  Some gentle streams there are,
That here, midst all this proud array,
  To me are dearer far.

I see them winding through the vales
  The Clover's breath perfumes,
Where, fluttering in the summer gales,
  The scented Wild Rose blooms ;
And where the Elms, with graceful ease,
  Their fringed branches droop ;
And where the tassell'd Alder trees
  To kiss their waters stoop.
While, glittering in the rosy light
  At day's serene decline,
They murmur onwards, calm and bright,
  Those pleasant streams of mine.

I see them from the mountain gush,
  Where wave the ancient woods
O'er rock and steeps impetuous rush,
  To blend their sparkling floods.
Now wand'ring through the forest glade,
  To sylvan lakes expand ;
In every form of beauty made,
  To bless the pleasant land.
And, midst the charms that greet me here
  Beside the swelling Rhine,
Their voices steal upon my ear,
  Those far-off streams of mine.

What though no ruins* rise above
　　My Country's pleasant streams ;
Nor legends wild, of war or love,
　　Invoke the Poet's dreams.
No lawless power can there disturb
　　The Peasant's tranquil sleep ;
No towers,† the free-born soul to curb,
　　Frown o'er each lofty steep—
Then, German, keep your Drachenfels,‡
　　Vine-clad and foaming Rhine,
The taint of bondage on them dwells,
　　Far happier streams are mine.
1838.

COMING HOME.

Mantled in snow, my native land,
　　I hail thee from the sea ;
Cheerless to others looks the strand,
　　But oh ! how dear to me.

My fellow-voyagers gaze and shrink,
　　As blows the breeze from shore,
With raptured pulse the air I drink—
　　The Northern breeze once more.

---

* The remains of the old feudal castles are seen in gr‚ , profusion, crowning the hills on both sides of the Rhine.

† A fortress, with a strong garrison, commands each large city on this river.

‡ The Dragon Rock, celebrated in Byron's *Childe Harold,* and which forms a noble feature of the Rhine's sublime scenery.

They, thinking of their Southern homes,
   And of the trellised vine ;
Wonder from icy shores there comes
   Excited thought like mine.

As landmarks, they, thy headlands view,
   Right glad to pass them by ;
To me they're pictures, stern, but true,
   That charm and cheer the eye.

They cannot see the scenes beyond,
   Of happy household mirth,
The skaters on the glittering pond,
   The children round the hearth.

They cannot hear the merry cheer
   Of coasters on the steep ;
They do not know how soundly here,
   The free and happy sleep.

They cannot hear the peasant's axe
   Sharp ringing through the groves,
Nor see the blazing fire he piles
   To gladden those he loves.

The sleighs go through the crowded street,
   Like swallows on the wing ;
Beneath the furs warm fingers meet,
   Hark ! how the sleigh-bells ring.

There's not a sound that cleaves the air
  But music has for me ;
Nightly the warm hearts beating there,
  Have blest me on the sea.

The stately piles of old renown
  With reverent thought I've trod,
Where noble hearts have laid them down
  With History and with God.

The crowded mart, the busy throng,
  The gay and brilliant halls ;
The tramp of steeds, the voice of song,
  The many-pictured walls,

Are all behind ; but, all before,
  My native land I view ;
A blessing on her sea-girt shore,
  Where toil the good and true.
January 25, 1862.

SATURDAY NIGHT AT SEA.

Sweethearts and Wives—the Goblet pass—
  A Bumper let it be,
Bright eyes are sparkling through each glass
  'Tis " Saturday night at sea."

The matron sits by her fireside,
  Her children at her knee ;
They're breathing prayers that we may glide
  In safety o'er the sea.

The maiden droops in her shady bow'r
  What cause of grief has she?
The heart that heeds not bird or flow'r,
  Is with us on the sea.

But, brighter hours are yet in store,
  From ev'ry danger free,—
We'll share the smiles of those on shore,
  We toasted on the sea.

THE STORMY PETREL.

Away—away—o'er the deep blue wave,
  I spread my froward wing,
And the Winter's gale as proudly brave
  As the balmy airs of Spring.

A venturous life and gay I lead,
  Whatever wind may blow,
There's a boundless sky above my head,
  And boundless seas below.

Let the Birds of Land to homes repair
  Beneath the greenwood tree,
The hunter's tube awaits them there—
  He dare not follow me.

I scorn the land and the landsman's hate,
  The sailor's Bird am I ;
My life is charm'd, for he knows the fate
  Of those by whom I die.

In shady groves and woodland bower,
  Let others rear the nest,
On the crested wave, in its wildest hour
  I fold my wing to rest.

Though the hedge may boast its perfumed rose,
  And clear the Streamlets-shine,
Oh! what are the joys of earth to those
  That ev'ry hour are mine?

The Linnet may list the Peasant's sigh
  At rosy eventide,
I catch the glance of the Rover's eye,
  As he clasps his sea borne Bride.

The Iceberg's dangerous track I mark,
  Till it wastes beneath the sun,
And I float above the ravening Shark,
  When his struggling prey is won;

I mark the sport, when the black cloud scowls,
  And the Tars aloft are sent,
And the sun-bleached sail, while the tempest howls,
  From their hands like chaff is rent.

When the pumps are choked, and the gallant ship
  Goes down to ocean's cave,
I flap my wing o'er her pennon's tip,
  Ere it sinks beneath the wave.

When embattl'd fleets, in fierce array,
  Their sulph'rous broadsides pour.

The varying fortunes of the day,
　　The belching cannons' roar,—

The dying groan—the rallying cry—
　　The Boarder's desperate leap,—
These are the scenes that glad my eye,
　　The wonders of the deep.

Then away —away—o'er the wave I'll rove
　　With restless wing and free,
The timid may seek the leafy grove,
　　Give me the stormy sea.

———

THE COASTER.

Though the idle may heed not, the wealthy despise
　　The race to which I and my fellows belong,
My voice o'er my own native waters shall rise,
　　And the deck of my shallop resound to my song.

Though my craft may be small, she is snug and she's trim,
　　And her crew are accustomed to battle the wave,
They are cheerful of heart, and athletic of limb,
　　And follow the business their bold fathers gave.

Through the storm and the sleet of the winter we sail,
　　While the rich and the feeble on couches repose ;
There is health in our toil, and a charm in the gale,
　　And our courage still rises the harder it blows.

Every harbor from Sable to Canso's a home,
  Every depth from the Banks to St. Lawrence we've
    tried,
And we care not though round Labrador we may roam,
  Or sweep on the strength of old Fundy's fierce tide.

Now wealth from the wave we draw forth with our lines,
  And now with a cargo of produce we're stow'd,
Or having a full freight of coal from the mines,
  We slowly sail on with our cumbersome load.

Though the Merchantman looks gay, her crew are but
    slaves
  And own not a stick of the vessel they steer,
Though the Frigate glides by, like the Queen of the
    Waves,
  We know that the cat and the bilboes are there.

Then who would exchange the rough life that we lead,
  Joint owners at sea, and free sons of the soil,
At the bidding of others to labor and bleed
  With but little of pleasure to sweeten our toil.

We build our own shallops, we rear our own crew,
  And life has for us sweet endearment in store,
For though luxury's fetters our souls never knew,
  Bright eyes bid us welcome when peril is o'er.

Thus we Coasters enrich the fair land that we love,
  And if danger should threaten, the cutlass we'd seize,
And our hearts and our sinews in battle should prove,
  That the spirit of freedom is nursed by the breeze.

THE SONG OF THE MICMAC.

Oh ! who on the mountain, the plain, or the wave,
   With the arm of the Micmac will dare to contend ?
Who can hurl the keen spear with the sons of the brave
   Or who can the bow with such energy bend ?

Who can follow the Moose, or the wild Cariboo,
   With a footstep as light and unwearied as he ?
Who can bring down the Loon with an arrow so true,
   Or paddle his bark o'er as stormy a sea ?

Who can traverse the mountain or swim the broad lake ?
   Who can hunger and thirst with such fortitude bear ?
Or who can the Beaver as skilfully take ?
   Or the Salmon so nimbly transfix with his spear ?

And if the wild war whoop ascends on the gale,
   Who can with the Micmac the tomahawk wield ?
Oh ! when was he known in the combat to quail ?
   Whoe'er saw him fly from the red battle field ?

Free sons of the forest, then peal forth the song,
   Till each valley and rock shall of victory tell,
And the ghosts of our heroes, while flitting along
   With triumph shall smile on the spots where they fell.

THE WILD CHERRY TREE.

Child of the wilderness—gladly I see
Thy blossoms unfolding on hill-side and lea ;
By streamlet and river thy white veil is spread,

Where the Witch Elm looks lovingly down on thy head;
In the depth of the forest the Moose turns aside
To gaze on thy branches with pleasure and pride;
And the Salmon leaps higher, if lit by the beam
Of noontide, you gracefully droop o'er the stream.
Oh! dear to all nature, but dearer to me
Is the pride of the Spring time—the Wild Cherry Tree.

Storm-tested, the Oak on the mountain top grows,
And the date of its seedling no living man knows;
The Maple, in Autumn, is lovely to view,
And the tremulous Aspen, that shakes off the dew;
Like a Temple the Pine Grove invites us to prayer,
And we worship 'midst beauty and solitude there;
By the Beech in the pastures, 'tis pleasant to lean,
And the Fir, through the snow wreath, looks cheery and
    green.
Though highly I prize them, yet dearer to me
Is the pride of the Spring time, the Wild Cherry Tree.

The Laurel's pink blossoms look gay on the moor,
The Larch's red berries droop round the church door;
The Alder Clumps, dress'd in their tassels, are fine,
And the Rockets, the Windfalls with beauty enshrine;
The wings of each zephyr the Bay-leaf perfumes,
And, rich in its odors, the modest Fern blooms.
Oh! countless the blossoms the woodlands display,
And varied the scents on the night air that stray—
From childhood I loved them—but dearer to me
Is the delicate flower of the Wild Cherry Tree.

J. blooms on the barren—it smiles through the grove,
It hangs o'er the path where the young lovers rove;
Like a sweet flag of truce, at the Pensioner's door,
It gladdens his eye when life's warfare is o'er; ;
Round the Emigrant's clearing, far back in the wild
It catches the eye of each frolicksome child,
And the Indian draws, in the gloomiest hour
New health from its bark, and gay thought from its
    flower.
And black eyes will sparkle, whenever they see,
Festoon'd round the Wigwam, the Wild Cherry Tree.

Fair child of the woodland, wherever I roam,
I ne'er can forget that you bloom'd round my home;
That the brow of that sister I've wept o'er for hours,
Was crown'd with thy berries, and wreath'd with thy
    flowers.
That the roads where we rambled, the knolls where we
    stood
While our voices in gladness rang clear through the wood,
That the spots which, love hallow'd, still verdant appear,
Unchanged in a feature—undimmed by a tear,
Were graced by thy presence, and come back to me
When Spring decks in blossoms the Wild Cherry Tree,

THE MICMAC.

  Though o'er Acadia's hills and plains
    The wand'ring Micmac listless strays,
  While scarce a single trace remains
    Of what he was in other days.

And though he now an outcast seems
    Upon the lands his Fathers trod,
And his dark eye no longer beams
    With pride which bent but to his God,—

Though the fire-water's deadly wave
    Which even pride could not control,
Has drown'd each feeling high that gave
    Such innate grandeur to his soul;—

There was a time when Nature's child
    With nobler port and manner bore him,
And ranged with joy his native wild,
    Or slept with Heaven's blue curtain o'er him.

Long ere the white man's axe was heard
    Resounding in the forest shade,
Long ere the rifle's voice had stirr'd
    The stillness of the Sylvan glade,—

Ere Science, with her plastic hand,
    And Labor, with his patient toil,
Had changed the features of the land,
    And dispossess'd him of the soil.

Then let fair Fancy change the scene,
    While gazing on the Micmac's brow,
And showing what he once has been,
    Make us forget what he is now.

MY FATHER.

[These lines were written at the age of 16, and published in the Weekly Chronicle, in 1821.]

His form, combining health and ease,
And features form'd by Heaven to please,—
His face is placid.   In his mien
Meekness and Charity are seen.
If you could view his polish'd mind,
Religion's self is there combined
With grace, and truth, and manly pride,
Which to Religion are allied,—
You'd find, if you his life could scan,
" God's noblest work, an honest man."

GLIDE MERRILY ON MY LITTLE SKIFF.

Glide merrily on, my little skiff,
  O'er waves lit up by Luna's smile,
There lies no shoal or rugged cliff
  Between thee and yon fairy Isle.

Skim lightly o'er the glittering tide,
  The stars shall be our lamp the while,
And bear me quickly to the side
  Of her I love on yonder Isle.

The Miser doats upon his store,
  And dreams the Warrior's heart beguile,—
If fate bestows, I'll ask no more
  Than her who lives on yonder Isle.

1827.

TO MY WIFE.

My gentle Wife, though girlhood's peach-like bloom
Perchance is passing from thy cheek away,
And though the radiance that did erst illume
Thine eye be temper'd by a milder ray ;
And though no more youth's airy visions play
Around thy heart, or flutter through thy brain,—
Still art thou worthy of the Poet's lay,
Still shall my spirit breathe the Lover's strain,
And, if approved by thee, not breathed perhaps in vain.

E'en as the Painter's or the Sculptor's eye
Dwells on some matchless vision which combines
All that they deem of Beauty, ere they try
By inspiration's aid, to catch the lines.
To deck earth's highest and her holiest shrines,—
So did I oft my boyhood's heart beguile
With one fair image,—and the glowing mines
Of Ind would have been freely given the while,
To bid that being live to glad me with her smile.

But when in maiden loveliness you came,
Giving reality to all the fair
And graceful charms that, blent with woman's name,
Had seem'd too rich for earthly forms to wear,
Yet stood beside me in the twilight there—
Then came the agony, to artists known,
The dread that visions so surpassing rare
May fade away, and ne'er become their own,
And leave their hearts to mourn, all desolate and lone.

Thou wert the guiding star whose living beam
Flash'd o'er Youth's troubled thoughts and vague
    desires ;
Something of thee was blent with ev'ry dream
That fed Ambition's fierce but smother'd fires.
The gentle fancies Poesy inspires—
The hopes and fears of Manhood's early dawn,
That lent their witchery to youthful lyres,
Were of thy guileless fascinations born,
And threw their spells around the fount whence they
    were drawn.

If in my youthful breast one thought arose
That had a trace of Heav'n, it caught its hue
From the instinctive virtue that o'erflows
Each word and act of thine,—and if I threw
Aside those base desires that sometimes drew
My spirit down to earth's unhallow'd bowers,
'Twas when I met, or heard, or thought of you,
Or roved beside you, in those ev'ning hours,
Beneath the boughs that waved wide o'er your Island
    flowers.

Thou canst remember—can'st thou e'er forget,
While life remains, that placid summer night
When, from the thousand stars in azure set,
Stream'd forth a flood of soft subduing light,
And o'er our heads, in Heaven's topmost height,
The moon moved proudly, like a very Queen,
Claiming all earthly worship as her right,
And hallowing, by her power, the peaceful scene
Spread out beneath her smile, so tranquil and serene

Then, as you wander'd, trembling, by my side,
Gush'd forth the treasured tenderness of years;
And your young ear drank in the impetuous tide
Of early passion—boyhood's hopes and fears—
Affirm'd with all the energy of tears.
And then love wove around our hearts a chain
Which ev'ry passing moment more endears—
Mingling our souls, as streams that seek the plain,
Through wastes and flowers to pass, but never part
      again.

Years have gone by since then—and I have seen
Thy budding virtues blossom and expand;
Still, side by side, amidst life's cares we've been,
And o'er its verdant spots roved hand in hand;
And I have marked the easy self-command
That every thought and movement still pervades—
The gen'rous nature and the liberal hand—
The glance that gladdens me, but ne'er upbraids,
And the confiding soul whose faith faints not nor fades.

Like to the young bard's Harp, whose magic tone
Delights, yet startles, when he strikes the strings,
And stirs his soul with rapture all its own
As an unpractised hand he o'er it flings,
Thy heart was once to me.   But now its springs
Of deepest feeling I have known so long,
Its treasured stores of rich and holy things,
Its sweetest chords round which soft accents throng,
That life becomes to me like one inspiring song.

Nor think, my love, that time can ever steal
Its sweetness from me.   Years may wander by,
Afid in their course the frolic blood congeal,
Or dim the lustre of that hazel eye.
But, even then, with proud idolatry
On that pale cheek and wasted form I'll gaze,
And wander backward to those scenes where I
Bent o'er them first, in youth's primeval days
Where memory all her wealth of hoarded thought dis-
    plays.

The lonely beach on which we often roved,
And watched the moonbeams flickering on the sea—
The ancient trees, whose grateful shade we loved,
The grassy mounds where I have sat by thee—
The simple strains you warbled, wild and free.
The tales I loved to read and you to hear,
With every glance of thine so linked shall be,
That every passing day and circling year,
Shall to my faithful heart my early love endear.

I'll paint you as you bloom'd in that sweet hour,
When friendly faces beamed on every side,
And, drooping like a frail but lovely flower,
'Fore God and man you claimed to be my bride,
Or, as you now, with all a mother's pride,
Fold to your beating breast your darling child ;
And thus, though years beneath our steps may glide,
My fancy still, by mem'ry's power beguiled,
Shall whisper: Thus she looked—'twas thus in youth
    she smiled.
    July, 1832.

TO MY SISTER JANE.

[Written at Musquodoboit, after the elections, in 1847.]

Sister mine, I'm home at last,
  Life's severest conflict's o'er,
The seals are set upon the past,
And, like a tempest-shaken mast,
That press of sail, and shot, and blast,
  Have spared to reach the friendly shore,
Conscious of neither warp nor strain,
And draped with bunting once again ;
Be mine, the task, my dearest Jane,
Forgetting ocean's helter-skelter,
'To deck the port I've toiled to shelter.

Sister mine, when April showers
  Strewed with buds each woodland glade,
Our hearts expanding like the flowers,
  A tryst betwixt us two was made,
How kept, you know ; or, by this token,
You rather know how it was broken.
When summer came, and you were free,
  No hour had I to call my own ;
And now the sunny hours have flown,
The cares of life environ thee.
Another year must pass, ere we,
With tearful eyes and full hearts yearning,
Our steps to keep that tryst are turning.
Would we had kept it, sister mine,
  And looked into each other's faces,
For I would mark, with jealous care,

The slightest touch, the faintest traces
That Time, upon that form of thine
    Hás left, and miser-like, compare
The treasure spared, with what I knew
When first his light wing o'er us flew.
We cannot meet, but yet our souls
    Ever commingle day and night,
The past our current thought controls,
    Our hearts are mutual in our dreams,
At times how sombre, then how bright,
    We climb the hills, and trace the streams
In which we used to take delight,
Recalling scenes receding ever,
And forms, to be forgotten—never !

    That circle first, beside the sea,
So dearly loved by you and me,
On which, as in Art's grandest themes,
The light of love divinely beams,
From one whose gracious presence seems
To bless the Earth, and charm the Air,
And shed effulgence everywhere.
Oh ! how we loved him, love him now,
Our noble Father.   By his side
My Mother, who my faults would chide,
With cares domestic on her brow,
More wayward, and of sterner mood,
But ever provident and good ;
Hating all shams, and looking through
The Beautiful, to find the True,

Sits knitting by the window pane,
Can you not see her, dearest Jane?

 The Cottage too, its ashes now
 Are borne on every idle wind,
The walls are down, and not a tree
 We loved remains, but yet how soon
We can replace it on the brow
 Of that sweet knoll, and, if inclined,
Restore it all, as you and me
 Prized it all earthly piles aboon.

 The dear old place, so quaint and queer,
Our home for many a pleasant year.
By Pine Groves from the world shut out,
And battlemented round about
With rude stone walls, that cleared the soil,
 And shelter to the bushes yielded,
Where grew our treasures, precious spoil,
 From cutting winds securely shielded.
The Lilac Hedge, rememberest thou,
 That wandering lovers used to rifle.
The Barn, and then the old red Cow
 That gave us syllabubs, and trifle?
See'st thou the Apple Trees in bloom,
 Or leaves with Cherries gaily braided?
The stiff old Poplars grim and high,
Like sentinels dropped from the sky,
 To guard the door they never shaded.

 Half hid 'neath Blackberries and Roses,
The crystal Spring is yet o'erflowing;

Unlike Narcissus, we can gaze,
And by the light of other days,
Find in its depths vain thoughts to smother,
And still more dearly love—each other.

The Lawn, with Oak trees round the edges,
  Sister mine, how oft we've trod,
North the Currants formed the hedges,
  South the Maples worshipped God ;
Lovely when the sap was flowing,
Lovelier still in Autumn glowing,
Smiling when the Sun caressed them,
When the Frosts in purple dressed them,
Smiling still as we should smile,
Looking heavenward all the while,
Though the Frosts have sometimes found us
With our kindred falling round us.

The " Arm," upon it be my blessing,
  Yet in beauty ebbs and flows ;
Labor's hands its shores are dressing,
Crime, upon its margin pressing,
  Sad purgation undergoes.
Carriage drives are formed and forming,
  Where our feet but pathways found,
And the Boutelliers * are storming
  With the pick our berry ground.
But the water yet remaineth
  Blue and cheery as before,
Not a cove but still retaineth
  Wavelets that we loved of yore,
    * A family living in the neighbourhood.

Lightly up the rock-weeds lifting,
  Gently murmuring o'er the sand,
Like romping girls each other chasing,
  Ever brilliant, ever shifting,
Interlaced and interlacing,
  Till they sink upon the strand.
  Sweet the voice of music sounds

On that lovely bay at night
When, as the oar the water wounds,
  'Tis bathed with phosphorescent light.
And the Indian's torch, afar
Glimmers like a fallen star.
Pleasant was it to behold
The veil of fog, at morning roll'd
By the sun from off that bay,
While it like a mirror lay ;
Bridal vesture drawn aside,
Never lovelier looked the bride.

Pleasant was it, Sister mine,
When the evening sun would shine
  Down the " Arm " in all his splendor,
Like a lover, warmer growing,
As the hour approached for going ;
  Then, as grew the tints more tender,—
Pleasant 'twas to see him fade
In rosy bowers his beams had made,
Lighting with his sweetest smile,
What appeared his funeral pile,
As the Monarch we are told
Midst " barbaric pearls and gold,"

On the couch his hand had fired,
Like a reveller expired.

Could we have kept our treasures round us
  Till the parting hour, dear Jane,
Oh how rich the year had found us,
  How exulting then the strain;
But of loving, count the cost
In the treasures we have lost.

Nearly all that stood around us
  In the sunlight on that shore,
All that to that Cottage bound us,
  To the grave have gone before.
As we gaze upon the Ocean,
  Calm and tranquil as it lies,
Who can check our souls' emotion?
  Who shall dry our tearful eyes?

  The sea has pictures, Art might sigh for,
  Grand and terrible and true,
Tableaux that our thoughts enthrall,
Scenes that Memory can recall,
Vividly each tint retaining
Till our senses, over-straining
  Clutch the very forms we view.
    Those we've nestled and would die for.
Two such pictures hang, unfading,
  In our hearts, my dearest Jane;
How intense the depth of shading,
  Every ray of light is pain;
But the pleasant faces round us,

And the happy homes we share
Win us from the thoughts that wound us,
  And forbid us to despair.

Sacred are the dead who've perished
  On the land and on the main,
Be their mem'ries ever cherished,
  But to Joy let's turn again ;
Good, and dutiful, and true,
Toil your girls to comfort you,
And my children full of grace
Make my Home a holy place,
Where work and study, thought and play,
Alternate, wile the hours away.
Come and see us, Sister mine,
  Welcome shall your footsteps be
Merry eyes will brighter shine,
  Eager arms be stretched for thee—
Come, and she, who, by my side,
From the hour I claimed my bride
Has bred my chicks, and made the nest
Ever jocund, ever blest,
Shall strain you to the heart I've proved,
And tell you how your brother loved.

TO SUSAN ANN.

Though but a few short days have flown
  Since down your cheek the tear drops strayed,
And round your neck my arm was thrown,
  And fond " goodbyes " were ling'ring said ;

And though 'twill not be long till I
  Shall bound again to your embrace;
When joy shall light your hazel eye,

  And banish sorrow's ev'ry trace.

At morn your look of love I miss—
  Your voice's music all day long;
At eve your chaste and balmy kiss—
  The touching music of your song.

The silent pressure of your hand,
  Your spotless bosom's gentle swell—
And wanting these, I long to stand
  Once more within their magic spell.

The Oak its branches flings on high,
  The lovely River rolls and shines,
The morning breezes softly sigh
  Among the stately forest Pines.

The Birds are pouring forth their lays,
  The wild Rose scents the balmy air,
And the bright Sun's unclouded rays
  Are shedding beauty everywhere.

Tho' grand the scenes, I tread the while,
  And fair the flowers o'er which I roam,
I long to meet your placid smile
  And sigh for Home—my happy Home.

OH THINK NOT THAT MY HEART CAN E'ER.

Oh! think not that my heart can e'er
   Before another's altar bow,
Or that you'll cease to be as dear
   To that fond heart as you are now.

Oh! think not when we shortly sever,
   Another's form will dearer be,
Oh! no,—'tis you—and you forever
   My bosom's idol still must be.

For while existence I can claim,
   In my heart's core you'll be enshrined,
In death I'll breathe your much loved name—
   The dearest, far, I leave behind.

You bid me think of you no more,
   But can I from my bosom tear
The thoughts of her I must adore,
   Whose image still lies buried there?

Oh! what is all this world can give
   Of riches, splendor, pleasure, pride,
If she, for whom alone we live,
   Her heart,—her smile—has still denied?

What are Ambition's charms to me?
   Altho' my mind they oft beguilé,
What are they all if wanting thee?
   What are they worth—without your smile?

Oh ! if your heart must ne'er be mine,
  To one more worthy be it given,
And that each blessing may be thine
  Shall be my constant prayer to Heaven.

1823.

NAY, CHIDE ME NOT.

Nay, chide me not, although I take,
  With trembling lip, one holy kiss,
For naught on Earth can e'er awake
  A throb of joy so pure as this.

One instant on those lips to dwell,
  Which none before have dared to press ;
One instant feel that bosom swell
  Responsive to my fond caress ;—

While in your mild, expressive eye,
  And on that beauteous brow of thine,
And on that cheek, where roses lie,
  I read, your trusting heart is mine.

Oh ! lovely are the mellow beams
  Of Summer's Sun at evening straying,
And soothingly the Moonlight gleams
  When o'er the sleeping Wave 'tis playing ;—

And beauteous are the Forest flowers
  When fresh from Flora's hand they spring,
And, dear are childhood's early hours
  Round which the memory loves to cling.

Yes, these have charms, yet purer still
   To youthful hearts a joy is given,
Which touches with a deeper thrill,
   Which, snatched on Earth, still tastes of Heaven.

Then chide me not, altho' I take
   With trembling lip one holy kiss
For naught on Earth can e'er awake
   A throb of joy so pure as this.
1827.

THE BEACH.

The Moonbeams slept upon the Wave
   Which scarce a wand'ring zephyr curl'd,
And with their silvery brightness gave
   Dreams of a fairer, holier world.

The distant Isles their shadows threw,
   Dark'ning the water's fair expanse,
While Nature's placid stillness drew
   By witchery forth the Soul's romance.

A rapture o'er our spirits broke
   Till that still hour unknown before,
And many a thought which love awoke
   Was utter'd on that lovely shore.

For wild and lonely was the scene
   On which the sacred beams descended,
Rock, Isle and Wave, and Forest green,
   In lights and shades were softly blended.

Along the pebbly Beach we stray'd,
  And gazed upon the shining Sea,
And rais'd our eyes to Heaven, and pray'd
  As bright and calm our lives might be.

The drowsy world had sought repose,
  No wandering footstep lingered near
To check thy song, which sweetly rose
  Like fairy music on the ear.

Your cheek was pillow'd on my breast,
  My arm around you fondly clung,
And, as the Bird bends o'er its nest,
  In hope and joy o'er thee I hung.

And from the glorious bright array
  Which Nature spread before the sight,
Turn'd, half unconsciously away,
  To watch your eye's unsullied light.

The Pilgrim, thus, 'midst fairest bowers,
  One cherish'd, deep sensation feels,
Nor heeds the rich and fragrant flowers,
  While to his guardian Saint he kneels.
1827.

THO' TIME MAY STEAL THE ROSEATE BLUSH.

Tho' Time may steal the roseate blush
  On which I now so fondly gaze,
Its sternest power can never crush
  The love which lit my youthful days.

Your cheek may blanch, your eye grow dim,
  Your clustering locks with sorrow fade,
But still you'll be as dear to him
  Who on your breast in Boyhood laid.

Who, o'er you bent whole happy hours,
  Or round your form enraptured clung,
While Love and Hope transformed to flowers
  The sharpest thorns that near him sprung.

Who, in his childish heart would cherish
  Bright thoughts that kindled at your name,
Who'd rather Life and Peace should perish,
  Than try to quench the glowing flame.

Who, when the warm and genial tide
  Of youthful blood, flowed fresh and free,
Was only happy by your side,
  Was never blest till loved by thee.

Time may steal on, and Age advance,
  Affection's rays will brighter beam,
I'll love your eye's mild mellow'd glance,
  As now I love its sparkling gleam.

And though the hand of Age may press
  Its furrows on your gentle brow,
In meek and faded loveliness
  'Twill be as dear as it is now.

The glow of Mind, the Spirit's light,
　Which Time or Age can never take,
Will still shine on, undimmed and bright,
　And many a holy rapture wake.

And Mem'ry will recall the hours
　When side by side we sought the grove,
And there in Nature's beauteous bowers,
　Poured forth our vows of mutual love.

While to my bounding heart I held
　All that to that fond heart was dear,
And your unsullied bosom swelled
　With Love, unchecked by doubt or fear.

And thus, while Mem'ry's power shall last,
　Time ne'er can break Love's flowery chain
That links the present with the past,
　And brings youth's pleasures back again.
1827.

SONG.

Oh ! calm be your rest—may the Spirit of Dreams
　In her gayest attire, steal over your brain,
Till the splendor of morning's enlivening beams,
　Awakes you with smiles to bewitch us again.

Oh ! calm be your rest—may each vision that springs,
　Be bright as the hues which o'er Eden were spread,
While Sleep, from his lightest and downiest wings
　Around you his slumber-steep'd poppies shall shed.

Oh ! calm be your rest—while your lids gently close,
  Like the leaves of the Lily when sunlight has flown,
And a flush, like the delicate tint which the Rose
  Wears at eve, o'er your cheek in its stillness is thrown.

Oh ! calm be your rest—may your thoughts steal along
  If in sleep they intrude, like some silvery rill,
Which at night never ceases to murmur its song,
  But wanders 'mid blossoms and flow'rets still.

Oh ! calm be your rest—but while kneeling in prayer,
  When the glow of devotion is kindled most bright,
Let a thought of your lover be lingering there,
  And his name, 'mid your orisons, fondly take flight.

—

THE BIRTH DAY.

Believe me, love, I've kept the day,
  But not with noise or glee—
I've cheer'd my heart, though far away,
  With quiet thoughts of thee.

I have not breathed thy name above
  The wine-cup's sparkling tide—
But oh ! I've dreamt of all the love,
  I've shared when by thy side.

The glowing picture of thy youth,
  In maiden charms attired ;
The vows of tenderness and truth
  Thy modest worth inspired,

The ardent hopes, the anxious fears,
    That mark our wedded lot—
The sweet delights of by-gone years—
    These have not been forgot.

But o'er my head, and on my brain,
    They've crowded thick and fast,
Until I've tasted o'er again,
    Each joy that crowned the past.

Then trust me, love, I've kept the day,
    But not with noisy glee—
I've cheered my heart, though far away,
    With quiet thoughts of thee.

May 12, 1834.

THE WEDDING DAY.

This sunny morn—this sunny morn,
    How fair a dream it brings—
How bright the thoughts, of Mem'ry born,
    It o'er the Spirit flings.

Methinks I still can see thee stand,
    With pure and stainless brow,
Methinks I press your plighted hand,
    And hear your nuptial vow.

While down your cheek the gushing tear,
    By mingled feelings stirred,
Rolled in its pearly brightness there
    At every solemn word

That broke the thousand sinless charms
　　Round childhood's dwelling thrown,
And took you from parental arms
　　To give you to my own.

Methinks your cheek this morn appears
　　To bear its bridal hue,
Your eye the soften'd radiance wears
　　That then it mildly threw.

Methinks the kiss your lip bestows,
　　Thrills through my spirit now
Like that, which, spite the blush that rose,
　　Then crown'd our marriage vow.

And though along Life's varied way
　　We've met some cares the while,
I still can see our Wedding Day
　　Reflected in your smile.

Though e'en the chilly hand of Death
　　Has crush'd one tender flower,
Its memory, like the perfume's breath,
　　But sanctifies this hour.

And still as time this morning brings,
　　May ev'ry year disclose
The depths of those unsullied springs
　　Whence young affection flows.

February 2nd, 1830.

TO ELLEN.

My gentle child—my gentle child,
   I scarcely knew how dear
Thou wert, while in my arms you smiled,
   Or laughed and gambol'd near.

But now, that thou art far away,
   And I am all alone,
I long to join you at your play,
   And catch each tender tone.

To hear you call " Papa !" once more,
   To dance you on my knee,
Or hear your whispered " yes !" breathed o'er,
   The tales I'd tell to thee.

I long around my neck to feel
   Your little hands entwine,
And from your lips sweet kisses steal,
   And pay you back with mine.

But many a vale and mountain wild,
   As here I sadly roam,
Divide me from my gentle child,
   And from my happy home.

A thousand infant forms appear,
   Lit up by laughing eyes,
But still my Ellen is not here,
   And still her father sighs.

I see the happy parent fold
    His darling to his breast ;
But when shall I my babe behold,
    My beautiful and blest?

A LOVE SONG.

My Mary's eyes—my Mary's eyes—
    What would I give, to be where they
Are looking blue as summer skies,
    And shedding joy with ev'ry ray?

And then her little rosy lip,
    That breathes my name with such a grace,
If I could now its nectar sip,
    T'would brighten up this lonely place.

There's music in her roughest tone,
    There's magic in her ev'ry motion.
I'd rather be with her alone,
    Than sailing on this tedious ocean.

Oh! could I fold her to my breast,
    And feel her arms my neck entwine,
I'm sure I'd be so nearly blest
    I would not, for a week, repine.

Perhaps you'll think, so warms my song,
    That I some naughty tricks have taught her—
But Mary is but *two feet long*,
    My smiling, darling, blue eyed, *daughter*.

THE UNSEEN BABE.

God's blessing on the Baby Boy
   Its Father ne'er caress'd.
How much of sadness and alloy
Are blent with every thrill of joy
   That agitates my breast,

While o'er earth's fairest scenes I roam
   And feast my raptured eyes,
As thoughts of thee unbidden come,
To win me to the quiet home
   In which the New Born lies?

What would I give, at this still hour,
   For but a glance at thee?
Hast thou a spell of magic power,
Thou delicate and fragile flower
   That sleeps beyond the sea,

That thus my waking thoughts you share,
   And mingle in my dreams?
For, like a Spirit of the air,
O'er all that's rich, and grand, and rare,
   Some fancied feature beams.

I stood on Snowdon's topmost height,
   And far beneath me lay
A thousand hills in all their might,
Tinged with the sunset's rosy light,
   A fair and proud array ;

But by thy cradle then to kneel,
  And gaze upon thy face ;
Thy little hand in mine to feel,
To make a Father's first appeal—
  Thy answering smile to trace—

Could I have turn'd, such bliss to know,
  To spend one hour with thee,
The splendid scene that lay below,
Loch, vale, and stream, and sunset's glow
  Few charms had had for me.

O'er sweet Killarney's placid breast,
  My bark this moment roves.
And never did my spirit rest
On scene, by Heaven more richly blest,
  With all the wand'rer loves.

But there's a chamber far away,
  A mother's glance of pride—
Familiar forms, that, wondering, pray
That they with " Brother " still may play,
  That haunt me as I glide.

And thus it is, go where I will.
  Where'er my footsteps roam,
A Cherub face is with me still,
Mingling with rapture's wildest thrill,
  And beckoning me home.

1839

TO JANE.

Sister mine, I'm on the sea
   In mid ocean once again,
Amidst the waves I think of thee,
   My ever noble Sister Jane.

Like a matron, myriad breasted,
   Ocean's billows rise and fall,
Roundly swelling, curled and crested,
   Heavenly blue o'er arching all.

Living seems the World of Waters
   Grandly throbbing 'neath the eye.
Waves on Waves, like Neptune's Daughters,
   Dance and frolic 'neath the sky.

Intensely varied the expression,
   Movements rapid as the wind.
Soaring thought and sad depression,
   Flying o'er the gazer's mind.

Mirror'd on the waves of Ocean,
   I my Sister's form can trace,
With reverent love and deep devotion,
   On the Clouds I see her face.

See her as I saw her first,
   Juno's form, and neck, and brow,
Then when Time has done his worst,
   I see her as I know her now.

Ever Queen like,—graceful—good
　Ruling gently all around,
As before my eyes she stood,
　On " the Arm's " enchanted ground.

As she stood beneath the Willow
　In the dear old poplin dress,
As she smoothed my nightly pillow,
　With thoughtful word and kind caress.

As, in white, she went that day
　From the scenes her girlhood knew,
Unconscious of the weary way,
　That Fate with carking cares would strew.

As, in matron pride, she shone
　When Johnny's cherub face was near,
As she mourned when he was gone
　The early lost—to both so dear.

As she looked when Sarah left us
　Ne'er to bless our sight again,
Dearly loved and early 'reft us,
　Doomed to die upon the main.

As she ever, Sister kindest,
　Bravest, best, has been to me,
Ever to my faults the blindest,
　Comes she now upon the sea.

Silver'd o'er the locks of raven
　Black that bound her youthful brow,
Lines of suffering, deeply graven,
　Change the sweet expression now.

But her form, erect as ever,
  And her gracious style and mien,
Time himself shall blight them never,
  She shall live and die a Queen.

Not like her who, sorrow stricken,
  Built her throne her knees beneath,
But howe'er the dark clouds thicken
  Crowned by Heaven with duty's wreath.

Yes! my dearest, thou hast ever
  Duty's pathway bravely trod
Swerving from the precepts never
  Of your Father and your God.

Like the billow's restless motion
  My unquiet life has been,
Grand and stormy as the Ocean
  Bits of blue and sun between.

With the tides of conflict swerving,
  High of heart and stern of will,
Thou, however tried, deserving
  Heaven's serenest pleasures still.

They are coming, Sister mine,
  Not on Earth they come to thee,
Hov'ring, now, thy Spirit fine
  From our midst prepares to flee

To the realm where half our treasures,
  Safely garnered in the sky,
Wait to greet with endless pleasures
  Her whose eyes were rarely dry.

TO SOPHIA.

Lady, the verse which I have promised long
And still delay'd—the Muse would gladly pay,
But, those bright thoughts which are the soul of Song,
Those feelings which inspire the Poet's lay,
With Boyhood's years have long since passed away,
And may not, cannot, be recalled again :
The busy World, and all its strange array
Of cares, hopes, labors, and excitements vain.
Weigh on the heavy heart, and overload the brain.

Else easy were the task, a Poet's dream
Might well be woven round a form like thine,
Well might his spirit, kindled by the beam
Of that dark eye, flash o'er the graceful line,
And all a Lover's hopes and fears entwine
With the bright flowers Imagination rears ;
An humble aim—such, Lady, shall be mine—
Though Friendship's lay more cold than Love's
    appears,
Oh ! may the prayer it breathes cling round thy future
    years.

May thy path onwards through the Vale of Life
Lie through its pleasant scenes where all is fair ;
May that pure spirit that now shuns the strife,
The converse, the contagion, and the glare
Of Fashion and her votaries—to share
The joys that from the heart more freshly spring,
Ne'er fade beneath the with'ring blight of care ;
May Peace, Love, Friendship, each their offerings bring.
And, round thee, gentle girl, their fairest treasures fling.

TO A LADY.

[In answer to a charge of Flattery.]

Oh ! 'tis not Flatt'ry—though I own
    That thus to ramble on with thee
(Save Nature's presence) all alone
    Has many a pleasing charm for me.

To watch the flush that feeling throws
    In roseate tints upon your cheek,
Or catch the unsullied thought that flows
    In every artless word you speak.

To mark the smile those lips impart—
    That bright and airy form to view
Or hold communion with a heart
    To Virtue's holiest impulse true.

Nay, there's a spell of secret power
    Charming each word and look of thine,
That haunts my Mem'ry since the hour
    Your eyes first opened upon mine;

A spell, that all my Spirit's Pride
    (Which fancied coldness once awoke)
With many a struggle strove to hide,
    But, never, for an instant broke.

A spell, which Time nor Absence ne'er
    Could for a single moment sever,
Which to my heart has grown so dear
    'Tis twined around its core for ever.

TO M. J. K.

High of Heart! though some may sneer,
Tread thy path and have no fear—
Bow thy thoughts to Life's dull duties,
Feast thine eye on Nature's beauties,
Brood not o'er thine hours of sadness
Till the soul is stung to madness—
Heavy clouds which hover o'er us
Tell of sunshine yet before us—
Without the Artist's depth of shade
No noble picture e'er was made—
Corn grows but on the furrowed soil
And Virtue springs from care and toil—
Then clear thy brow oh Maiden fair
And tune thy Harp to lighter air.

I, like you, have mourned the Dead,
Scalding tears have o'er them shed ;
Noble stems have fallen round me
Rending ties which strongly bound me
To Life's dear departed hours—
Delicate and fragile flowers,
On my breast, have drooped and paled,
Till their fragrance had exhaled,
And gently to the skies ascended
With Heaven's incense meekly blended.

Bowed, and crushed, and hardly knowing,
While my cup was overflowing,
If my Soul its depths could drain
And wake to Life and Joy again.

I have stood the Dead beside
And my tears of sorrow dried,—
Gazed upon my broken tree,
O'er my flow'ret bent the knee,
Till high Resolve has come like balm
The bruised Spirit's pulse to calm,
And voices whispered from on high
" Thy Native Country cannot die."

These still survive, nor e'er can perish
The feeling which her offspring cherish
For every wild and rocky strand,
Which girds and guards our Native Land.
For every hill-top, forest-crowned,
For every stream which winds around
The Cottage Homes that deck the vale,
For every white adventurous sail
That cheers the blue surrounding sea,
And wafts the children of the free.

Be thine the task, whate'er betide,
To dash the gushing tear aside,
To raise the rich ennobling Song
Such hallowed feelings to prolong—
To turn, from musing on the Dead,
To paint the charms around thee spread—
To let thy gentle Spirit beam
On forest tree, and sparkling stream ;
Till as the Sunbeam woke of old,
Soft music in the Statue cold,
Thy Genius with its touch of fire
Shall patriotic thought inspire,

> To every scene new charms impart,
> And melt in Song the coldest heart.

June, 1845.

———

TO MARY.

Oh ! blame me not, Mary, for gazing at you,
  Nor suppose that my thoughts from the Preacher
    were straying.
Tho' I stole a few glances—believe me 'tis true—
  They were sweet illustrations of what he was saying.

For, when he observed that Perfection was not
  To be found upon Earth—for a moment I bent
A look upon you—and could swear on the spot,
  That perfection in Beauty was not what he meant.

And when, with emotion, the worthy Divine
  On the doctrine of loving our neighbors insisted,
I felt if their forms were as faultless as thine,
  I could love every soul of them while I existed.

And Mary, I'm sure 'twas the fault of those eyes—
  'Twas the lustre of them to the error gave birth—
That, while he spoke of Angels that dwelt in the Skies,
  I was gazing with rapture at one upon Earth.

TO ANN.

It is said in the Scripture, who weds will do well,
  But who does not is certain of bliss ;
Yet believe me, dear Ann, if the truth I must tell,
  You will gain very little by this.

You have spread every lure and left nothing untried,
  A helpmate to gain it is true ;
And although no fond partner reclines by your side,
  Living single's no Virtue in you.

OH ! IT WOULD MORE THAN TRANSPORT BE.

Oh ! it would more than transport be,
  That light and airy form to press
At midnight hour, when none but me
  Were near to own its loveliness.

While all those rapture-giving charms,
  Which well might lead a Saint astray,
Were circled in these trembling arms,
  Or on this beating bosom lay.

To meet that eye's warm, glowing glance,
  To feel that cheek on me recline,
And, to complete the blissful trance,
  Your sweet lips gently press'd to mine.

Oh ! Pleasure should our Idol be,
   And Love would every Joy refine—
Our sighs, breathed short and rapturously,
   The incense offered at her Shrine.

To pass an hour of bliss—of love—
   Of rapture—on that beauteous breast ;
Oh ! nought on Earth and nought above
   Can form so sweet a place for rest.

While Cynthia's mild and soft'ning beam
   Would heighten all our ecstacies ;
For never shone her silver gleam
   On fairer form or brighter eyes.

Oh ! let the Eastern Sages tell
   Of Joys their Paradise contains,
Where Love and Peace together dwell,
   And ever-varying Pleasure reigns.

Where all is fresh—and fair—and lignt,
   While sweetest fragrance fills the air,
And all that's beautiful and bright
   Is delicately mingled there.

To me your eyes are brighter still,
   And what so fragrant as your sighs ?
Let Orientals dream at will,
   Thy breast shall be my Paradise.

LINES WRITTEN IN AN ALBUM.

If, on the page where Beauty's gaze
  A new attraction still discovers
In Friendship's dearly valued praise,
  Or tributes from more ardent Lovers;

A Stranger, dare a thought to trace,
  A hasty stanza rudely wreathe,
Before he leaves thy dwelling place,
  For thee, fair Jane, a prayer he'll breathe.

He will not praise the youthful form
  Where health is blent with fairy lightness,
Nor linger, with a verse too warm,
  Upon that eye's unclouded brightness:

The lip, like some sweet instrument,
  That music gave whene'er 'twas stirred—
The gentle soul, that feeling lent
  To every gay or thoughtful word;

All these to younger Bards belong,
  Whose hearts are fresh, whose hands are free,
The burthen of the Stranger's song,
  Shall only be a prayer for thee.

Oh! may the gracious God above,
  Who reared so sweet a forest flower,
For Age to bless, and Youth to love,
  Protect thee to thy latest hour.

May smiles still deck that speaking face,
  And, if, at times, a tear should start,
Let it leave no unlovely trace
  .To show there's sorrow at the heart.

That Peace and Love your path may strew,
  The World its brightest aspect wear,
And Hope and Joy still smile on you,
  Shall be the Stranger's fervent prayer.

*TO VALENTINE

Not with the general crowd, behind thy bier,
  In mourning weeds, lost Artist, could I tread,
Nor can I now enforce one fruitless tear,
  Though standing by thy moist and narrow Bed.

I would not, if I could, thy Form restore,
  To toils that task'd it far beyond its strain ;
Nor win thy Spirit back, now free to soar,—
  To struggle in the world's harsh strife again.

Unfitted thou the thorny steeps to dare,
  Where Lucre dazzles, and where Fame is won,
Not thine the vaunt that makes the vulgar stare :
  Art's unpretending, artless, genuine son.

Self-taught, without the coarseness which betrays
  The sturdy nurture humble life imparts ;
Self-poised, yet shrinking from the flickering rays,
  Which Fortune flung thee but by fits and starts.

* The Artist who painted his Father's Picture.

Loving the Pencil for its innate power,
  To seize and consecrate what others love—
Pure thoughts, and childlike, were thy richest dower,
  Thou noble man, yet gentle as the Dove.

Poor Valentine ! The easel vacant seems,
  A Rembrandt shadow clouds thy dwelling place,
But, breaking through, a light from Heaven still beams
  To soothe us with the blended tints we trace.

Thou art not lost : like odors breathing round,
  Thy modest virtues still shall grace thy home ;
And praise of thee shall ever sweetly sound
  To those you cherish'd wheresoe'r they roam.

What they have lost, perhaps, I better know
  . That o'er me bends the Father's face and form
You rescued for me, many a year ago,
  Benignly smiling through Life's ev'ry storm.

Would I could trace a likeness that should last,
  For them to gaze upon in after years,
For then the bitterness of Death were past
  And Hope would spring exulting from their tears.

TO —————————— .

[Written for a lady whose only brother was about to sail on a long voyage.]

Farewell ! my Brother, since 'tis so—
  Our hearts must bend to Fate's decree ;
But, when to brighter shores you go,
  And sunnier climes—still think of me.

When tost upon the stormy wave,
  Or when 'neath spreading Palms you roam,
Recall the kiss your Sister gave,
  And let it turn your thoughts to Home.

Where swiftly flew our childhood's hours,
  When side by side we fondly strayed,
And culled Acadia's simple flowers,
  Or, on the greensward, thoughtless played.

Where oft you've lain upon this breast,
  And often I've reposed on thine—
Where oft my lips that cheek have press'd,
  And yours have fondly dwelt on mine.

If I was sad,—my transient grief
  Whate'er its cause—was felt by you,
If you were pained,—'twas some relief,
  To know your Sister shared it too.

Still hand in hand, we roved along,
  Or sat beside our cheerful board,
Together heard the Linnet's song
  Of love, at rosy morning poured.

Together pluck'd the Evergreen,
  And round our brows its foliage wreathed,
Together knelt, when, all unseen,
  Our evening orisons were breathed.

Together marked the billows' foam,
  The southern gales would fling in air.

Nor dreamed I then, that far from Home
  The Wave my Brother's form would bear.

But, since we part, farewell ! farewell !
  Yet ere from my embrace you break,
To tempt the Ocean's fearful swell,
  A Sister's parting blessing take :—

Oh ! may that Eye which beams above,
  Still watch your path upon the Main,
And, to the few you dearly love,
  Light you in Health and Peace again.

FAREWELL.

[A word that must be. *Byron.*]

Farewell to thee Sister, it may be forever,
  These moments of Friendship perhaps are our last,
And our hearts, by the framing of Fortune, may never
  Be blest with one hour like those which have pass'd.

Farewell !—though each feeling of Love and Affection,
  Which Friendship has taught in our bosoms to swell,
And which long have encircled our youthful connexion,
  Should burst at our parting, dear Sister, Farewell.

TO SARAH.

Forgive me, Maiden, if a word of mine,
  One idle word has caused a moment's pain,
And take this hasty, penitential line
  In pledge your friend will ne'er offend again.

Perhaps, the sweet familiar name you wear,
 Prompted a brother's free and careless tone,
Perhaps, presuming on the love you bear
 To one who from my childhood I have known,

I chafed your spirit with a thoughtless jest,
 And made you sad when most I wish'd you gay,
And scarcely felt how much my words express'd,
 Till more was said than e'er I meant to say.

But oh! forgive me—though the time is past,
 When I could worship such a form as thine,
For love like yours set Life upon a cast,
 And all Ambition's dreams and cares resign.

To kiss that polish'd, intellectual brow,
 That speaking eye's mild radiance to behold,
And hear, from lips like thine, the maiden vow,
 To youthful hearts more dear than Ophir's gold.

Though these are not for me, I still revere
 The form of beauty and the soul of grace ;
In such an eye I would not wake a tear,
 Or cast one shadow over such a face.

THE BIRTH-DAY.

My Birth-day is it ? Take a kiss,
 Thou junior of my line ;
The thirteenth ! yes, by George it is ;
 And I am fifty-nine.

Come hither, Boy, and let us dream
  Of birth-days long gone by;
Cloudless and merry many seem,
  And some that make me sigh.

My first was stormy, wind North-west
  The gathering snow-drifts piled;
But cosy was the Mother's breast,
  Where lay the new-born child.

And ever kind and ever true
  That Mother was to me,
As yours has ever been to you,
  And will for ever be.

And thirteen times the day came round,
  Within that happy home;
The " North West Arm's " enchanted ground,
  Ere I began to roam.

'Midst Trees, and Birds, and Summer Flowers,
  Those fleeting years went by;
With sports and books the joyous hours,
  Like lightning seemed to fly.

The Rod, the Gun, the Spear, the Oar,
  I plied by Lake and Sea—
Happy to swim from shore to shore,
  Or rove the Woodlands free.

To skim the Pond in Winter time,
  To pluck the flowers of Spring,
'Twas then I first began to rhyme,
  And verses crude to string.

You see the Picture o'er the fire,
      That smiles upon us now,
The pleasant face we still admire—
      The broad and noble brow

Stamp'd by the Maker's hand with lines,
      That he who runs may read,
The Christian Patriarch, there he shines,
      In thought, in word, in deed.

He was my playmate in those years,
      My Father, friend, and guide,
I shared his smiles, and dried his tears,
      Was ever·at his side.

And oh! my boy, when Death shall come
      And close my eyelids dim,
May you, where'er your footsteps roam,
      Love me as I loved him.

My next ten Birth-days Labor claimed,
      And hard I work'd, my son ;
But still at something higher aimed
      Whene'er my toil was done.

I work'd the Press from morn till night,
      And learn'd the types to set,
And earn'd my bread with young delight,
      As you will earn it yet.

In the dull metal that I moved
      For many a weary hour,
I found the Knowledge that I loved,
      The Life, the Light, the Power.

But something more turned those young days
  Of steady toil to joy—
Something we both may kindly praise,
  Your Mother's smile, my Boy.

And now that I am growing old,
  My Lyre but loosely strung,
For God's best gift my thanks be told,
  I loved while I was young.

For five-and-thirty years that love
  My varied life has cheer'd,
Through all its mazes deftly wove,
  The light by which I steer'd.

Each birth-day brought its glad increase,
  Whatever fortune came ;
In storm or sunshine—war or peace,
  That smile was still the same.

Birth-days there were when both were sad,
  When loved ones went to Heaven ;
On this, thank God, our hearts are glad,
  To Joy let this be given.

And, youngster, when in after years,
  Your son sits on your knee,
Half smiling through the starting tears,
  Then think of '63.

Dec. 13, 1863.

WRITTEN IN A BIBLE.

[Given to Georgina Osmond, daughter of my landlady in Sloane
Street, London, for whom I was persuaded to stand Godfather in
1851.]

When you can read, my Georgie dear,
　This Book I hope you'll prize,
And then, though I should not be here,
You'll learn to love, and duly fear,
　God—Father in the skies.

TO WOMAN.

There is a flower whose never-fading bloom
Cheers man's rough path from childhood to the tomb;
In simple loveliness its fragrance throws
Alike o'er India's sands, and Zembla's snows;
In every valley of Earth's varied breast,
On ev'ry mountain high, and rocky crest,
Fragrant, in spotless purity it springs,
And o'er the heart its softening influence flings.
That flower is Woman—first in Eden's bowers
She lent her smile to cheer Man's lonely hours;
And when Transgression forced him to the wild,
He still forgot his woes when Woman smiled,
And wiped away the unavailing tear
When her soft accents broke upon his ear.
And still she cheers and charms—her soothing voice
Still breathes delight to bid our souls rejoice;
And cares and griefs, like morning vapors, fly
Before the magic of her radiant eye.

Touched by her plastic hand, Life's sharpest stings
Are turned to harmless, if not holy, things.
And where could Man his fevered temples rest,
Or seek repose, if banished from her breast?

How many lingering recollections play
Around the heart, of Childhood's early day,
Like music wafted from a distant shore
Where we once trod, but ne'er can visit more.
How oft in thought we meet that wakeful eye
Which watch'd our slumbers!—hear the heavy sigh
That told an anxious Mother's hopes and fears,
Or feel our cheeks still moisten'd by her tears!
Who that around a Mother's neck has clung
Can e'er forget the thrilling airs she sung,
While on her lap, in sportive mirth reclined,
Her matron locks about his finger twined,
She fondly clasped her dear delighted boy,
Her full heart bounding with a holy joy,
And her raised eye, so eloquently mild,
Asked of her God a blessing for her child?

And oh! how long a Sister's silvery tone
Hangs round the heart with music all its own.
Years may sweep on, her rosy cheek may fade,
In the cold earth her youthful form be laid,
The heart which throbbed against our boyish breast
Be seared and broken—still, like something blest,
Her image, conjur'd up by Memory's spell,
Comes from the tomb, of happier hours to tell,
Of scenes of innocent and early joy,
Unstained by aught of passion's base alloy,

Of looks of love, and words of fondness spoken
Long, long, before that tender heart was broken.

Oh ! lovely Woman, 'tis to thee we owe
Each charm that robs the world of half its woe ;
Thine is the smile that gilds our early days,
Thy accents form our Manhood's noblest praise ;
Thy gentle hand, when Age has stolen our bloom,
Can strew with peace the borders of the tomb.
Who deem thee false, have never felt the power
Of Woman's faith, in Sorrow's darkest hour—
Have never known how steadfastly she clings
E'en round the basest and the worst of things ;
Nor flies, though all beside the world have fled ;
Nor shrinks, though death hangs o'er her by a thread.

WHAT IS A FRIEND?

What is a Friend ?   A being who
    Through all the changes Time may bring,
E'en though our joys may be but few,
    Will still around us fondly cling.

Who on Youth's bright and brilliant morn,
    A dearer charm to pleasure lends ;
Whose smile can sweeten and adorn
    Each gift that Heaven so kindly sends.

Whose approbation onward cheers
    Our souls in Manhood's busy strife,
Through scenes of toil, and woe, and tears,
    Gilding the darkest shades of Life.

Who shares our joys if Fortune smiles,
  And shrinks not should she darkly low'r,
But with a hallowed balm beguiles
  The anguish of each trying hour.

And if we win a wreath from Fame,
  Whose heart with joy and pride will thrill ;
And e'en through guilt, and sin, and shame
  Will shield, excuse, and love us still.

And when by Death we're called away
  From all our joys and sorrows here,
Will often to our Mem'ry pay
  The tribute of a burning tear.

THE PROMISE.

[While rambling through the County of Sydney, I was forced, by heavy rains, to seek shelter in a Log House, with a family who had seen better days, but who, from the pressure of misfortune, had been obliged to settle in the forest. From the old lady, who was at her wheel, I learned the family history. Three of her daughters had married within a few months after the clearing was begun. "While we were all together," said she, "we were company for each other—but when the girls were married, the old man began to lose heart—for he thought the others would go too, and we should be left alone in the wilderness. But Agnes cheered him up, and promised to stay with him three years at least. That time is past—but she has kept her word, though she might, if she chose, have been married long since." There was something to my mind, exceedingly touching in this voluntary surrender of the prospécts and pleasures of youth, for the solace and support of age; and if I have not done justice to the subject, it is certainly not because it is unpoetical.   I had passed the place some years before, about the time when it is probable the promise had been made.   On my second visit, the hopes which I have attributed to the girl had been partially realized, and a few years more will probably place the family in a situation of great comfort and independence.]

Nay, do not droop, my Father, I will stay,
Though all should leave thee midst the black'ning trees ;
I will not go, though better prospects tempt
To homes where less of hardship and of toil   -
Perchance await me.   I will not forsake
The hut, which Age and Fortune's sad decline
Forced thee within the Wilderness to rear.
Then do not droop, my Father—check the sigh
That o'erwrought feelings, woven from former wrecks
And present desolation, vainly prompt.
We may be happy here—and that which seems
A curse, may yet o'erflow with lasting joys.
Trust me it shall—though now our clearing wears
A dreary aspect—though burnt logs and stumps
Deform the scene, and leave but scanty space .
On which the grain its treasures may unfold,
(Our only hope when Summer's past away ;)
Though our Log Hut but poor defence affords
Against the rain, or Winter's searching blast,
(Unlike the ample home of other days,)
Yet never droop, my Father ; we will toil
With steady aim, and meek undaunted hearts,
Until the Wild shall "blossom as the rose,"
And plenty crown our hospitable board.

From morn till eve shall Agnes at your side
Your spirit soothe and every labor share ;
Attentive still, each step, each thought to save,
And chase the shadows from thy anxious brow.
Over the wounds that Poverty inflicts
Upon the noble mind, I'll pour the balm
That from youth's sanguine disposition springs,
And catch each fugitive delight, and bid
It nestle where Despair so lately dwelt.

Though no society, nor books, nor friends,
Here in the Wilderness their pleasures strew,
We'll have no lonely hours—nor ever sigh
For what, by Providence, has been denied.
The sense of mutual cares, and toils, and hopes,
Our hearts shall knit, with an enduring tie
Promiscuous friendships never yet could boast ;
And as we meet beside the Winter fire,
You shall dispense, from out your ample stores,
Instruction to your daughter ; by whose smile
All that you've seen and read, shall be revived.
Thus I shall grow in knowledge, while you learn
In turning o'er the leaves of Mem'ry's tome
To sweeten every bitter thought they yield,
By glad recurrence to the present joy.
Then do not droop, my Father.

THE THREE FLOWERS.

Flowers strew the earth, as stars the sky,
And on them rests the human eye
  With exquisite delight.
Their perfume haunts the air we breathe,
And graceful hands their petals wreathe
  Round fairy forms at night.
The glowing forest's solemn shade,
  The rugged mountain's brow—
Where Man, of Nature half afraid
Allured and charmed, but yet dismayed—
Flora with graceful skill can braid
  As only she knows how.

Around the mansions of the great,
  Festooned with artful care :
Lending their sweetness to the weight
  Of fetid city air.
They tempt the lily heads of those
Whose blush might almost shame the rose ;
They win the wandering outcast's gaze
To rural scenes and brighter days,
  And hang like Spirits every where.
Between the gentle and the vile,
  On human pride, and sin, and care,
  On pampered ease, and gaunt despair,
    With equal grace they smile.

Note. This was simply introductory; the intention being to present three flowers as types of three fair woman.

Of all that ever smiled on me,
　Three Flowers I still retain;
In an old volume lie the three,
　Crushed, faded, scentless, ne'er again
To court or charm the wanton air;
Unconscious why I keep them there
As is the volume, quaint and old,
Whose leaves their pretty wrecks enfold.

Wrinkled and dusty, old and brown,
Three times a year that book comes down
　And rests upon my knee;
And when with moist and thoughtful face,
I rise to put it in its place,
　I feel as sad as you will be,
When I have shook your tears in showers,
By telling what the faded flowers
　So often tell to me.

TO Mrs. NORTON.*

[At Lady Palmerston's Soiree.]

Lady, how eagerly I thread the maze
Of rank and beauty, 'till thy noble form
Stands full before me—'till at last I gaze,
In joy and thankfulness, to find the storm
That shook the fruit profusely, spared the tree;
To realize my dreams of time and thee—

* Mrs. Norton was a Granddaughter of Richard Brinsley Sheridan
and Aunt to the present Earl Dufferin.

To find the eye still bright, the cheek still warm,
The regal outlines swelling, soft and free,
And lit by luminous thoughts, as I would have them be.

Unconscious thou, how, far beyond the wave,
The lowest murmur of thy softest strain
In early life articulate music gave
To thousands, who, when agony and pain
Shook every tremulous string, yet sigh'd again,
That ever sorrow should the notes prolong.
Unconscious thou, that 'midst the light and vain,
The Stranger turns him from the glittering throng,
In Mem'ry's stores to hoard the graceful Child of Song.

How oft, in weariness, we turn away
From what we've sought, from picture, fane, or
    stream ;
But well dost thou the ling'ring glance repay
With full fruition of the fondest dream ;
The light that o'er the billows used to beam,
Lodged in a stately tower.   The minstrel's smile
Is sweeter than her Song—the playful theme
Of early genius, even less versatile
Than are the matron charms that Soul and Sense
    beguile.

The Maple, in our Woods, the frost doth crown
With more resplendent beauty than it wears
In early Spring.   Its sweetness cometh down
But when the Woodman's stroke its bosom tears.
And thus, in spite of all my doubts and fears,
I joy to see thy ripened beauties glow

'Neath sorrow's gentle touch that more endears ;
To feel thy strains will all the sweeter flow
From that deep wound that did not lay thee low.

——

TO FANCY.

Oh! come, fair Fancy, dwell with me,
    Thou airy, lovely child of Heaven !
Let all thy brilliant witchery
    To soothe and cheat my soul be given.

Come from your dwelling in the skies,
    Your ever-varying beauteous home ;
Which the mild rainbow canopies,
    Round which bright wayward Planets roam.

Oh! take my heart, and bind it still
    With thy deluding rapturous spell ;
You know each chord that makes it thrill,
    And you alone can touch them well.

Come let us rove together now,
    Too soon, I fear, we'll have to part,
When sorrow stamps my boyish brow,
    And chills the current at my heart.

——

THE BLUE NOSE.

AIR.—*Bumper of Burgundy.*

Let the Student of Nature in rapture descant
    On the Heavens' cerulean hue ;

13

Let the Lover indulge in poetical rant,
  When the eyes of his Mistress are blue.

But fill high your glasses—fill, fill to the brim,
  I've a different toast to propose :
While such eyes, and such skies, still are beaming for him,
  Here's a health to the jolly Blue Nose.

Let the Frenchman delight in his vine-covered vales,
  Let the Greek toast his old classic ground ;
Here's the land where the bracing Northwester prevails,
  And where jolly Blue Noses abound.

Long—long may it flourish, to all of us dear,
  Loved and honored by hearts that are true ;
But, should ever a foe chance his nose to show here
  He shall find all our Noses true Blue.

FRIENDSHIP'S GARDEN.

'Twas on a lovely summer day
  Folly, Philosophy, and Reason,
To Friendship's Garden took their way,
  Where fruits and flowers were in season.

All that the nicest taste could please,
  All that the eye could fancy fair,
Was hanging on the bending Trees,
  Or sprung in rich profusion there.

Philosophy, with cautious eye,
    Could neither fancy fruit or flower—
In all the last, he thorns would spy,
    And all the first, he fear'd were sour.

And Folly rambled on the while,
    Each gaudy flow'ret heedless choosing;
Plucking each fruit that seem'd to smile,
    Unconscious she her time was losing.

But gentle Reason smiling went
    And chose the flowers that grew retired;
Whose leaves a pleasing perfume lent,
    To heighten what their charms inspired.

When Friendship mark'd them onward straying,
    Her arm round Reason's neck she threw,
And press'd her to her bosom, saying
    My bowers are only meant for you.

TEARS.

Tears glisten in our infant eyes
    When first upon the light they break;
Tears flow, as, ere the spirit flies,
    A last leave of the world we take.

Tears trickle o'er the cheek of age,
    When, looking round for those who shed
Sweet flowers to cheer his pilgrimage,
    He finds them number'd with the dead.

Tears flow, while at the sacred shrine
In Bridal vestments Beauty bows,
And calls on Heaven, with rites divine,
To listen and record her vows.

Tears tremble in the Mother's eyes
While bending o'er her infant sleeping,
His Father's smile she fondly spies,—
This is the luxury of weeping.

Tears start, when at Fate's stern command,
From those we love we're forced to part,
And wander to some distant land
With heavy and repining heart.

And Oh! what tears of joy bedew
The wanderer's eyes when safe returning,
He clasps the loved, the hallow'd few,
And sees his Cottage fire still burning.

And there are tears—yes, bitter tears,
Which, like the torrent, fiercely roll,
Telling of guilt, remorse, and fears,—
The burning lava of the soul.

THE TRAVELLERS.

As gallant Barks, on Ocean's tide
When summer breezes blow,
Oft meet and journey side by side,
Communing as they go ;

But soon, by varying wind and wave,
  Are parted on the Main,
The stormy seas alone to brave,
  And never meet again.

So we, by happy fortune thrown
  On Pleasure's crowded ways,
While brilliant scenes around us shone,
  Have spent some joyous days.

But soon to different havens bound
  A separate course we steer,
And where shall meet, in life's dull round,
  The circle gather'd here?

We may not meet, but yet those hours
  So blest to each and all,
So strew'd with variegated flowers,
  The spirit may recall.

On distant shores, when memory warms
  Till life's unsunn'd decline,
We'll round us bring the friendly forms,
  That parted on the Rhine.

TO THE MOOSE.

[In the Jardin Des Plantes.]

Wild native of the western woods,
  I grieve to see thee here,
Far from the hills, and groves, and floods,
  To both of us so dear.

What evil stroke to bondage gave
 That gaunt but agile frame?
Curse on the mercenary slave,
 That sold thee to this shame.

Wast thou in full career 'o'erthrown,
 Wounded, but not to die,
Or, lured by notes adroitly blown,*
 Didst read the sylvan lie?

Or wast thou caught in tender years,
 And brought from o'er the sea,
To grow, in agony and tears,
 The idler's sport to be?

Poor captive!—would that we had met
 Upon our native hills;
But here—to see thee thus beset,
 My soul with sorrow fills.

The tiger roars within his cage,
 The lion shakes his mane,
And tries the bars with baffled rage,
 Then sinks to sleep again.

In far off scenes, I never scann'd,
 These monsters pant to roam,
But thou art from my own fair land,
 And speak to me of home.

---

* A Common mode of luring the moose is to imitate the call of
his mate by blowing through a trumpet made of birch bark.

We've roamed beneath the same tall trees,
  Plunged in the same bright streams,
Both hear the murmur'd tones of these,
  And see them in our dreams.

Thy thoughts, like mine, are far away,
  By western lake and grove,
Where, free as air, we loved to stray,
  Where now our kindred rove.

I go once more those scenes to tread,
  But, thou a prisoner here,
Must heave the sigh and droop the head,
  And feel the captive's fear.

Be mocked by idlers every hour,
  That dare not, in the wild,
Unarmed, attempt to show their power,
  Or check the forest's child.

Farewell—poor Moose—I would my hand
  Could set the captive free—
But often in our own dear land,
  My thoughts shall turn to thee.

1838.

THE TALBOTS.

[The French were engaged in the siege of Castillon, when Talbot
marched against them. His first approach drove in the Franc
Archers. This success emboldened him to attack the intrenched
camp of the French. Though now eighty years of age, Talbot on

foot led his men of arms to the assault. The fight was bravely
sustained on both sides, until the English General was struck
down by a culverin. His son, Lord Lisle, flung himself on the
body of his parent. "Fly, my son :" said the expiring Talbot, "the
day is lost. It is your first action, and you may without shame
turn your back to the enemy." Lord Lisle, nevertheless, with thirty
nobles of England, was slain before the body of Talbot.— *Crowe's
History of France.*]

"Fly, fly my son," old Talbot said,
  " The day can ne'er be ours ;
" I feel 'tis not for us to spread
  " Our banner o'er yon towers.

" Then fly, you can without a stain,
  "You're but a youthful Knight,
" And yet may live, renown to gain,
  " In many a gallant fight.

" Your Mother sits within our Hall,
  " Your Sister at her knee ;
" And tho' on this rough field I fall,
  " They still can cling to thee.

" For thou canst arm my Yeomen bold,
  " And bid my hearthstone blaze ;
"And Talbot's name and power uphold,
  " In England's happier days.

" I will not fly," the youth replied,
  " No tongue shall ever say
" That while my Father bravely died,
  " I turned and fled away.

" Could all the fame of after years
   Efface so deep a stain ?
" Could piles of dead, and streams of tears,
   "Bring honor back again ?

"Thy dying breath wouʌd curse thy son
   " My Mother's tearless eye
" Could ne'er, in gladness, look upon
   " The Knight who feared to die.

"My Sister's hand would seize the blade
   "Which I had thrown aside,
" And come t'appease thy gallant shade,
   " And die where you had died.

" Then fare thee well, my noble Sire,
   "But ere your eyelids close,
" Mark Talbot's sword and soul of fire
   "Deal vengeance on your foes.

" Our blood in France may mingle here,
   "Our whit'ning bones decay ;
" But English hearts shall aye revere.
   "The mem'ry of this day.

" Then raise my banner proud and high.
   " Strike Knights, and Yeomen true ;
" Let England be our battle cry—
   "Once, more, brave Sire, adieu."

He said—and o'er his Father's form,
   He stood in youthful pride,

And braved the battle's fiercest storm,
  And still the foe defied.

His eye was like a beacon fire—
  His sword the lightnings beam,
That bade the daring foe retire,
  Or die beneath its gleam.

Then backward rolled the power of France,
  A moment kept at bay—
But soon unnumbered hosts advance,
  And join the fatal fray.

Shadow'd by swords—encompass'd round
  By many a levelled spear,
He died within the human mound
  His arm had toiled to rear.

1827.

CORNELIA'S ANSWER.

To the Campanian Lady, who, after making an ostentatious display of her jewels, expressed a wish to see those of the Roman matron.

Oh ! precious are the brilliant things
  That in earth's peaceful bosom lie,
And bright the beams the Diamond flings,
  In radiant lustre on the eye.

Rich are the Ruby's dazzling gleams,
  And pure the Pearl's unfading ray,
And mellow are the golden beams
  That round the costly Topaz play.

There's light in many a sparkling gem,
  And wealth in many a precious stone,
But let them deck the diadem,
  And blaze around the monarch's throne.

Cornelia never casts a thought
  On baubles valueless as these,
Such gems by Monarch ne'er were bought
  As nightly deck Cornelia's knees.

Elastic forms, bright eyes of flame,
  And souls lit up by Nature's fire,
Which point the glowing path to fame
  And still to glory's meed aspire.

Hearts that through battle, toil or death,
  In virtue's cause would nobly stand,
And proudly yield their latest breath
  To guard their own, their native land.

Such are the gems Cornelia owns,
  From such she claims her dearest joys,
For what are all earth's precious stones,
  Compared with these—my Boys—my Boys?

1827.

CINCINNATUS.

The purple robe was o'er him flung—
   They hail'd him Chief in Rome—
But yet a tear unbidden sprung,
   He sigh'd to leave his home.

He look'd to Heaven—it sweetly smiled,
   He look'd to Earth—and there
The flowers of Spring, untrained and wild,
   Shed fragrance on the air;

A stream beside his Cottage stray'd,
   And murmur'd as it went;
The Birds, in varied plumes arrayed,
   Their gentle music lent.

All Nature seem'd at peace,—the breeze;
   That lightly wander'd by,
Scarce shook the foliage of the trees,
   'Twas soft as Beauty's sigh.

" And who would leave a scene like this,
   " To tread the battle field,
" And change life's peaceful hours of bliss,
   " For all that war can yield !

" There's music in the charging note,
   " To Warrior's spirits dear ;
" But sweeter airs at evening float
   " In mingled softness here.

" The shouts of triumph—loud and long,
  " May ring o'er earth and sea :
'· But yet Attilia's evening song
  " Has sweeter charms for me."

'Twas no unmanly childish fear
  That bade his spirit sigh ;
But thoughts like these, which swell'd the tear,
  That dimm'd the Roman's eye.

TO THE MAYFLOWER

Lovely flow'ret, sweetly blooming
  'Neath our drear ungentle sky—
Shrinking, coy, and unassuming
  From the gaze of mortal eye.

On thy bed of moss reposing,
  Fearless of the drifting snow,
Modestly thy charms disclosing,
  Storms but make them brighter glow,

Spring's mild, fragrant, fair attendant,
  Blooming near the greenwood tree,
While the dew-drop, sparkling, pendant,
  Makes thee smile bewitchingly.

Oh! I love to look upon thee,
  Peeping from thy close retreat,
While the sun is shining on thee,
  And thy balmy fragrance greet.

View exotics, proudly growing
  On the shelter'd, mild parterre,
But, if placed where thou art blowing
  Would they bloom and blossom there?

April's breeze would quickly banish
  All the sweets by them display'd,
Soon each boasted charm would vanish,
  Every cherish'd beauty fade.

Scotia's offspring—first and fairest,
  Nurst in snows, by storms caress'd
Oh! how lovely thou appearest
  When in all thy beauty dress'd.

Red and white, so sweetly blending.
  O'er thy fragrance throw a flush
While beneath the dew-drop bending,
  Rivall'd but by beauty's blush.

Welcome little crimson favor
  To our glades and valleys wild
Scotia ask'd, and Flora gave her,
  Precious boon, her fairest child.

TO THE LINNET

Oh! fear me not, sweet little Bird,
  Nor quit the bough for me,
But let your evening song be heard
  Of artless minstrelsy.

Think not I wish to do you harm
　　Or drive you from the spray,
In hopes your song my thoughts may charm
　　I'm listening to your lay.

Oh! sing the saddest, wildest strain
　　You've e'er been taught by grief,
And chaunt it o'er and o'er again
　　'Twill give my soul relief.

If you have watched a Parent dear
　　Whose life was on the wane,
The mournful song pray let me hear,
　　You sang to soothe his pain.

If you have seen his eyelids close
　　Without the power to save,
Warble the lay, 'twill bring repose,
　　You sang beside his grave.

How oft by yonder aged tree,
　　My Father at my side,
I've listen'd many an hour to thee
　　At silent eventide.

For then, the merriest roundelay
　　You sang on summer eve
Was welcome, to a heart so gay
　　It knew no cause to grieve.

E'en yet your simple strain I love
　　Altho' by care oppress'd,

To hear thee warbling as I rove
  Relieves my aching breast.

Then fear me not, sweet little Bird
  Nor quit the bough for me,
But let your evening song be heard
  Of artless minstrelsy.

TO THE FIRE-FLY.

Little Insect, brightly gleaming
  Through the murky shades of night,
Most assiduously beaming
  All around thy transient light.

Still at eve, through air careering,
  Though the scene be e'er so dark,
Yet your little light appearing,
  Shines a gay resplendent spark.

Shine again, thou pretty meteor,
  Though the night be drear and damp,
Lovely, lucid, speck of Nature
  Light again thy little lamp.

Spread again thy airy pinion,
  Let thy ray once more appear,
Come, dame Fortune's favor'd minion,
  Learn a moral lesson here.

Lull'd on luxury's lap supinely,
  What avails your worldly pelf,
Though through life you glide divinely,
  Yet you live but for yourself.

View this little Fly, commencing
  Undisturb'd, his evening flight,
To proud man a ray dispensing—
  Gen'rous Fly—to guide him right.

With the little God has given,
  And to worldly troubles blind
He lights his taper up at even,
  Sparkles, flies, and is resigned.

THE DESERTED NEST.

Deserted nest, that on the leafless tree,
  Waves to and fro with every dreary blast,
With none to shelter, none to care for thee,
  Thy day of pride and cheerfulness is past.

Thy tiny walls are falling to decay,
  Thy cell is tenantless and tuneless now,
The winter winds have rent the leaves away,
  And left thee hanging on the naked bough.

But yet, deserted nest, there is a spell
  E'en in thy loneliness, to touch the heart,
For holy things within thee once did dwell,
  The type of joys departed now thou art.

With what assiduous care thy framers wrought,
  With what delight they viewed the structure rise,
And how, as each some tiny rafter brought,
  Pleasure and hope would sparkle in their eyes.

Ah! who shall tell when all the work was done,
  The rapt'rous pleasure that their labors crown'd,
The blissful moments Nature for them won,
  And bade them celebrate with joyous sound.

A Father's pride—a Mother's anxious care,
  Her flutter'd spirits, and his gentlest tone,
All, all, that wedded hearts so fondly share,
  To thee deserted nest, were surely known.

Then though thy walls be rent, and cold thy cell,
  And thoughtless crowds may hourly pass thee by,
Where love, and truth, and tenderness did dwell,
  There's still attraction for the Poet's eye.

TO A ROSE.

[On an Opera Dancer's Skirt.]

Sweet Rose that each voluptuous whirl
  With deeper blushes dyes,
As soars yon frail but lovely girl
With locks of jet and teeth of pearl,
  Before our wondering eyes.

I wish thy leaves had perished where
  In innocence they bloom'd,

Wasting upon the desert air
Their charming tints and perfume rare,
  Nor to this fate been doom'd.

How oft upon the Rose I've dwelt
  With exquisite delight,
How oft to catch its odor knelt,
But ne'er the mix'd sensations felt,
  It conjures up to-night.

I've seen it nestling in the lace
  The timid Maid had thrown
Above the snowy orbs of grace
Where sin had found no resting place,
  Nor broke the virgin zone.

Above the Bride's unsullied brow
  I've seen it lightly wove,
While solemn word and whisper'd vow,—
The cheerful scene's before me now,—
  Gave latitude to love.

I've seen it scatter'd o'er the tomb
  Where little children lay,
Type of their beauty and their bloom,
Their withering charms and early doom,
  As fair and fleet as they.

Whenever met, the Rose has been
  My cherish'd fav'rite flower ;
The ornament of every scene,
With vermeil tint and foliage green,
  And beauty for its dower.

But, dangling to that gauze-like dress
　　That scarce a limb conceals,
That woos, in very wantonness,
The fetid zephyr's rude caress,
　　And every charm reveals.

It seems to feel the sad disgrace,
　　And blushes deeper red ;
Another round it may not trace,
Its leaves, dishonor'd, o'er the place
　　In parting showers are shed.

1838.

THE WREATH.

Yes, keep the Wreath, and let it be
　　'Twixt you and me a gentle token
Of sunny hours, spent joyously,
　　And merry thoughts, in friendship spoken ;

Of bursting buds, and opening Spring,
　　Of flowers round our footsteps wreathing ;
Of Robin Red Breasts on the wing,
　　And trees balsamic odors breathing.

Of gushing streamlets, winding down
　　The mountain sides as we ascended,
Sparkling their last, before the brown
　　And turbid waters with them blended.

Of starlight night, and homeward ride
Beside the lonely Avon River,
Then keep the Wreath, whate'er betide,
And sometimes think upon the giver.

Falmouth, May 10. 1869.

TO THE TOWN CLOCK.

Thou grave old Time Piece, many a time and oft
I've been your debtor for the time of day;
And every time I cast my eyes aloft,
And swell the debt—I think 'tis time to pay.
Thou, like a sentinel upon a tower,
Hast still announced "the enemy's" retreat,
And now that I have got a leisure hour,
Thy praise, thou old Repeater, I'll repeat.

A very *striking* object, all must own,
For years you've been, and may for years remain,
And though fierce storms around your head have blown,
Your form erect, and clear and mellow tone,
Despite their violence, you still retain.

A "double face," some foolishly believe,
Of gross deception is a certain sign;
But thy *four faces* may their fears relieve,
For who can boast so frank a life as thine.
You ne'er disguised your thoughts for purpose mean,
You ne'er conceal'd your knowledge from the crowd,
Like knaves and asses that I've sometimes seen,
But what you knew with fearlessness avow'd.

Time, with his scythe, could never mow you down,
  Though you could cut him up in fragments small—
Showing his *halves* and *quarters* to the town,
  Old *Quarter* Master General for us all.
Though unambitious, still the highest place
  All ranks and classes cheerfully resign,
And " looking up to thee," feel no disgrace
  If to " look down on them " thou dost incline.
While some the Graces seek,
  And others love the Muse's rosy bowers,—
Thou art content from week to week,
  To revel with the ever fleeting Hours.

How many curious scenes and odd displays
  You've gazed upon, since first you took your stand ;
How many sad, how many brilliant days,
  You've had a *hand* in—Oh ! that you could hand
      Your knowledge down—
Your Log—your Album—all your observations,
  Jokes and remarks, on what you've heard and seen ;
If besides "note of time," your cogitations
  On all the doings that in time have been
      You had recorded,
No book would sell so well
      About the town,
  Nor any author be so well rewarded.

What various feelings, in the human heart,
      Thy tones have stirred ;—
  How hast the Lover curs'd thee, when he heard
Thy voice proclaiming it was time to part.
      With what a start

Of quick delight, about to be set free,
The schoolboy heard you say that it was *three;*
But then, next morning, how he'd sigh and whine
When you as frankly told him it was *nine;*
Oh! cruel Clock! thus carelessly to shout it,
   If e'er you'd play'd
At Ball, or By the Way, on the Parade,
You never would have said one word about it.

To wretch, condemn'd for flagrant crimes to swing,
What horrid anguish would thy clear tones bring,
   Telling his hour!
But, to the pilloried scoundrel, placed on high,
Round whom stale fish and rotten eggs did fly—
   A fearful shower!
Whose dodging shoulders, and averted eye,
Half uttered prayer, or sharp and piercing cry,
  Betray'd his fears;
Who thought "his hour" would surely last all day,
Sweet was thy welcome voice, when it did say
   The storm about his ears
Should cease and die away.

How oft hast thou observ'd the hapless wight,
Who'd toil'd, and raked, and scraped, from morning
    light,
   Till nearly *three;*
And yet had not enough his Note to pay,
   Turn round to thee;
While throbbing brow, and nervous gait did say,
Hold—hold—good Clock, another quarter stay—
 For if I cannot raise, or beg or borrow,

My credit will have died before tomorrow,
For this I do assure you's, my "last day."
The Sun *stood still*, at Joshua's command,
Oh ! be as kind, or I can never *stand;*
Ah ! do—if you of pity have one drop,
If you "go on," by Heaven I'll have "to stop,"

How many dashing blades have gone to pot,
   Who sought on Folly's files the first to be ;
But never one, of all the precious lot,
   Could live, old friend, so long "on tick " as thee.
The cunning fellows, too, thou put'st to shame,
   Who scheme, and plot, and plan from morn till eve ;
Thy "wheels within wheels " always go the same,
   While they, some "screw loose " failing to perceive,
On ev'ry side their wreck'd machinery leave.

     A good example
To all the idle chaps about the town,
     Who trample
On precepts by economists set down,
     You always gave ;
Your "hands " were going night and day ;
From year to year you toil'd away
     Like any slave ;
Your limbs from heavy weights no hour were free
And " Sunday dawned no holiday to thee."
You " the whole figure " went while others faltered,
And howsoe'er times changed, your time ne'er altered.

A TOAST

Here's a health to thee Tom,* a bright bumper we drain
  To the friends that our bosoms hold dear,
As the bottle goes round, and again and again
  We whisper "we wish *he* were here."

Here's a health to thee Tom, may the mists of this earth
  Never shadow the light of that soul
Which so often has lent the mild flashes of mirth
  To illumine the depths of the Bowl.

With a world full of beauty and fun for a theme,
  And a glass of good wine to inspire,
E'en without thee we sometimes are bless'd with a gleam
  That resembles thy spirit's own fire.

Yet still, in our gayest and merriest mood
  Our pleasures are tasteless and dim,
For the thoughts of the past, and of Tom that intrude,
  Make us feel we're but happy with him.

Like the Triumph of old where the *absent one* threw
  A cloud o'er the glorious scene,
Are our feasts, my dear Tom, when we meet without you,
  And think of the nights that have been.

When thy genius, assuming all hues of delight,
  Fled away with the rapturous hours,

* "Tom" was Judge Haliburton, better known as Sam Slick the Clockmaker.

And when wisdom, and wit, to enliven the night,
  Scatter'd freely their fruits and their flowers.

When thy eloquence played round each topic in turn,
  Shedding lustre and life where it fell,
As the sunlight, in which the tall mountain tops burn,
  Paints each bud in the lowliest dell.

When that eye, before which the pale Senate once quailed
  With humor and deviltry shone,
And the voice which the heart of the patriot hailed,
  Had mirth in its every tone.

Then a health to thee, Tom, ev'ry bumper we drain
  But renders thy image more dear,
As the bottle goes round, and again, and again,
  We wish, from our hearts, you were here.

THE FANCY BALL. No. I.

Oh ! were you at the Fancy Ball,
  Or did the pastime see, man—
The stately old Masonic Hall
  Lit up with life and glee, man ?
How lived you through the waltz's whirl,
  Or stood the Polka's tread, man—
Is not some gay, bewitching girl,
  Still dancing in your head, man?

I've just escaped, as well I might,
  I fled the scene uproarious—
As many a stalwart, thirsty wight,

Was fast becoming glorious,
With life I fled—but jupons court,
  Symmetric limbs revealing,
And busts, where Love himself might sport,
  Yet through my brain are stealing.

The music's wild voluptuous swell
  My waking senses scatters,
And my poor heart, by many a Belle,
  Is torn all into tatters.
I've kept the field, with sword in hand,
  When bullets round me hurtled ;
But how the devil could I stand
  Limbs so adroitly kirtled.

Eyes "raining influence," were there,
  And cheeks that shamed the roses ;
With sylph-like forms, surpassing fair,
  Small feet, and powdered noses.
Old maids, well rouged, I might defy,
  Their airs and vain pretences—
From Mrs. R's bewitching eye
  The soul has no defences.

The Quakeress—a thought too old,
  Howe'er the spirit move her—
But Jessica's bright eyes are roll'd
  And all the world must love her.
Of little girls, a score I passed,
  They put me in a flutter,
With budding charms, expanding fast,
  They " smelt of bread and butter. "

A Knight of Malta struts along,
　　And makes the heathen stagger—
I'll back against his weapon strong,
　　That dark eyed maiden's dagger.
Sarmatia's widow, young and fair,
　　Could I her fate control—
I'd revel in those beauties rare,
　　Nor rove from Pole to Pole.

Bluff Harry, every inch a King,
　　A pair of black eyes prizes,
And quits, full oft, the glittering ring,
　　And to the dais rises.
Crush'd by his helmet, staggers round
　　The Trooper young and slender,
And ever looking on the ground,
　　Revolves the young Pretender.

Prince Hal, with sprightly step, goes down,
　　And well sustains his part—
But girls beware, who stole a Crown,
　　Perhaps may steal a heart ;
A Cossack bold, with visage grim,
　　Looks at the dance Shakspearian,
When supper's served—just look at him,
　　He'd pass for a *Hungerian.*

Good Fisherman, with sky-blue shirt,
　　Thy net is wanted here,
To guard each enterprising Flirt
　　From " loose fish " wandering near.

But faith I'm off—my brave Maltese
Before I quit the scene,
  Some scarlet skiffs are on the seas,
Just watch that Algerine.

—

THE FANCY BALL. No. 2.

Joy rules the hour—the Fancy Ball
  Invites us all to pleasure—
Who would not answer to the call,
  And tread one jocund measure.

Ten fathoms deep let Care go down
  Beneath the sparkling tides
Where Strife and Envy sink and drown,
  And Beauty's smile presides.

The lamps are lit, and Music's swell
  Voluptuous fills the Hall,
And, yielding to the magic spell,
  Let's view the Fancy Ball.

Not Xerxe's eye, from Salamis,
  Such countless tribes discerned—
Not Peter's army equall'd this,
  Nor Joseph's coat when turned.

Turks and Albanians, Suliotes, Poles,
  And Indians from the mountain,
They gleam and rush and past us roll,
  Like bubbles in a Fountain.

Who have we here, bold " Robin Hood,"
    Array'd in kirtle green ;
But Cupid has a shaft as good,
    Young ribs to glance between.

John Chinaman, in rich costume,
    To trade comes o'er the sea ;
Heart whole he paces round the room,
    Yet does it to a T.

With stalwart limbs and ample chest,
    Springs forth the Matadore,
No bull he fears, but by my crest,
    He can't abide a bore.

Well dress'd and stately, Charles sustains
    With ease, his kingly part,
His head is safe, but faith he strains
    That blonde too near his heart.

What ho! Sir Miner, pick in hand,
    You're countermined, I fear,
The Safety Lamps of all your band
    Could not protect you here.

Of proud Venetia's noblest son
    Behold the stately mien,
Joy comes, but when the revel's done
    His heart's not in the scene.

The Course is clear—who'll win, who'll win ?
    A Gallop—off they roll—

Good Jockey hold that Filly in—
　　She'll bolt, upon my soul.

See, see, they fly,—round, round, they go,
　　Some lady's lost a garter ;
That girl, who thinks she's caught a beau
　　Has only caught a Tartar.

Sage William Penn must go the pace,
　　That brawny maid will prove him,
Who'll take the odds, he'll win the race
　　For flesh and spirit move him.

Bright Flower Girls, full half a score,
　　Exhibit Fancy's freaks,
We prize above their gather'd store
　　The roses on their cheeks.

With " Jupon court and juste corset,"
　　Yon Regimental daughter,
Whene'er she turns her eyes this way,
　　Dooms all our hearts to slaughter.

Perhaps I might withstand her glance,
　　Her smile I do not dread,
But, whirling in the mazy dance
　　Her foot just turns my head.

Art, o'er that antique Dame has thrown,
　　The air of days gone by,
Yet cannot curb the heaving zone
　　Nor cloud that rolling eye.

Young Demoiselle, from Chizetcook,
 To sell your egg prepare,
I'll buy it spite your merry look,
 If you the yolk (yoke) will share.

The Queen of Sheba—Queen of Love,
 May joy and bliss betide her;
But Charlie boy be on the move,
 There's Solomon beside her.

See gentle Night, our hearts assail,
 So modest, yet so gay,
If shadow'd by her mystic veil
 Who'd ever wish for day?

February, 1850.

TOM'S APOLOGY.

[The son of Judge Haliburton (The Clockmaker) very early
evinced a taste for musical composition, so strong, that he deserted
all the sports of boyhood to sit for hours at the piano. This
decided bias towards a pursuit but little adapted to the circumstances of a new country, occasioned much parental anxiety. The
following verses were written for Tom, on his presenting the
writer with an original air :]

Oh! tempt me not with meaner joys,
 Nor frown, if I decline
The sports so lov'd by other Boys—
 The World of Sound is mine.

I care not for the busy crowd
  Where noisy mirth prevails,
Where peals of laughter, long and loud,
  Swell Pleasure's glittering sails.

The idle jest, the vacant mind,
  Let others freely share,
In Music's spells I still can find
  Delights more rich and rare.

Oh! let me yet each note prolong,
  And treasure every tone
That haunts the magic realms of Song
  And make them all my own.

Just as the birds that Heavenward soar
  The troubled earth above
From brighter regions catch and pour
  The simple strains they love.

ONCE MORE I PUT MY BONNET ON.

Once more I put my bonnet on,
  And tie the ribbons blue,
My showy poplin dress I don,
  That's just as good as new,
And smooth and stately as a swan
  Go sailing to my pew.

Once more, Ah ! me, how oft, how oft,
   Shall I the scene repeat ?
With graceful ease and manner soft
   I sink into my seat,
And round the congregation waft
   The sense of odors sweet.

A finer form, a fairer face
   Ne'er bent before the stole,
With more restraint, no spotless lace
   Did firmer orbs control,
I shine, the Beauty of the place,
   And yet I look all soul.

When to the sinful people round
   My pitying glances rove
The dewy tints of Heaven's profound
   Seem in my eyes to move,
Too sorrowful their hearts to wound,
   And hardly asking love.

And thus for four long years I've sat,
   My gloves without a crease,
For two of them I wore a hat,
   For one a blue pelisse,
When will the wicked know what's what,
   The weary heart have peace ?

My head gear twenty times I've changed,
   Worn Paris flowers in Spring,
Wheat ears in Autumn, re-arranged,
   Tried birds of every wing,

Bade that from Paradise estranged
　Its lustre o'er me fling.

But yet, as "nether millstones" hard
　The hearts of men appear,
Smooth shaved, " or bearded like the pard"
　They're worse from year to year.
My " virtue is its own reward,"
　I'm sitting single here.

The Rector's eyes, a brilliant pair,
　Lit up with love divine,
Beaming with inspiration rare,
　And phrenzy very fine,
Like nestling birds from upper air,
　Would gently droop to mine.

What could I think, as day by day
　His gaze more earnest grew,
Till half the girls began to say
　He neither cared nor knew,
Though all the Church should go astray
　If he could save my pew.

I read divinity by reams,
　The Bible got by heart,
I studied all the Church's "Schemes,"
　Prepared to play my part
Of Rector's wife, as well beseems
　A lady of high Art.

But, let the truth at once be told,
  Religion's cause was nought,
For Twenty Thousand Pounds in gold
  The Rector's heart was bought,
And I was most completely sold,
  The Blackbird was not caught.

The Curate's hair was crisp and brown,
  His color very high ;
His ample chest came sloping down,
  Antinous-like his thigh,
Sin shrank before his gathered frown,
  Peace whispered in his sigh.

So young ! I hoped his steps to guide
  From error's devious way ;
By bad example sorely tried,
  I feared the youth might stray ;
To life's allurements opening wide
  Become an easy prey.

I did my best, I watched and prayed,
  His ardent soul to save,
But by the sinful flesh betrayed,
  What could I do but rave ?
Ten stone of blonde, in lace arrayed
  Walked with him down the nave.

If Gospel truth must now be told
  I've selfish grown of late,
The Banker next though somewhat old,

And limping in his gait,
And quite as yellow as his gold,
   I thought to animate.

I'm sure my Note he would have "done"
   With "two good names" upon it;
I do not think he ever run
   His eye glass o'er my sonnet,
Or counted, in the morning sun
   The feathers in my bonnet.

The widowed Judge I next essayed,
   His orphans kindly viewing,
Read Blackstone nearly through 'tis said,
   All gaudy dress eschewing;
But, am I doomed to die a maid?
   Not yet he comes a wooing.

Once more I'll put my bonnet on
   And tie the ribbons blue;
My showy poplin dress I'll don,
   That's just as good as new,
And smooth and stately as a swan
   Go sailing to my pew.

Merchants and Lawyers, half a score,
   Bow on their hats to pray,
Tho' scattered round, I'm very sure
   They always look my way.
I'll re-appear, encore! encore!
   Who shall I catch to-day?

A NEW MEMBER.

[During a discussion in the House of Assembly a large dog made
good his entrance and walked about the House, apparently
astonished at the singularity of his situation.   The following lines
were suggested by the incident.]

'Why, Rover, by what wily art
　　Did you get entrance here?
By playing well a Patriot's part,
　　And wasting bread and beer ?

By kissing each Elector's wife,
　　And flirting with his sister,
And swearing that, upon your life,
　　Your heart could ne'er resist her ?

Did you shake many a voter's hand,
　　And tell full many a story—
For days upon the hustings stand,
　　And bow to Whig and Tory?

While *rights*, and *liberties*, and *laws*
　　Were always on your tongue,
Enlisting hundreds in your cause,
　　You'd just as soon have hung?

And now you're here, come tell us, pray,
　　Which side you mean to sit—
What part do you intend to play,
　　A Dummy or a Wit ?

Will you seek fame like H. and B.,
　　By making lengthy speeches,

Or range upon the side of D.
   When 'gainst our punch he preaches?

And will you kick, and bark and bite,
   When Road Votes come before ye,
Or put the Council all to flight,
   Whene'er the fit comes o'er ye?

Will you stand up, ten times at least,
   To speak on every question,
And give the House a glorious feast,
   Enough to check digestion?

Or will you sit your sixty days *
   For Five-and-Thirty Guineas,
And ne'er attempt your voice to raise
   Like many other ninnies?

----

*Formerly members of the House of Assembly received 35 guineas for the session, which was supposed to last 60 days,

EPIGRAMS.

[On being told by a Lady that the face was an index to the mind.]

Although you protest it again and again,
　　I still must believe you are jesting,
· For what must thy exquisite volume contain
　　When the Index is so interesting?

———

PATIENCE.

, Tim says that the maid who first kindled a flame
Of desire in his heart was called Patience by name,
But at length Tim discovered this beautiful creature,
Who was patience by name was impatience by nature.

———

THE ROSE AND THE THORN.

Thy vermeil cheeks, Janette, I swear,
　　Deep blushing as the morn,
Like two fair *rose buds* do appear,
　　Thy nose portrays the *thorn*.

TO A LADY.

[Whose eyes were remarkably small.]

Your little eyes, with which, fair maid,
   Strict watch on me you're keeping,
Were never meant to *look*, I'm 'fraid
   They're only fit for *peeping*.

PRECEPT AND EXAMPLE.

Renounce the world, old Cassock cries,
   With vice and folly it abounds ;
But yet, in worldly vanities,
   Cassock spends Twenty Thousand Pounds.

ON A MISER. .

[Who was very ugly.]

" He grinds the faces of the poor,"
   Said Ned with solemn tone.
" Does he ?" said Dick. " I'm very sure
   He'd better grind his own."

ESSAYS.

SHAKSPEARE.

[An Oration delivered before the St. George's Society, Halifax, N. S. April 23, 1864.]

Not quite two thousand years ago, in a small village of Judea, a poor Carpenter's wife was blessed with a son, who grew to manhood beneath his reputed father's roof —who wrote nothing which has been preserved, who died young, and who but for four or five years appeared conspicuously on the stage of public life.

This divine man so lived, for that short space of time, that by the dignity of his person—the grace and fascination of his manner—the purity and simplicity of his life—the splendor of his eloquence—the novelty of his doctrines—the miraculous power which he displayed, he so alarmed the hierarchs and bigots of his day, that they put him to death, to extirpate what they conceived to be a pestilent heresy dangerous to existing institutions.

A few short discourses—one new commandment— some exquisite parables—a few noble bursts of righteous indignation—a fervent prayer here and there—two or three touching lamentations—some simple reproofs— and a few beautiful illustrations of his courtesy to women and children, and of his sympathetic consideration for the wants and weaknesses of his fellow men, are all that remain to us of the Biography and recorded speech of this poor youth.

Yet every Sabbath, all over the Christian world, millions of people assemble to do honor to this person

—to repeat his words—to ponder upon his life, and to endeavour to mould the growing generations by his example. We, in view of the miracles he wrought and of the wisdom of his teaching, acknowledge his divine origin and attributes; but millions, who regard him only as a man, are yet won to daily and weekly recognition of the holiness of his life—the wisdom of his words, and of the self-sacrificing spirit in which he died for the redemption and security of his fellow-men.

How many Emperors, Kings, Conquerors, Tyrants, have lived and died within these two thousand years, for whom no festivals are kept—whose example no man quotes—whose wisdom no man ponders. Their mailed figures, as they appear in history, seem to shake the earth, their pride to flout the skies—their policy to cover the globe. Yet there they lie, the best of them with their marble or bronze hands folded on their stone sarcophagi, looking up to the Heaven they outraged, and challenging from the earth which they devastated but scanty notice or recognition. From all which we gather, shutting divinity out of the question, that the world knows and will ever know its benefactors from its oppressors—that the beauty of holiness outlasts mere earthly splendor—that the still small voice of wisdom will go echoing through the hearts of successive generations, whom the hoarse command of authority cannot stir.

A little more than a century ago, a child was born in the cottage of a poor Scotch peasant in Ayrshire, and but a few years have passed since the Centennial Anniversary of that boy's birth was kept throughout the civilized world. You kept it here. I was not present, but I read the account of your celebration with interest and pride. Throughout the British Empire—all over this continent, wherever the British races mingle and British literature is read, bonfires blazed and cities were illuminated—Balls were given, and Dinners and Suppers were enlivened by the songs of Burns, or by sentiments uttered in his praise. I happened to be in Boston, the city that, next to Halifax and London, for many reasons, I like the best, and where I feel the most at home. Two festivals were held, one at the Revere House by the North British Society, the other at the Parker House, by the leading literati of New England. I was honored by invitations to both, and at both witnessed the enthusiasm of the hour, and the intellectual affluence of the community. The Governor of the State, the Mayor of the City, the leading Merchants and Bankers, the Professors of Cambridge, Whittier and Emerson, Holmes and Hilliard, Fields and Whipple, and a score more of men who give animation to the social, and fire to the public life of the old Bay State, were there ; and we all lifted our voices to honor the memory of that poor Scotch Peasant, and bowed our heads in reverential thankfulness above his literary remains. What we were doing in Boston, you were doing here, and the intellectual and appreciative all over the world were doing in the same spirit on the same occasion.

Now, how did it happen that the noble and the high-born, the Scholar, the Novelist, the Historian, the Statesman, the Poet, all mingling with the joyous acclamations of those wider classes that come more nearly down to his own worldly station, gave point and significance to festivals got up to honor the memory of a poor Ploughman a century after he had passed away? The man was no saint—sharp of speech, and loose of life, at times he had tried the patience of many friends, and made many enemies. He had lived and died in poverty; his errors, whatever they were, being veiled by no drapery of convention, nor refined away by the ordinary accessories of elegant self-indulgence. He left behind him no relatives who could defend his memory—no sect to battle for his opinions—no wealth to purchase venal advocacy—no station or organized influence to disarm independent criticism. How was it then, that all the world, by a simultaneous impulse, moved as one man to do honor, on the same day, to the memory of this poor Scotch Ploughman?

It was because, long after he was dead, and his faults and follies were forgotten, it was discovered (as it had been before by a few keen sighted and appreciative friends who knew and loved him) that in this man's soul there had been genuine inspiration—that he was a patriot—an artist—that by his genius, and independent spirit, he had given dignity to the pursuits by which the mass of mankind live, and quickened our love of nature by exquisite delineation. It was found that hypocrisy stood rebuked in presence of his broad humor—that he had put one lyric invocation into the mouth of a dead warrior that would be worth to his country, in any emergency, an army of ten thousand men—that he had painted one picture of his country's rural life, so touching and so true, that it challenged for her the respect of millions who knew her not; and gave character and refinement to the thoughts of those who knew her best.

What has become of the wrangling race of bloody Chieftains, whose mutual slaughter and mutual perfidy, Tytler so well describes? With the exception of Wallace and Bruce, we would not give the Ayrshire Ploughman for a legion of them. What has become of the drowsy Holy Willies, whose interminable homilies made the Sabbath wearisome, in Burns' time, and the gospel past finding out? They are dozing in the churchyards, as their congregations dozed in the churches ; and no one asks to have them waked up by a festival ; yet the man they denounced, and would have burnt if they could, shows his " Cottar's Saturday night" to the admiring world and puts them all to shame.

Three hundred years ago (1564) William Shakspeare, whose Birth Day we have met to celebrate, was born, of comparatively obscure parentage, at Stratford-upon-Avon, a small English village.· His father John Shakspeare, dealt in wool, and though at one period of his life he had been better off, was, before the Poet's death, so poor as to be exempted from the payment of local assessments. His mother, Mary Arden, was descended from a family some members of which had served the office of Sheriff, and brought to her husband, as dower, 65 acres of land and £6 13 4 in money. Our Poet was the eldest of ten children. Before he was three months old the Plague ravaged his native village, carrying off a seventh part of its population, but seems to have spared his family. He was educated at the Free School of Stratford, till withdrawn to assist his father, whose circumstances were becoming straitened. At eighteen he married Anne Hatheway, and commenced business for himself, but, being arrested with some other youngsters for Deer Stalking in Sir Thomas Lucy's Park, to escape the law he fled, to London, and joined a company of Players. He became an Actor, a Dramatist, a Poet, a Theatrical Manager, won the favor of the Earl of Southampton, and of Queen Elizabeth. He earned a competence, and after the death of the virgin Queen retired to his native village, where he purchased a handsome house and enjoyed an income of £300 a year. He had three children. He died on his birth-day, the 23rd of April, at the early age of 53.

This is nearly all that is known, with certainty, of the marvellous man whose Tri-Centenary we have met to celebrate. The very acute editor of one of the latest and finest collections of his works, thus mourns over the paucity of material for any authentic and enlarged Biography:—"That William Shakspeare was born at Stratford-upon-Avon; that he married, and had three children; that he wrote a certain number of Dramas; that he died before he had attained to old age, and was buried in his native town, are positively the only facts in the personal history of this extraordinary man, of which we are certainly possessed; and if we should be solicitous to fill up this bare and most unsatisfactory outline, we must have recourse to the vague reports of unsubstantial tradition, or to the still more shadowy inferences of lawless and unsatisfactory conjecture."

Whether Shakspeare actually held gentlemen's horses at the door of the Theatre before he became an Actor —how much or how little he knew of Latin or Greek, or of any foreign language ; to what books he was indebted for his plots, his conceits, or his imagery, are questions which we linger not to-day to ask or to answer. Have not these, and other kindred themes of speculation and conjecture, for more than a century furnished employment for ingenious critics and commentators ? We must brush them aside. If we stood by the grave of Richard Cœur de Leon, we should not pause to enquire who taught him tricks of fence, or of what nutriment his muscle had been formed ; and, standing beside the grave of this great Englishman, it is enough for us to know that he lived, and died, and made the universe his heirs.

This man founded no sect, sat on no throne, conducted no government, led no army, upheaved no ancient dominion. How is it, then, that three hundred years after he has been dead and buried, in a Province of which he never heard—which was a wilderness for two hundred years after he was born—how happens it, that in a city not founded for a century and a half after he was in his grave, we are assembled to hold high festival on this man's natal day? How does it occur that the highest in military rank and civic station comes here at the head of all that is distinguished by culture and refinement, to do honor to the memory of Shakspeare? that the Parliament adjourns—that the Courts are closed—that business is suspended—that the place where "merchants most do congregate" is deserted and that all ranks and classes, by a common impulse, have gathered here to do honor to this man's memory? As your procession moved through the streets, the scene was most imposing, and now I can scarcely see your heads for banners consecrated to every branch of our nationality, and to every form of Christian benevolence. Faces as fresh as Rosalind's, and eyes as bright as Juliet's, smile approbation or rain influence on this scene, until the heart dances at the sight of an intellectual community doing homage to Genius by methods the most graceful, and with a unanimity that is marvellous.

On Saturday evening this Hall resounded with the music interspersed through Shakspeare's Plays. Mr. Passow will presently delight us with some readings. We shall plant an Oak on the sunny side of our Provincial Building, in commemoration of this Tri-Centenary celebration, and close the day with the "feast of reason and the flow of soul." To-night we re-assemble here, to enjoy a second time the delightful entertainment which the Officers and Soldiers of the garrison have kindly consented to repeat.

But, after all, what is our poor Festival, rich in sincerity and enthusiasm though it be, compared with what we know will elsewhere make this day memorable. All over the British Islands, all over the British Empire, it will be kept as a holiday, and enlivened with all that intellect of the highest order can contribute, or art the most chastened, yet elaborate, combine.

In the great Metropolis of the World, whose financial pulsations are marked by millions—where war or peace for half the universe, trembles in the hourly vibrations of human thought—where men battle for wealth, and distinctions and worldly power, with an intensity proportioned to the value of the prizes to be won; even there on this day the great heart of the Empire will be stilled for a time, that all the world may witness how profound is the impression which the genius of Shakspeare has made in that Imperial City, where for centuries his Dramas have nightly contributed to the intellectual life of the population.

At Stratford, the Birth Place of the Poet, a Pavilion has been erected which will hold 5,000 people—550 musicians have been engaged; and Concerts, Oratorios, Balls, and Theatrical performances, will gather together, for a week's unmixed enjoyment, an assemblage not more distinguished by wealth and station, than remarkable for intellectual culture and shrewd knowledge of books and men.

But not only in England will this day be kept. In Ireland, where the memories of her Poets, and Dramatists, and Orators are treasured as the richest element of national life, the great Englishman, who was loved and honored by them all, will be this day crowned with the deepest verdure, and hailed by universal acclamation. Scotland will put aside her theology and metaphysics, and the fiery cross, with Shakspeare's name upon it, will be sped from city to city, and from mountain to mountain, rousing the clans to rivalry with all the world. Bonfires will blaze upon Ben Nevis and Ben Venue; and the bones of her great Poets will stir beneath the marble monuments that national gratitude has reared above them, in recognition of the merits **of** this great master of our tongue.

All over the Empire—in the great Provinces of the East—in the Australian Colonies—at the Cape—in the West Indies—in the neighboring Provinces of Canada and New Brunswick no less than in the Summer Isles, where, if Prospero's wand no longer waves, we have Moore's warrant, and our own experience, to assure us that Miranda's fascinations may yet be found ; wherever British communities have been formed, and British civilization has been fostered, will this day be honored, and the memory of this great man be " in their flowing cups freshly remembered."

If our American cousins, North and South, do not keep this Festival as they kept that in honor of Burns, it will not be from want of inclination, or from ignorance of the merits of the great Dramatist whose works they read, appreciate, act, and quote, with an admiration as intense and with a familiarity as ready as our own.   Engaged in these " great wars," which, from their magnitude of proportion, ought "to make ambition virtue," and which another Shakspeare, half a century hence, will be required to illustrate, they may not have leisure for any but military celebrations ; but of this we may be assured, that Shakspeare has gone with the camp furniture of every regiment, into the field, whether North or South of the Potomac ; and that his glorious pages have cheered the bivouac and the hospital, whenever the tedious hours of inaction were to be wiled away, or the " ills that flesh is heir to," and which combats surely bring, have had to be endured.

Nor will these manifestations be confined to the lands which the British races inhabit. All over the continent, where Shakspeare is known as we know Goethe or Voltaire—where his works have been translated and illustrated by men the most discriminating and profound, this day will be honored, and his name, making the circuit of "the great globe itself," will not only awake the "drum beat" which indicates the waving lines of British power and dominion, but the echoes of warm hearts and sympathetic natures in every quarter of the earth.

Shakspeare left behind him, when he died, thirty-seven Dramas, and a few Poems. Upon these his reputation rests; but it is curious to reflect how tardy the world, now so unanimous in its verdict, was in recognizing its benefactor. That Queen Elizabeth, and the brilliant men by whom she was always surrounded, applauded his Plays in the old Globe Theatre which he managed, and enjoyed his Poems in their studious hours, we have authentic record. That the sturdy middle-class of English society for whom his Plays were written, wept and laughed three centuries ago, exactly as we weep and laugh, no man can doubt. That the critics in the pit wondered then, as now, at the fertility of his invention, while the gods in the gallery roared at his inexhaustible humor, are facts which we may assume to lie upon the surface of all safe speculation. But how did it happen, that for more than a century his works appear to have passed from the minds of men, and that his reputation, like the aloe, took a hundred years to bloom? Who can safely answer this question?

For more than two centuries, the European races trod
the soil of Nova Scotia without perceiving the gold that
lay beneath their feet ; the Temple Church was buried
in rubbish for more than a ·century, till its beautiful
proportions, and elegant ornamentation were redeemed
and restored by a tender and loving process, akin to
that by which the Dramatic Works of Shakspeare have
been redeemed and illustrated.

The Poet appears to have taken but little pains to
ingratiate himself with posterity. Though he published
his Poems, which went through several editions, during
his lifetime, but few of his Dramatic Works were
printed, while he lived. The whole were collected and
published by his fellow comedians seven years after his
death.

But in 1623, the year in which they were published,
the world was beginning to be busy·about other things
than stage plays and dead Poets. That great Historical
Drama, in many Acts, of which England was to become
the Theatre, was in course of preparation. James the
First, with his pedantic learning, haughty favorites, and
high prerogative notions, was passing away, amidst a
storm of Parliamentary Eloquence more intensely exciting even than Dramatic Literature. Elliot and Pym,
Hampden and Vane, were unfolding the grievances of
England as Mark Antony bared the wounds of Cæsar
in the forum. The first Act closed with the death of
James two years after the publication of Shakspeare's
Plays, and Charles the First ascended the throne in
1625.

Bye and bye money was wanted for foolish Continental

wars, and the Commons of England were determined that the redress of grievances and supplies should go together. The Star Chamber was busy with arrests and thumbscrews, and Laud was busy dictating to all earnest-minded Englishmen how they should worship God, and what they should believe. The "times are out of joint," and sweet Will Shakspeare must wait awhile for recognition

> " Till the hurly burly's done,
> And the battle's lost and won."

Then Ship Money is demanded and resisted, and Charles comes down to seize the members in the Commons House of Parliament. Then Prynne's ears are cut off in the Pillory, and the leaders of the people are fined and imprisoned ; and now the action of the great Drama becomes intensely exciting—the Counties begin to arm, and Hampden lives in the saddle. The King's Standard is set up, and a rough looking soldierly man, with broad shoulders, a huge head, and some pimples on his face, begins to attract attention, as Washington did long after when a man of action was required. By 1642, nineteen years after Shakspeare's Plays were printed, the Cavaliers and Roundheads are fairly at it. Then come Edgehill, Marston Moor, and Naseby. Hampden and Falkland are dead, Laud and Wentworth executed. People are too busy making history to care much about representations of it, and Shakspeare must sleep on.

The slovenly looking soldier with the broad chest has come to the front, and, at the head of a marvellous regiment of cavalry, has trampled down, on every battle field, everything opposed to him. People may be excused for not thinking of Shakspeare, with such a phenomenon as Cromwell, in living flesh and blood, treading the stage before their eyes.

Then come the capture of the King and his execution—Irish and Scotch wars, Drogheda and Dunbar, more materials for History rapidly accumulating. Then there are pestilent Dutchmen—Von Tromp, De Witt and De Ruyter, in the Channel with 120 ships, prepared to land and burn all the Theatres and other property of the nation; and Shakspeare must be quiet while Monk and Deane, and other gallant Englishmen, sweep this nuisance out of the narrow seas. And swept it was by the besom of destruction, and no brooms have been hoisted in the Channel since.

And bye and bye there is peace at home and abroad, and the Lord Protector, with John Milton for his Secretary, and John Howe for his Chaplain, is standing on the place where the Throne of England stood, known of all men as a redoubtable soldier and a most wary politician. But Oliver, though he loved a grim joke at times, and could snatch off his son Richard's wig at a wedding, or smear Dick Martin's face with ink after signing the Death Warrant, was no favorer of stage plays, and it behoved Will Shakspeare to be quiet until he had made his exit.

England was parcelled out into Districts, and a stern Major General of the true Cromwellian stamp, ruled over each, with orders to pull down the May-poles, close up the Theatres, and set amusing vagabonds in the stocks. "There were no more cakes and ale," and if "ginger" was "hot" in anybody's "mouth" the less he said about it the better.

But England is nothing if she be not "merrie." She had prayed and fought her way to freedom, as she thought, but here were new forms of restraint, and a tyranny more irksome than that from which she had escaped. Better pay Ship Money, and lose an ear once in a while, than have no more village sports and city recreations. The Queen has been in mourning but for two short years, yet John Bull grumbles at the gloom. All places of public amusement have been open, and everybody, outside of the Royal circle, has done just as he pleased; yet something was wanting while the Queen was sad, and a cheerful Sovereign is as necessary to England as a Free Press and a Free Parliament. Cromwell, with all his sagacity, and bewildered in the theological fogs of the period, did not understand this. He died, and "apres mois le deluge." The reaction of cheerfulness came with the Restoration—the Theatres were re-opened and the May-poles went up again. And now, one might fairly assume, that Shakspeare's hour had come. But it did not.

Charles, who had been twelve years an exile, if he had not lost his English cheerfulness, had become a foreigner in all his tastes. The men who had shared his expatriation, had learned to speak and write and think in French and other foreign languages; and foreign literature—dramatic literature especially, which day by day beguiled the tedious hours of banishment,

had become a necessary of life. Foreign tastes came
back with the Court, and were of course cultivated by
the higher classes.

How was it with the great body of the people? The
Wars of the Roses had ceased to interest them. They
had had a Civil War of their own, brought home to their
very doors with stern reality.   What were the fictitious
sorrows of dethroned monarchs, compared with the
real tragedy behind Whitehall? The ravings of Mar-
garet and the lamentations of Constance were forgotten
in presence of Henrietta Maria, with her children in
her hand, taking leave of the Royal Husband she was
to behold no more.   The men who had seen a charge
of the Ironsides were not easily stirred by a flourish of
trumpets on the stage; and those who had seen Hampden, Rupert, Essex, Ireton, and Desborough, in the
saddle, required no poet to show them what the men
and horses were like that broke the French at Agincourt
and Poictiers.   And so sweet Will Shakspeare slept on
through the Restoration as he had done through the
Protectorate, until the Court of England was composed
of men and women who had been bred at home—who
could relish English humor and English sentiment;
and a sturdy middle class had grown up, who had
wondered at Milton and laughed at Hudibras till they
were weary of both; and had begun to long for something less exaggerated, and more germane to the realities
of every day human life.   The Puritan Warriors and
Cavaliers had passed off the scene; and, to the new
generation, who knew them not, both Civil Wars were
alike historical: while the Feudal chivalry of York and

Lancaster, as drawn by Shakspeare, seemed, of the two battalia, the most picturesque.

Another King had been driven out—the people had seized the purse strings—Responsible Government was established—"the liberty of unlicensed Printing" had been secured, and glorious John Dryden, Prior and Ben Johnson, had taught the People of England the flexibility and music of our mother tongue; and Bunyan, Locke, De Foe and Addison, had shown how all-sufficient it was for the expression of arguments the most subtle, and for the highest flights of the most luxuriant imagination.

Then the discovery was made that a dead Englishman, who had been buried a hundred years, had left to his countrymen a literary treasure of inestimable value. What was Cæsar's legacy of seventy-five drachmas to each of the citizens of Rome?—here was a treasure inexhaustible, and capable of sub-division among the British races to the end of time. What were Cæsar's

> "walks,
> His private arbors, and new planted orchards,
> On this side Tiber?"

Here were the gardens of the Hesperides, richer in enchantment than the bowers of Calypso and Armida —orchards, where "apples of gold in pictures of silver" were hung within the reach of all—arbors that a Mussulman warrior would die to inherit, with Imogene and Thasia, Cressida and Titania, Portia and Jessica, Helena, Cordelia, Olivia and Beatrice, flitting through the foliage, with fascinations ever varying, and smiles that could never fade.

With a spirit of deep reverence and unselfish love did the great Poets and Critics of modern England address themselves to the task of exhuming this treasure, and making known to their countrymen its extent and value. Foremost in this good work were Rowe and Theobold, Pope, Warburton and Johnson ; and after them have come critics and commentators by the score, till every obsolete phrase has been explained, every old work translated into current English, every blemish detected, every beauty brought to the surface. In this labor of love, Goethe, and Schlegel and Voltaire, and the finer minds of Continental Europe, have labored with diligence and often with keen discrimination, until the subject has been exhausted, and now no wise man looks for a new fact or for a plausible suggestion.

A brillant series of great actors and actresses have devoted their lives to the study of Shakspeare's Plays, and have won fortune and high distinction by their illustration. Garrick, Mrs. Siddons, the Keans and Kembles, Macready, and many other brilliant Artists, have, for a hundred and fifty years, presented to succeeding generations the master-pieces of this great Dramatist. Yet "custom cannot stale his infinite variety," and still "excess of appetite grows by what it feeds on."

During these hundred and fifty years the genius of Shakspeare has kept possession of the public mind, appealed to by rivals in every walk of literature, and it may be safely said that no book except the Bible, has taken a hold of it so universal and so firm. Tried by every test, read in the light of ancient and modern literature, Shakspeare has not only held his own, but has steadily risen in general estimation.

Within the period which has passed since he lived and wrote, the Classics, redeemed from the wrecks of ancient civilization, have been edited with care and elegantly translated into every modern language. Æschylus and Euripides, Plautus and Terence, can now be read with as much facility as Shakspeare. The great dramatists of France, appealing to a population to whom theatricals and bread are the necessaries of life, have constructed Tragedies of stately severity, and lighter pieces in every vein of humor. Alfieri, in Italy, and Calderon and Lope de Vega, in Spain, have presented their master-pieces to the admiring world. Schiller's great Dramas, beautifully rendered into English by Joanna Bailley, have enriched the literature of Germany; while in our own country Addison, Congreve, Younge, Home, and Otway; Byron, Shelley, Talfourd and Knowles, with all the phases of modern civilization expanding before them, with free access to all the treasures of ancient and modern literature, and with the "moving accidents by flood and field" which history and biography have accumulated in those three hundred years, have done their best; and each has won a place in the loving hearts touched by their genius and refined and elevated by the exquisite harmony of their verse. But which of all these men would we venture to put beside Shakspeare? If they were all assembled here to-day, they would confess their several obligations to the great Poet, who "exhausted worlds and then imagined new," and join with us in crowning him as the great master of their art.

Now what is the secret of this great success—of this universal homage? Who shall give the answer? The ocean with its majestic waves, fathomless depths, and ever receding outlines, who can measure or define? The starry heavens are incomprehensible to the astronomer, who can weigh the planets, as to the peasant who, in simple love and reverence, sees them shine above his head. The incendiary, who destroyed the Temple of Diana, could not comprehend the secret of that universal admiration which made his act a sacrilege and a crime. We stand beside Niagara, or beneath the dome of St. Peter's, or St. Paul's, and are overpowered by a sense of sublimity and beauty, for which we thank God, but which it is extremely difficult to analyze. We hang over a beautiful statute, or gaze at a fine picture, but are lost and bewildered when we come to describe why it touches our feelings, or excites our involuntary admiration.

If the phenomena of nature, the sublimities of architecture, and the miracles of high art, thus impress and confound us, we can readily understand how it is that we stand awe-struck and bewildered in presence of a writer who is at once a creator and an artist ; at whose command " cloud-capped towers and gorgeous palaces '' spring out of the earth—who sets the sublime "artillery of Heaven " to music—who presents to our admiring gaze forms that would defy the chisel of Canova or the pencil of Sir Peter Lely ; who sketches scenery with the warmth of Claude and the dripping softness of Gainsborough ; who reasons like a philosopher, speaks like a statesman, and jests like a King's fool ; who infuses life into the dead bones of History : clothes Warriors and Kings and Prelates with living flesh and blood ; and makes them unfold their policy as though he had been familiar with their counsels, and act and speak as though a Photographer and Reporter had been present all the time. We accept this man as a gift from the all-bountiful Creator, but we cannot comprehend him, or fathom the secret springs of his ascendancy and power.

The reason why Englishmen should love him, as the Scotch do Burns, and the Irish Moore, may not be far to seek. He has won the first place in universal literature for his country, and he has won it, so far as any body can discover, without ever having been out of England. He seems to have been beloved by his cotemporaries, and those who knew him best. Though honored with the favor of his Sovereign and the patronage and friendship of Southampton, he was not spoilt. "I loved the man," said old Ben Johnson who knew him well, "and did honor his memory, on this side of idolatry as much as any. He was indeed honest, of an open and free nature, had an excellent fancy, brave notions and gentle expressions." "Gentle Shakspeare," the "Swan of Avon," "Sweet Will"— these were the endearing names given to him by his cotemporaries, and they have come down to us as the best evidence that can be furnished of the personal qualities he displayed.

That he was a dear lover of his country who can
doubt? With what pride and exultation and entire
confidence he speaks of her fortunes and her future, at
a time when her great career of conquest and of Empire
had hardly begun :

> "This royal throne of kings, this sceptred Isle,
> This earth of majesty, this seat of Mars,
> This other Eden, demi-paradise ;
> This fortress, built by Nature for herself
> Against infection and the hand of war ; '
> This happy breed of men, this little world ;
> This precious stone set in the silver sea,
> Which serves it in the office of a wall,
> Or as a moat defensive to a house,
> Against the envy of less happy lands ;
> This blessed plot, this earth, this realm, this England,
> This nurse, this teeming womb of royal kings,
> Fear'd by their breed and famous by their birth ,
> Renown'd for their deeds as far from home,
> (For Christian service and true chivalry,)
> As is the sepulchre in stubborn Jewry
> Of the world's Ransom, blessed Mary's son,
> This land of such dear souls, this dear dear land,
> Dear for her reputation through the world."

Again, he calls her " our sea-walled garden," which
she has remained, thank God, to this hour. And
again :

> "That water-walled bulwark, still secure
> And confident from foreign purposes.
> This England never did (nor never shall)
> Lie at the proud foot of a conqueror."

Shakspeare had seen the proud Spanish Armada, with
its 130 ships of war, its 2,650 "great guns," and

30,000 men, scattered by the hand of Providence, and by the valor of Drake and Howard ; and he might well exult in the valor of his countrymen and in the impregnability of the "little island" that he loved. Could he see her now, with her 670 war ships, her well disciplined army and her 150,000 volunteers, he would not be less confident in her destiny.

How like the blast of a trumpet has the magnificent speech which Shakspeare puts into the mouth of our Fifth Harry on the eve of the Battle of Agincourt, rung through the hearts of Englishmen in all parts of the world! At Torres Vedras, at Waterloo, at Inkermann, at Lucknow and Delhi, wherever our countrymen have been far from home and hard bestead, Shakspeare's glorious thoughts have been uppermost in their minds.

The time may come, in these British Provinces, when we may be called upon to test the purity of our lineage and "the metal of our pastures ;" and when it comes, let us hope that Shakspeare's invocation may not be lost upon us. Our volunteers and militiamen show well upon parade, in their "gayness" and their "gilt," but when the "working day" comes, and they

> "are all besmirch'd
> With rainy marching in the painful field,'

let us hope that they will emulate the valour of the Mother Isles, without a Westmoreland wish to have "more men from England.

Shakspeare's National Dramas are a valuable addition to the History of our country. An Admiral of some celebrity declared that he read nothing else. I have read nearly all the works of our popular Historians, but how few of them paint the scenes they describe with the vividness of Shakspeare? and where is there one that presents the men of by-gone periods with the same dramatic power? Hundreds of illustrations could be given. Take Hume's account of Buckingham's intrigues to secure the Throne for Richard, with that which the Duke himself gives of the scene at the Guildhall ; or contrast his description of the murder of the young Princes with that in which Shakspeare shows us how

"the murderers,
Albeit they were flesh'd villains, bloody dogs,
Melting with tenderness and mild compassion
Wept like two children, in their death's sad story,
"O thus," quoth Dighton, "lay the gentle babes,"—
"Thus, thus," quoth Forrest, "girdling one another
"Within their alabaster innocent arms :
"Their lips were four red roses on a stalk
"Which in their summer beauty kissed each other.
"A book of prayers on their pillow lay ;
"Which once," quoth Forrest, "almost changed my mind,"
"But, O the devil "—there the villain stopped ;
When Dighton thus told on—"we smothered
"The most replenished, sweet work of nature,
"That, from the prime creation, e'er she framed."
Hence both are gone, with conscience and remorse
They could not speak ; and so I left them both
To bear these tidings to the bloody king."

Here we have the whole scene. This is 'the picture that all Painters copy, and when we visit the Chamber in the Tower, or recall this touching event in English History, it is with Shakspeare's and not Hume's language in our thoughts.

The same may be said of the ten National Dramas,

including seven Reigns, and spreading over a period of three hundred years. The portions of History which Shakspeare has illustrated are invariably those into which we have the clearest insight, and to which we return again and again with interest deepening as we read.

Of Queen Elizabeth we have only the Christening benediction and a fine foreshadowing at the close of Henry the 8th, but what would we not give for a Drama by Shakspeare, in which the two rival Queens, with Cecil and Walsingham, Raleigh and Essex, Bothwell and Rizzio, were sketched with the distinctness of the Yorkists and Lancastrians of an earlier period? And coming down to the later Civil Wars, how hard we find it, without Shakspeare's guidance and portraiture, to gather from all the historians and biographers (and they are numerous enough) the same vivid realistic notions of Cromwell and Monk, of Rupert, Ireton, Waller, Fleetwood, and other Cavaliers and Parliamentarians, that he has given us of Hotspur, Falconbridge, Warwick, or John of Gaunt.

But we are not only indebted to Shakspeare for clearer views of English History, but for some marvellous delineations of stirring events and portraitures of remarkable men in times more remote. Plutarch and Livy are highly dramatic and picturesque, and yet we rise from the perusal of their charming volumes with a dreamy and indistinct impression of the scenes they describe, and of the characters they portray. There is a haze of remote antiquity which we cannot completely penetrate; and the stately language they employ, while it fascinates, often elevates us above the range of practical business, and the point of view from which a clear insight can be had into the affairs of common life.

Shakspeare, in Julius Cæsar and Coriolanus, takes us to Rome, and gives us the very spirit of the scenes that he animates with real bustling human beings. We hear the mob roaring in the streets—the orators speaking in the forum—we almost touch their robes and feel their warm breath upon our faces. The topics are different, but the men are perfectly present to our senses, as an English mob would be shouting in Charing Cross, or Lord Derby or John Bright speaking in Parliament. His Greeks are just as life-like. When an Englishman reads Homer, though he is charmed by the rapidity and variety of movement, and by the exquisite skill of the versification, the celestial machinery is a sad drawback. We should take but little interest in a charge of cavalry at Balaclava, or in a fight between King and Heenan, if Juno were to interpose a cloud, or catch up a pugilist, when the Russians or the American were getting the worst of it. In Troilus and Cressida there are no Gods and Goddesses: but Greeks and Trojans, so life-like and natural, that we hear them rail, and jest, mourn, and make love, as though our own blood relations or familiar friends were conducting the dialogues; and when the combats begin, whether single or general, it is stern, English, hand to hand fighting, by the heady currents of which we are swept along, till we almost bet the odds, and clap our hands with excitement, as the blows are struck or the charges are delivered and sustained. By the aid of Shakspeare I can see the burly form of Ajax, in action or repose as distinctly as I can see Shaw the Life Guardsman. Hector's plume is as much a reality to me as General Doyle's, and Astyanax, introduced by the Bard of Avon, is a genuine English Baby.

But wherever he wafts us it is the same. We revel in the warm air of Cyprus and drink the Greek wine with Cassio—we float down the Nile with Cleopatra—or stand upon the blasted Heath with Macbeth ; and our difficulty is not so much to realize the scene as to get back to full possession of our identity, and to be sure that we are not a part of it.

Of the Dramas which are not simply historical but "of imagination all compact," I have left myself no time to speak. But what could I say if I had the whole afternoon? Volumes have been written about them, and the subject is still fresh and new. " To gild refined gold, to paint the lily or add a perfume to the violet," we have warrant for believing " is wasteful and ridiculous excess." All I will say is, that from boyhood upwards these great masterpieces have been a study and a delight. They have won me from the distraction of State cares when these were most perplexing—they have charmed the evil spirit out of me often when I would have hurled a javelin or launched a sarcasm. Their harmonies have interlaced the wildest discords, and lent a silver edging to the darkest clouds of a somewhat stormy life.

Shakspeare's minor poems would form a charming subject for a separate paper. They are less known than his Dramas, but are not less deserving of constant study by all who desire to comprehend the whole scope of the great Artist's power, or who desire to enjoy the mellifluous sweetness and flexibility of "our land's language."

But it may be asked, of what use are these celebrations? They have many uses. Wherever God, for his own wise purposes, has endowed a human being with great powers, and these have been wisely used, it behoves us reverently to discern and to acknowledge the Divine afflatus. It is becoming and proper also that we should offer up the tribute of grateful hearts to the mighty dead whose works live after them. More people have seen Shakspeare's Dramas acted than now inhabit the British Islands ; and millions, who have perhaps never entered a theatre, have yet read his works with infinite instruction and delight. Is it too much, then, to dedicate one day in three centuries to mutual felicitations for this special gift? The Bird, that hangs by our casement, charms us twenty times a week, by his sweet notes, to involuntary gratitude to the Creator, who smoothed his plumage and made his voice so clear ; and shall we not be thankful for that sweet Songster, whose music has been throughout life a solace and an inspiration? Oh ! yes, ingratitude was the sin by which the Angels fell ; and if, as a people, we would prosper or aspire, let us not be ungrateful.

If it be permitted to the Bard of Avon to look down upon the earth this day, he will see his " sea-walled garden " not only secure from intrusion, but every foot of it embellished with all that wealth can accumulate or art display. But he will see more—he will see her "happy breed of men" covering the seas and planting the universe ; rearing free communities in every quarter of the globe ; creating a literature which every year enriches ; and moulding her institutions to the easy government of countless millions by the light of large experience. He will see more. He will see the three kingdoms, hostile or disjointed at his death, united by mutual interests, and forming together a great centre of power and dominion ; bound in mutual harmony and dependence by networks of iron roads and telegraphic communications, and by lines of floating palaces connecting them with every part of the world.

He will behold, wielding the sceptre of this wide dominion, a Lady to whom his own panegyric on his great Patroness, may, without flattery, be applied—

She shall be

A pattern to all princes living with her,
And all that shall succeed.   Sheba was never
More covetous of wisdom and fair virtue
Than this pure soul shall be.   All princely graces
That mould up such a mighty piece as this is,
With all the virtues that attend the good,
Shall still be doubled on her.   Truth shall nurse her,
She shall be loved and feared ; her own shall bless her ;
Her foes shall be like a field of beaten corn.
And hang their heads with sorrow,   Good grows with her ;
In her days every man shall eat in safety,
Under his own vines, what he plants, and sing
The merry songs of peace to all his neighbors.
God shall be truly known ; and those about her
From her shall read the perfect ways of honor,
And by those claim their greatness, not by blood.

19

He will see no barren virgin on the Throne, but a Queen whose children are to embellish the courts of Europe, and to whose bright succession there is a princely Heir in whom all his mother's graces and his father's virtues are combined.

Seeing all this, and knowing that the races, by whom this Throne is upheld, have lived upon his thoughts, and more than realized his patriotic prophecies, it is fitting also that Shakspeare should know that his intellectual supremacy is acknowledged—that, as civilization widens his fame extends ; and that, committed to the keeping of an enterprising and energetic people, his memory will follow the course of Empire till time shall be no more !

14
A TOAST

Here's a health to thee Tom,* a bright bumper we drain
   To the friends that our bosoms hold dear,
As the bottle goes round, and again and again
   We whisper "we wish *he* were here."

Here's a health to thee Tom, may the mists of this earth
   Never shadow the light of that soul
Which so often has lent the mild flashes of mirth
   To illumine the depths of the Bowl.

With a world full of beauty and fun for a theme,
   And a glass of good wine to inspire,
E'en without thee we sometimes are bless'd with a gleam
   That resembles thy spirit's own fire.

Yet still, in our gayest and merriest mood
   Our pleasures are tasteless and dim,
For the thoughts of the past, and of Tom that intrude,
   Make us feel we're but happy with him.

ELOQUENCE.

[A Lecture delivered before the Literary Society, Halifax N. S.
September, 1845.]

Mr President,—I come, in obedience to the expressed
wish of this Society, to offer my contribution to the
common stock of knowledge.   While others have given
of their great abundance, I, like the widow in Holy Writ,
must claim to have the insignificance of my offering
pardoned, for the cheerfulness and sincerity with which
it is bestowed.

At the early meetings of this Institution, I was an
occasional attendant ; and although of late, pressed by
other avocations, I have been something of a truant, I
have constantly heard of its well-doing, and have never
ceased to feel an interest in its progress.

The design of its formers was I believe to establish
a school of Eloquence, in which young men of the
Industrial Classes might meet, on leisure evenings, to test
each other's powers, and improve each other's minds.
Such objects would seem to be praiseworthy ; and your
experience proves, that to a reasonable extent, they have
been attained.   Truth has often been struck out here
by the collision of opinion—the imagination has spread
its noblest plumage, when fluttered by the breath of
generous emulation ; and the untutored have sometimes
risen to a height of genuine Eloquence, prompted by
innate good taste, and the impetuous feelings of the
heart, often without any strict analysis of the rules by

which the emotions they felt enabled them to act upon the understandings and the feelings of others.

Thus far then your meetings have been productive of pleasure and improvement. But that you may elevate the standard both of recreation and utility, it is necessary that you should ever have before you a clear perception of the true nature of the art you assemble to cultivate ; and have deeply engraven upon your minds a few simple principles which are too apt to be overlooked amidst the jargon of rhetorical speculations. It would seem to be not an inappropriate occupation of your time to call your attention to these at the opening of a new course ; and to endeavor to invite enquiry, rather by the simplicity than the profundity of my illustrations.

But first, it may be necessary to vindicate our claim to deal with such topics as these—to assert our right to study and employ the art which is to become our theme.

There may be some here, there certainly are many elsewhere, who believe that Eloquence is above the sphere of the mass of mankind, who belong to the industrious and productive classes. These in *their* social and political system, they condemn to a life of labor ; and if they call them from it, for a moment, it is but as listeners, to be moved or influenced by the Eloquence of the more favored classes—to wonder at their wisdom and to bow to their commands. The Deity, however, has made no such partial subdivision of his gifts. Man, by the strong hand of power, or the accidental arrangements of society, may divide the earth, but the realms of intellect and knowledge are the undivided property of all. The facts, treasured by the industry of the whole human race, are spread like a repast, before the human family. Individual use or appropriation, increases rather than diminishes the common· stock: the poor man may become rich in knowledge, while the wealthy is poor indeed; he who owns a fertile country may be unable to reckon his income, while the poorest man upon his estate can measure the heavens and calculate the contents of the earth. The sensibilities of the elevated in rank, may be deadened and obtuse, while the peasant's heart may respond to the most delicate and kindly emotions. The inspiration, which cometh from on High, may fail to unlock the icy egotism of a haughty soul (as the sun-burst thaws not the lofty mountain peak) while it wakes the lowly nature to enthusiasm, to eloquence, to song.

Thanks be to God, then, that, in treating of Eloquence—in tracing it to its sources—in employing its powers, to elevate and improve each other, we are not exceeding our privilege, or committing an intellectual trespass.

But, it may be said, if Eloquence be of a nature so catholic and universal, how does it happen that so few orators have appeared in any age or nation. The answer is simple, but yet does not circumscribe our common rights. Eloquence, like Poetry, in its higher moods, is the gift of Heaven, and the gift is too precious to be profusely squandered. There may be few poets and fewer orators in any age or nation, but these few may spring from the industrial classes, and therefore have they a common interest in the discovery of this great gift, and a common right to improve it by assiduous and successful cultivation.

But, assuming that to these classes Eloquence was to be a gift denied, still they would have a deep interest in the study of it—in the correct appreciation of the nature and value of those tests by which its genuine character may be ascertained. Eloquence influences more or less, every moral, economic, and political question, which involves the welfare and security of those who live by labor. By one speech each man's worldly possessions may be swept away—by one speech his country may be involved in irremediable ruin ; and one sermon, showy, declamatory, but unsound, may shatter his nerves, or cloud his reason. Those whose temporal and eternal welfare may be so largely influenced by Eloquence, even though they may never become eloquent themselves, ought to learn to judge of the performances of others by whom they may be safely guided or egregiously misled. The Lo ! here, and the Lo ! there, of oratorical pretence, is sounding continually in the people's ears. There is as much spurious oratory passing current in the world, just now, as there is spurious coin. The ring of true metal almost every ear can detect ; nor would it be much more difficult, even for simple people to judge of genuine Eloquence, were the laws by which they are urged to decide less voluminous and contradictory. But there is no end to the making of laws, nor to the confusion which the manufacture produces. The laws of Rhetoric have increased in proportion to all the others ; until, while rules for making good speeches have been steadily accumulating, the number of good ones made is proportionally on the decrease.

An old friend of mine, alluding to the increase of the Statute Book, which he declared his inability any longer to cope with, observed, laying his hand on his heart, "but I have a little law-maker in here, and I must trust "to him to keep me out of law." I must confess that when sometimes seeking for the sources of true Eloquence and puzzled with the logicians and rhetoricians, and sophists, I have been tempted to close the books, and turning in upon my own thoughts, to seek for some simple standard, by which to form my own taste, and find my own way. Many of you, I doubt not, have done the same ; but there may be others to whom a very simple rule may be of service, if, upon reflection, it is found to be of any value.

If asked then by any youth in this assembly, how he should become an effective, and impressive public speaker, I would answer—

"Speak the truth—and feel it."

I know of no rule better than this—I know of none so good. I think it is fortified by all the best examples, and includes the pith and essence of all that has been written by the best critics.

A practiced speaker may utter what is untrue, and may not feel at all; but the impression he makes will be in proportion to the probability of the facts he assumes, the plausibility of his reasoning, and the apparent earnestness of his manner. So universally is this the case, that the very exceptions may be said to prove the rule, and may embolden any man, however unskilful, who is strong in the truth, and really in earnest, to beat down all the guards, and finally overcome the most cunning rhetorician. The actor, it may be said, declaims what has no foundation in fact, and cannot believe in the reality of what he utters; but, it will be found, that, just in proportion as the scene is true to nature, the sentiments noble and elevated, and the actor is really convulsed by the passion he delineates, will be the depth and overpowering character of the impression made upon the audience. The orator must really feel what the actor feigns, or he must become an actor, and feign so adroitly what he ought to feel as to create the belief that he is indeed in earnest. This will ever be a task of great difficulty and delicacy; the safer course, for plain men dealing with the practical business of life, is—

"To speak the truth—and feel it."

Let it not be supposed that this rule is too simple, and includes too little of labor and research. There may be cases, in which a few words, embodying an important truth, or a noble sentiment, and spoken with dignity and force, may carry a point more surely, and produce a more powerful effect, than the most skilful and elaborate oration. Of this character was the address of Rochejacquelaine to the Vendeans :—

"If I advance, follow me—if I fall, avenge me—if I fly, slay me."

That of Hegetorides, the Tharian citizen, who at the risk of his life proposed the repeal of an impolitic law.

"Fellow Citizens, I am not ignorant of the fate which awaits me; but I am happy to have the power to purchase, by my death, your preservation. I therefore counsel you to make peace with the Athenians."

That of Scævola, to the King of Tuscany, when his hand was burning:

"Learn how little those regard pain who have before their eyes immortal glory."

Volumes of words could not have produced the effect of these short sentences, which any man of ordinary intellectual powers, without study or premeditation, might have uttered. Whence the electrical effects, precipitating masses of half armed Peasants upon the bayonets of disciplined Soldiery, in the one case; and in the others, preserving the lives of the speakers, doomed to apparently certain death? These men spoke the truth, or showed, by their courage and elevation of soul, by the imposing energy and earnestness of their elocution, that they felt what they said—that they were in earnest.

What a noble sentence was that spoken by Nelson, from the masthead of the Victory, when going into action: "England expects every man to do his duty;" and every man did it. Why? Because he knew that Nelson was in earnest; that he felt what he said; that he would lead the way into the thickest of the fight, and lay down his life for his Country. That bit of bunting, then, was truly eloquent, because he who hoisted it was a man to suit the action to the word. But suppose it to have been hoisted by a poltroon—a man of no mark, or likelihood or experience; though none could have objected to the sentiment, very few could have been warmed by its utterance. Its influence was electrical, because every sailor in the fleet saw Nelson standing on the quarter-deck, his eye flashing with patriotic ardor, and his shattered frame ready to enforce the signal with its last pulsation.

You will perceive then, that something more than mere earnestness of manner is required to give effect even to such short sentences as these. To attain their object, there must be something in the life, the position, the achievements, of the party who speaks, to give to his audience a guarantee of earnestness and sincerity. For the absence of these nothing can compensate. So live then my young friends, that when a great truth, a noble and elevated sentiment, rises to your lips, it may find an audience predisposed to feel that it is not out of place.

It is a mistake to suppose that genuine Eloquence is confined to the Pulpit, the Forum, or the floors of Parliament. There are a thousand situations in which a good and a brave man, by a few words well chosen, spoken with earnestness, and deriving weight from personal character, may serve himself, his neighbor, or his country. Treating of the most ordinary of these occasions, Bacon hath well said : " Discretion of speech is more than eloquence ; " and " to speak agreeably to him with whom we deal, is more than to speak in good words or in good order." There is room for the best kinds of oratory in pleading the cause and stating the claims of the humble in the ordinary affairs of life. How often will a word flash truth into the coarse or selfish mind; a look, or a gesture, put aside some petty oppression. And, in these cases, what weight is given to words by a conviction of earnestness, of deep feeling, by the guarantee of an upright and guileless life.

There is room for Eloquence by the fireside, and in the social circle, in soothing the infirmities of age, and in opening the minds and stimulating the ambition of the young. To my eyes there is no more beautiful picture than that of "an old man eloquent," pouring, with all the fervor of affection, the treasures of experience into the minds of children clinging round his knees, in whose transparent features he reads the story of his early love and of his checkered life. Yes, there is perhaps a picture more attractive; it is that of an ingenuous youth, who, as that old man declines to second child-hood, rouses his dormant powers by apt discussion, or new intelligence; and supplies from his teeming stores the oil, without which the flickering lamp of intellect would scarcely shed a ray.

How weightily fall that old man's words, when his children feel that he is in earnest, and that they have the pledge of a well-spent life for the sincerity of his convictions. But who shall paint the smile which lights up that venerable countenance, as the patriarch, straining each rigid sense, recognizes in every tone and gesture, in each elevated sentiment and well selected fact uttered by the boy, indications of intelligence and enthusiasm, which assure him that the fire of his intellect and the manly qualities of his nature, will survive, for the use of his country and the illustration of his name, when his bones are mouldering in the grave.

There may be few, here, who are born to be great orators. I trust there are many who will realize these pictures ; and some, who, if occasion present themselves, will show how truly eloquent men become, who, in a good cause, back their words with heroic self-devotion.

You will expect me to apply my rule to Eloquence in its more extended sense, and I shall endeavor to do so bye and bye ; although I must confess that I love to linger upon the less pretending, domestic, and, if you will, inferior departments of the art. Perhaps it may be that I feel my inability to cope with critics by whom the high road has been beaten, and am more at my ease in the byways. It may be that I would rather have you all good men and true, able " to give a reason for the faith that is in you," and to speak a word in season, without dissimulation and without fear, than have two or three of you distinguished rhetoricians, able to maintain either side of any question, and not much caring which side you take. It may be that I overvalue this essential element of sincerity ; but I cannot bring myself to believe that there is any true Eloquence without it. I would rather listen to Sterne's Starling, mournfully singing, " I can't get out," than read the most pathetic description of unreal misery that rhetorician ever uttered.

I will not go to the length of saying that Lord Nelson was a greater master of Eloquence than Demosthenes, although I might almost prove it, from the rhetoricians themselves, who define oratory to be " the art of persuasion." It was the design of the great Athenian to persuade his countrymen to win battles, not to lose them ; to secure the liberties of Athens against the encroachments of Philip, not to fall, after a few vain struggles, prostrate at his feet. In all the great objects for which he spoke, passing over the temporary excitement which he created, Demosthenes signally failed. It is almost profanation to say, that he was not in earnest in anything, except in the desire to make good speeches, which he did ; but that if he had spoken less, and died on the Macedonian spear, with one terse, vehement, national sentiment on his lips, in all probability the liberties of his country would have flourished half a century longer. Demosthenes filled his mouth with pebbles, declaimed by the sea shore, gesticulated with drawn swords suspended above his shoulders, but threw his shield over his head and fled, when his sincerity, the real depth of his feelings, came to be proven. The Athenians admired the orator, but could not depend on the man ; and probably thought that if they were all slain in defending the liberties of their country there would be nobody left to admire the next oration, in which Demosthenes should undertake to persuade the people to do what he shrunk from doing himself. Lord Nelson would have spoken a single line, but he would not have left Philip a single sail in the Classic seas. With that line spoken in earnest and backed by his own high spirit, he would have accomplished more than Demosthenes with his studied orations.

If then, Campbell is right in saying, that "Eloquence

in its greatest latitude, denotes that art or talent by which a discourse is adapted to its end;" or if the object of oratory be the "production of belief;" or if rhetoric be "the art of persuasion;" in either or all of these cases, Nèlson may, perhaps, be considered the more eloquent of the two. At all events, if I had my choice, I would rather have one practical and sincere man, like Nelson, in Nova Scotia, with his heart on his lips, and his life in his hand, than a dozen Rhetoricians, with mouths full of pebbles, uttering "sound and fury, signifying nothing."

This may be a harsh judgment of Demosthenes, whose speeches are the highest models of rhetorical composition—worthy of all imitation and all praise. He doubtless was a sincere man, to the whole extent that he knew his own nature; but incapable of that heroic self-devotion which he inculcated as a duty upon others, which was the true Eloquence his country required, and without which she could not be saved. To give full effect to the Eloquence, not only the action of the body, but the action of the life must be suited to the word. Elliot, dying in prison, pleaded more eloquently for the liberties of England, than Elliot declaiming in the House of Commons. Chatham, falling in the House of Lords, touched the hearts of his countrymen more keenly than his noblest passage, delivered in the plenitude of his matchless powers. Had Demosthenes rounded his periods with a heroic death, his name would have "fulmined over Greece" with a majesty which even his oratory, almost divine as it was, could never reach.

Take a few more instances of the effect of sincerity, as an essential element of successful oratory. Some of the most beautiful are to be found in Holy Writ.

When Nathan spoke these words to David, there was something exquisitely touching in the picture which he drew ;

" There were two men in one city ; one rich and the other poor."

"The rich man had exceeding many flocks and herds."

" But the poor man had nothing, save one little ewe-lamb, which he had bought and nourished up ; and it grew up together with him and his children ; it did eat of his own meat, and drink of his own cup, and lay in his bosom, and was unto him as a daughter."

"And there came a traveller unto the rich man, and he spared to take of his own flock, and of his own herd, to dress for the wayfaring man that was come unto him ; but took the poor man's lamb, and dressed it for the man that was come to him."

There may be finer things than this in classic oratory and poetry, but I must confess that I know not where to find them. Who can wonder while he beholds in his mind's eye, " the little ewe lamb," lying in " the poor man's bosom," that David was moved to terrible indignation, and said :—

" As the Lord liveth, the man that hath done this thing shall surely die."

All this is beautiful, and natural ; but when the poor Prophet, moved by a sense of duty, and holding his life in his hand, as the gauge of his sincerity and deep conviction turns to the great King, and pointing his finger at him, pronounces these terrible words, "Thou art the man !" the whole scene rises in oratorical sublimity, to the level of any passage, in any language.

Why is this? Because Nathan risks all—dares all, from a sense of moral obligation, because he "speaks the truth, and feels it." Because to him, whatever men most value, the pride of place, the favor of a mighty monarch, nay, life itself, are perilled by the expression of virtuous emotion, and a vindication of the eternal principles of justice.

We have had some dissolute monarchs on the throne of England, and I have searched among the divines for parallel reproof to this, but I have looked in vain ; and therefore it is, that while this short sermon has lived for centuries, and will be read to the end of time, many of their gilt-edged volumes of discourses, perfect in rhetorical proportion but which they did not feel, are mouldering on the shelves.

It may be said that Absalom defeats my theory, for though a dissimulator from the first, "he stole the hearts of the men of Israel." He did, but it was by a consummate imitation of truth, aided by elevated rank, and the most rare intellectual and physical endowments. Absalom was the Alcibiades, the George the Fourth of his day with "fascination in his very bow."

"In all Israel there was none to be found so much praised as Absalom, for his beauty ; from the sole of his foot to the crown of his head there was no blemish in him."

When such a man, the heir apparent, stood in the

King's gate, descanting on the grievances of Israel, shaking hands with the Jews, and regretting that he was not a judge, it is not to be wondered at that he had influence. But this proves, not that he was an orator, but that the people had not the sense to detect the artifices of the showy and plausible rhetorician. Had they applied the true tests to Absalom ; had they asked, —Has not this man slain his brother?—Is he not stirring up sedition against his father ?—Can a monster, so unnatural, be a safe leader, and a good judge ?— Absalom would have exhausted his rhetorical arts in vain.

There is a fine oratorical scene in the Old Testament, where Solomon, having completed the Temple, "stands before the Altar of the Lord in the presence of all Israel, and, spreading forth his hands to Heaven," beneath that gorgeous structure, which had cost him eleven years of toil and anxiety, upon which thirty thousand men had labored ; which had exhausted the forests of Lebanon and the gold of O'phir, puts up that memorable prayer, filled with devotion to his Maker, and solemn admonition to his people. Here, again, it is his sincerity, the utter negation of self, which is most to be admired, and gives the highest charm to the performance. Though he has just reared a noble pile, the wonder of his age and nation, and was about to sacrifice two and twenty thousand oxen, and one hundred and twenty thousand sheep to distinguish its dedication, not a vainglorious word escapes him. He even attributes the original design to his parent ; and when invoking the presence and the benediction of his Heavenly

Father, and contrasting the eternal temples, not made with hands, with his highest architectural conception, he checks himself and exclaims :—

" But will God indeed dwell on the earth?   Behold the heaven, and heaven of heavens cannot contain thee ; how much less this house that I have builded?"

There are few things finer than that burst of Job's, whose sincerity we cannot doubt, where, after portraying the abject misery of his present condition, he turns, with the eye of faith, to the promises of a Saviour :—

" Know now that God hath overthrown me and hath compassed me with his net."

" He hath also kindled his wrath against me, and he counteth me unto him as one of his enemies."

" He hath put my brethren far from me, and my familiar friends have forgotten me."

" They that dwell in mine house, and my maids, count me as a stranger : I am an alien in their sight."

" I called my servant, and he gave me no answer ; I entreated him with my mouth."·

" My breath is strange to my wife, though I entreated for the children's sake of mine own body."

" Yea, young children despised me ; I arose, and they spake against me."

" All my inward friends abhorred me ; and they whom I loved are turned against me."

What a picture of utter loathsomeness and personal desolation is here.   How strangely it contrasts with Nathan's sketch of the poor man, surrounded by all the kindly charities of life, with the pet lamb lying in his bosom.

Yet, when Job rouses himself, and peering through the darkness of his present condition, beholds the brightness of the Saviour's glory, there is an oratorical elevation in his hope, which casts even Nathan's indignation into the shade. We no longer see a broken-hearted old man, covered with sores, but behold a Prophet of the Lord, glowing with holy inspiration :—

" Oh, that my words were now written ! Oh, that they were printed in a book ! "

" That they were graven with an iron pen and lead in the rock forever."

" For I know that my Redeemer liveth, and that he shall stand at the latter day upon the earth."

" And though, after my skin, worms destroy this body, yet in my flesh shall I see God."

But, it may be said, what have these passages to do with oratory? Much ; the painting in both is admirable, and the rhetorical bursts taken in connection with the positions of the speakers, are magnificent. Besides : it may be as well to show that the sermons of those who boldly reprove great men live longer than the fulsome adulation of the sycophant ; and that there is no situation, however loathsome or abject, to which a human being may be reduced, to which strong inspiration and elevated sentiment may not lend dignity and grace.

In reading the New Testament, how often we are struck with fine oratorical passages and imposing positions. How often is the interest deepened, if not wholly created, by a conviction of perfect earnestness in the speakers. The Apostles were no mere teachers of rhetoric, visiting different cities, to display their skill in reasoning upon indifferent topics with equal ability and ease. They were men dealing with the highest interests of humanity—who " spoke the truth, and felt it." There is no mannerism, no mere tinsel ornament, no shrinking, no fear. Whether surrounded by the infuriated Jews, or the wondering Gentiles—in the synagogues, on the hill side, or before the judgment seat of Kings, we find them self-possessed and eloquent. It may be said they were inspired—I grant it: but I hold that a firm conviction of the importance of great truths, ever has brought, and ever will bring, sufficient inspiration to make men eloquent in their promulgation and defence. I say a firm conviction, because men may accept truth, without feeling its value very intensely, and such will ever lack the inspiration to proclaim it—to suffer —to die for it. Such may be cold rhetoricians and elegant mannerists, but they will never be eloquent, or produce any enduring or permanent impression.

Let us test the correctness of this observation by reference to some of the successors of the Apostles, who were no otherwise inspired. Show me a successful preacher of the Gospel, who has produced any remarkable effect in the religious world, and I will show you a man thoroughly in earnest. Take St. Patrick for an example, and you will find that he was not only eloquent, but that his oratory gushed out from a heart, filled to overflowing with fervent piety, in which reverence for the Most High was blent with an enlarged philanthropy ; so that every word he uttered was enforced by purity of life, and nobleness of soul. Think you, if he had been a mere rhetorician—apt at scholastic disputation, but

living, like many a modern prelate, in luxury and profusion, on princely revenues, drawn from the sweat of
poor men's brows, that he would have converted a
kingdom to Christ? No: hundreds who may have
believed the truth, but did not feel it, have tried that
experiment, and what is the result? That the people
have left the trained rhetoricians, with their senior
wrangler's diplomas in their pockets, and have gone to
hear genuine Eloquence, from the poor self-denying
priest, or dissenting clergyman, over the way.

What was the secret of John Knox's success in Scotland? Again the answer is,—he was in earnest: so
much in earnest, that even the first principles of
rhetorical science were constantly violated by the coarseness and intemperance of his manner. To him the
delicate proprieties of life, the artificial divisions of
society, the triumphs of architecture, "thrones, principalities and powers" were as nothing, when they
appeared to dam up, or discolor the waters of life. It
was in vain that the clang of murderous weapons broke
upon his ear—that glaived hands menaced, and noble
brows were bent. "Wist ye not that I must be about
my Father's business," was the prevailing sentiment of
the enthusiast, as he turned from or defied such vanities
as these. The smile of that royal beauty—so winning
and resistless, which, faintly reflected by the pencil,
we love at this very hour, fell on the torrent of Knox's
eloquence, as the sunbeam falls upon Niagara ; revealing
it may be, its depth and volume, but powerless to change
its current, or quell the deafening thunder of its roar.

The Scottish hills were filled with orators of this

class during the persecutions; whose spirit and whose principles survive them, and whose memories will probably haunt the heather while it grows. These were no subtle schoolmen, trained to artistic disputation —they were men who had "embraced the truth, and felt it;" who preached upon the hillside where they were prepared to die; who poured forth the truths they felt with beautiful simplicity, with the bay of the slot hound, and the tramp of dragoons, sounding in their ears. These men were listened to, believed, and loved, because they were in earnest; and many became orators, as the dumb son of Crœsus learned to speak, from the strength of the domestic affections, and the perils of the hour. So it ever will be. Eloquence must gush out of the warm heart. We drink the water that is trained through leaden pipes; but when a country is to be irrigated, or overflowed, the supply must come from the heavens, or well from the fathomless fountains which no human eye can trace.

How was it that John Wesley created, not a mere contemptible schism, but a great moral revolution in the Protestant Church? That he founded a new order of Christian ministers, and sent them, not only all over the civilized, but into the remotest corners of the heathen world? How is it that his hymns were sung this week by millions of people called by his name, in thousands of churches that were not in existence when he was born? How is it that an organized church government, perfect in all its parts, radiating from a common centre, and including members of every clime and country, bids fair to perpetuate his system and immortalize his name ? You may tell me because he was a great scholar, and a great orator, but I tell you it is because JohnWesley was in earnest ; because he felt the truths he preached ; because he strictly conformed to the requirements of the system he promulgated ; because in the whole tenor of his life, he suited the action to the word.

To him it could never be said :—

> " But, good, my brother,
> Do not, as some ungracious pastors do,
> Show me the steep and thorny way to Heaven,
> Whilst like a puff'd and reckless libertine,
> Himself the primrose paths of dalliance treads,
> And recks not his own rede."

Take another instance. The captivity of the Holy Sepulchre, and the cruelties practised by the Saracens upon Christian pilgrims, were truths known to all Europe in 1092. Peter the Hermit was not the only man who knew them, but he was perhaps the only man who felt them deeply ; who made them the subject of his daily thought, and nightly meditations ; who, not only comprehended the whole scope and nature of the grievances, but had the courage, and energy, and self-devotion, to grapple with it. With such a theme, little more was required to make him truly eloquent ; and, by the united testimony of cotemporaries, truly eloquent he was. The man was in earnest ; he felt the truths he uttered. His very earnestness and enthusiasm supplied all deficiencies. He was the true fiery cross ;

and, as he passed from city to city, and country to country, the souls of men kindled, until Europe was in a flame. The Peasant beat his ploughshare into a weapon ; the Baron ceased from rapine and violence, to assume the symbols of Salvation ; and Monarchs left their Kingdoms to the government of Heaven, while they crossed the seas, to purchase eternal life by the thrust of lance and stroke of sword. Peter was no cold and formal rhetorician, but a man of action and desperate courage ; ready to lead the way he pointed, to do what he advised should be done. His very defects, as a warrior and leader, arose from the excess of those qualities which made his oratory so over-whelming ; a disregard of difficulties, in his reverence for his cause, and his firm reliance upon the direct interposition of Providence. If his sermons have not been preserved, history records, on many a sad and many a brilliant page, the singular effects they pro-duced. Fleets were constructed, and armies marshalled, as if by magic ; the best blood of Europe was poured out like rain upon the sands of Palestine ; the enthusiasm of the Moslem was met by enthusiasm higher than his own ; a new road to Heaven was opened, by which "strong･men armed" might enter. Thrones were shaken, and Principalities founded ; and out of this military chaos, with its worldly policy blent with religious excitement, came more extended know-ledge, and the nascent principles of freedom and civilization. We turn back to trace the origin of these mighty movements, and we find a poor monk, with a coarse frock over his shoulders and a rope around his waist, but with his whole frame convulsed with the reality of his emotions, and his whole soul speaking, with what Shakspeare calls—

"The heavenly rhetoric of the eye."

I doubt if Wolsey was ever so truly eloquent as after his fall; when on that journey to York, which was to be his last but one, he preached to the people, and blessed the little children who flocked around him. While struggling up the steep ascent of worldly great-ness, he had been—

> "Exceeding wise, fair spoken, and persuading.
> I' the presence
> He would say untruths, and be ever double
> Both in his words and meaning."

Genuine Eloquence wants no such aids, and eschews such practices. But when he fell, when he had exclaimed,-

> "Vain pomp and glory of the world, I hate ye.
> I feel my heart new opened;"

he rose in eloquence as rapidly as he declined in power, and he who was deemed no longer suitable for an earthly minister became a true minister of Heaven. Then it was that he gave such lessons as these :—

> "Love thyself last; cherish those hearts that hate thee;
> Corruption wins not more than honesty.
> Still in thy right hand carry gentle peace,
> To silence envious tongues. Be just and fear not,

Let all the ends thou aim'st at, be thy Country's,
Thy God's—and Truth's."

Then it was, that, as the courtiers fled his presence,
the people gathered round him ; to hear those precious
words of wisdom in which there were no double
meanings ; to be moved by Eloquence, bursting from
an overcharged heart, and pregnant with the realities
of vast experience, and moving vicissitudes of fortune.

Thus far I have drawn my illustrations from the
Sacred Volume, and from the lives of those who have
been its distinguished expounders.   I have done so
without reference to the sub-divisions of the Christian
family ; thank God, there is nothing sectarian in
oratory.   The fountain from which true Eloquence
flows, is not part of the Church property of any
denomination.   One spire after another may attract the
lightning, or be shaken by the thunder, but the home
of both is in the cloud which floats above them all ; so
is it with that Divine afflatus, that kindling inspiration,
which descends at times for the purification of all
sects, but which no sectarian can confine in the hollow
of his hand.

If it should not seem out of place, nor savor of
irreverence, I would pause for a moment to consider
the Great Founder of the Christian Family, in the
purely oratorical phases of his earthly story.   Veiling
our eyes for a moment to his Divine perfections, to his
astounding miracles, let us regard him as a man,
reasoning with men, and influencing them, through the
senses, by the power of language.   I must confess that

judging from the scanty memorials that remain to us, I have ever regarded Christ as the Prince of orators; and, reflecting on the limited amount of these, when I have heard persons mourning over the loss of classic treasures, coveting a book of Livy, or a speech of Bolingbroke, I have involuntarily sighed for the lost biography and oratory of our Saviour.

What we have is all-sufficient to enable us to judge of the rest. Like the fragments of a noble statue, the lines of beauty we can trace determine the exquisite character of the whole. But one saying of Jesus is recorded until his baptism by John. Yet we are told by Luke, that—

"The Child grew, and waxed strong in the Spirit, filled with wisdom, and the grace of God was upon him."

How often, among his youthful companions, and in the domestic circle, must that strong spirit have flashed out, and that knowledge have overflowed! Yet the apples of wisdom, borne by the green tree, are forbidden fruit to us. None have been preserved. What they were like, however, we may gather from that most touching incident of His early life, when, about twelve years old, Joseph and Mary lost Him, and turning back to Jerusalem, "found Him in the Temple sitting in the midst of the Doctors both hearing them, and asking them questions. And all that heard Him were astonished at His understanding and answers." What a scene; what a discussion must that have been, where the Jewish Doctors were confounded by a child of twelve years old! From this period till He was thirty, all His eloquence is lost to us ; though it is recorded, that He "increased in wisdom and stature, and in favor with God and man."

The power of His eloquence may be judged by the fact, that, after the Temptation, while we behold him in his mere human and intellectual character—"there went out a fame of Him through all the region round about Galilee, and He taught in their synagogues, being glorified of all." Talk of the lost treasures of literature, I would give the whole, and a cartload of sermons into the bargain, for but one of these discourses to the Galileans. The burden of but one is preserved by Mark ; and when I have sought to call up before my mind's eye the figure of a perfect orator, I have imagined Christ with the Divine inspiration shining through those noble features, and animating that graceful form to which the highest skill of the artist can do but feeble justice, and an awe-struck auditory clustering round, as those fearful words, uttered as He only could pronounce them, sounded in their ears :

"The Kingdom of God is at hand. Repent ye, and believe the Gospel."

His subsequent discourses, which have been preserved, to say nothing of their Divine wisdom and inspiration, and regarding them in their rhetorical character, are masterly specimens of oratory: the purest morals being adorned with the highest imagination, without one violation of good taste, or one superfluous word. Though we might dwell on this theme for hours, and illustrate it by the whole New Testament, I shall content myself with two extracts.

The first is the opening passage from the Sermon on the Mount :—

" Blessed are the poor in spirit: for their's is the kingdom of Heaven."

" Blessed are they that mourn : for they shall be comforted."

" Blessed are the meek, for they shall inherit the earth."

"Blessed are they who hunger and thirst after righteousness : for they shall be filled."

" Blessed are the merciful : for they shall obtain mercy."

"Blessed are the pure in heart : for they shall see God."

" Blessed are the peacemakers : for they shall be called the children of God."

" Blessed are they which are persecuted for righteousness' sake : for their's is the Kingdom of Heaven."

We, who have had this message of mercy sounding in our ears from childhood, till constant familiarity has partially deadened our perception of its spirit, condensation, energy, and beauty, can form no idea of the feelings which it was calculated to excite in the poor and unlettered auditory, whose country was groaning under a foreign yoke ; whose city was torn by factions ; and whose minds were perplexed by the rhetorical flourishes of the teachers of rival sects, who were equally blind guides to the people ; and who only agreed in making them toil, that those who perplexed their understandings, might sit in the uppermost seats at feasts, and revel in the odor of a sanctity that was assumed.

When, turning upon these blind guides, how fearful is that burst of oratory, in which they are denounced! Cicero's, " How long, O Catiline," sinks into insignificance before it :—

" Woe unto you, Scribes and Pharisees, hypocrites! for ye shut up the Kingdom of Heaven against men : for ye neither go in yourselves, neither suffer ye them that are entering, to go in.

" Woe unto you, Scribes and Pharisees, hypocrites! for ye devour widow's houses, aud for a pretence make long prayers; therefore ye shall receive the greater damnation.

" Woe unto you, Scribes and Pharisees, hypocrites! for ye compass sea and land to make one proselyte; and when he is made, ye make him twofold more the child of hell than yourselves.

" Woe unto you, Scribes and Pharisees, hypocrites! for ye pay tithes of mint, and anise, and cummin, and have omitted the weightier matters of the law, judgment, mercy, and faith.

" Woe unto you, Scribes and Pharisees, hypocrites! for ye are like unto whited sepulchres, which indeed appear beautiful outward, but are within full of dead men's bones and all uncleanness."

In the whole range of human invective, where shall we find such terrible oratory as this? And when thundered, for the first time, in the ears of men swollen with pride and self importance, strong in their mere worldly wisdom, and mistaking their ceremonial observances for genuine piety, the scene must have been one to which our feeble imaginations can never do justice.

In passing from the oratory of the Saviour, I need hardly remind you that his example confirms, rather than weakens, the maxim with which I set out. Who can doubt that he was ever in earnest? That he spoke the truth, we know ; that he felt it, a Christian audience will not readily disbelieve.

Two questions will probably arise in many minds :— But WHAT IS TRUTH? and

How far may Art assist Nature, in rendering its utterance pleasing and impressive?

To answer these questions, we should require to enter upon the broad field of oratory, redolent of perfume, and cultivated to luxuriance by the sister arts of rhetoric and logic. This task will probably be assumed by some more experienced guide ; if not, we may devote to it some other evening. To essay it now, would be to violate a fundamental rule of the art we seek to teach, by trespassing on the time of an audience already sufficiently weary.

THE MORAL INFLUENCE OF WOMEN.

[A Lecture delivered before the Halifax Mechanic's Institute, September 1836.]

I trust that my fair countrywomen will not suppose that the idea of preparing a paper, addressed especially to them, originated in a disparaging estimate of their understandings ; or in any distrust of their inclination and ability to partake largely of the wholesome philosophic and literary fare furnished by those who cater for the weekly feasts provided at this Institute. I hope also that they will not suspect me of a design to waste this leisure hour in vain trifling, and mawkish compliment—foreign to the avowed objects for which we meet, and insulting to the good taste of such an audience as is here assembled.

My object in appearing before you this evening is very different. The design of this paper originated in a conviction of the immense moral influence which females as a class possess ; in a high appreciation of this power, and a desire to give it a bearing, so far as circumstances permit on the character and prosperity of our common country. Pardon me, if I venture to assert, that there are many females in Nova Scotia—nay, that there may possibly be some in this audience—who are not duly sensible of the extent of this influence, nor of the paramount obligation which it imposes.' Nor is this surprising. The recognition of great principles, the growth of public spirit, (the want of which in this community has often been lamented here) is generally slow in a new country. Men themselves are often but tardy scholars of what they should learn and practice without delay; and though each may not be indisposed to "do the State some service," their collective duties to society are often ignorantly or indifferently put aside; while their vague designs, and languid determinations, assume no palpable or profitable form.

If this be true as respects the lords of creation, to whom the portals of colleges are open, whose self-examinations are prompted by the seclusion of academic groves, whose minds are informed, and faculties quickened, by those studies and that training which are essential to success in the professions, or in the active business of life,—how much more may "gentle woman" be excused for a less early appreciation of her moral power in the State, and of the high duties imposed by its possesion. But in a new country, as I have often told you, much depends on early impressions and determinations; and the sooner both sexes understand the natural boundaries of their influence and their obligations, and become feelingly alive to the reputation and advancement of the land in which they live, the sooner will it flourish; the more rapid will be the growth of that public spirit, or rather public virtue, the fruitful parent of high thoughts, amiable qualities, noble actions, and valuable institutions.

Strongly impressed by this belief, I endeavoured some year or two ago, to kindle the fire of honorable enterprise in the minds of my young friends of my own sex, by a few simple appeals and historic illustrations. The same motives which induced me to address them, urge me now, ladies, to address you; and to solicit your attention to some views, which, if not novel, are well meant; and in the exhibition of which I have studied simplicity rather than effect—the ornament of common sense, rather than the pomp and grace of language.

It is a common error,—one extensively propagated by the overbearing and self-sufficient of our sex—that women's thoughts should be bounded by her household cares; that these alone should engross her time; and that all matters of literature, science, politics, and morals, should be carefully eschewed—as any infringement on man's exclusive monopoly of these, would at once detract from the softer graces of the female character, and endanger the balance of domestic subordination. On the other hand, the more reckless and daring apostles of the rights of women, have contended for a measure of liberty so large, for a participation in masculine thoughts and employments, so extensive and so gross, that they have made but few converts to their theories, and are not likely ever to persuade a whole people to bring them into practice.

Let us not be led away by either extreme; but while we preserve inviolate the delicacy and freshness of the female character, that which is the presiding spirit of domestic life, and gives to it its holiest and most inexpressible charm; let women exercise that legitimate and rational influence on all the great interests of society, to which they are entitled, by their knowledge, their talents, and their virtues; and especially by the deep stake they have in the general happiness and prosperity, not only now but in all succeeding times.

Before explaining how I think this influence may be brought to bear on the advancement of our own Province, let me turn your attention to the direction of the Female character in other countries; to its bearing on their history and institutions; to the excitements it held forth to genius and valor; and the fidelity with which it followed out the great objects and prevailing impulses of the age. .

The favorite pursuit, the passion, the business, if you will, of most ancient, and indeed of most modern nations, of which we have any authentic accounts, appears to have been War. However the motives may have varied, or the principles on which these contests were conducted may have differed; vibrating as they did, between the bloody exterminations of the Scythian and the courtly politeness of Chivalry; still War was the great end and aim of life; the highest honors of the State were to be won in battle; a man's wealth was estimated by the wounds upon his body, or the numbers he had slain. So prevalent and so exciting was this warlike spirit, that no nation was secure that did not possess courage, discipline, and experience, superior to its immediate neighbors. Wars were continually declared or courted, in order to acquire or test these qualities; and the whole system of education was framed to prepare youth for the tented field, and teach them that it was more honorable to die fighting bravely in their ranks, than to live a life of cowardice and ease, earning for their families no honor, and performing no service to their country.

Remember that we are not now approving of the conduct of these semi-barbarous ages, but looking at their spirit and institutions, in order to trace the influence of the female character upon them, and to show how much they were indebted to that influence for, the self-devotion they exhibited, and the glory they achieved. It would not be wise, because it would not be delicate, to examine minutely the bearing of ancient laws and customs on the liberty and privileges of the female sex; but this I think I may venture to assert, that in ancient, as in modern times, the influence which women exercised upon the spirit of their age, on the character and fortunes of their country, was in exact proportion to the consideration in which they were held, and the rational freedom they enjoyed.

When treated as slaves and inferior beings, they have invariably degenerated, as man himself does when so treated, in body and in mind. But when regarded as rational beings ; as the friends and companions of the other sex; as the wives and mothers of warriors and statesmen ; they have constantly shown an elevation of soul ; a susceptibility to the impressions of patriotism and national glory; a readiness to sacrifice even the heart's best affections to the interests of their country, and the reputation of those they loved, which justifies the high place that they occupy in the history of the more civilized nations of antiquity ; and satisfies us, that had the general mind in some of them had a wiser and less sanguinary direction, female influence would have fostered the arts of Peace as assiduously as it cultivated and transmitted the sentiments and impressions essential to a state of War.

How much of the spirit of ancient Sparta breathes, even at this day, from the noble answer of the mother of Cleomenes, when her son had been promised succor by Ptolemy, King of Egypt, on condition that he would send his parent and children as hostages. After much irresolution and visible sorrow, he ventured to communicate the sad alternative, when she replied — "Was this the thing which you have so long hesitated to communicate? Why do you not immediately put us on board a ship and send this carcase of mine where you think it may be of most use to Sparta, before age renders it good for nothing and sinks it in the grave?" Being on the point of embarking, she took her son alone into the Temple of Neptune, where, seeing him in great emotion and concern, she threw her arms about him and said—"King of the Lacedæmonians, take care that when we go out no one perceives us weeping, or doing anything unworthy of Sparta. This alone is in our power; the event is in the hand of God." After her arrival in Egypt, hearing that Cleomenes, though desirous to treat with the Achæans, was afraid to put an end to the War without Ptolemy's consent, she wrote to desire him " to do what he thought most advantageous and honorable for Sparta, and not for the sake of an old woman and a child to live in constant fear of Ptolemy."

Though often apparently wrapt up in the honor of

the individual they loved, there was, in the breasts of these Spartan dames, a regard to the reputation of the State, triumphing over every feeling of mere family pride. The Mother of Brasidas, enquiring of some Amphipolitans whether her son had died honorably, and as became a Spartan, they loudly extolled his merit and said there was not such a man left in Sparta: upon which she replied—"say not so my friends; for Brasidas was indeed a man of honor, but Lacedæmon can boast of many better men than he."

When their city was threatened by Pyrrhus, and the Lacedæmonians proposed to send off their women to Crete, Archidamia, entering the Senate with a sword in her hand, complained of the mean opinion which they entertained of the women, if they imagined that they would survive the destruction of Sparta. This appeal prevailed, and as soon as the works necessary for defence were commenced, the matrons and maids devoted themselves to labor. Those that were intended for the fight, they advised to repose themselves; and, in the meantime, they undertook to finish a third part of the trench, which was completed before morning. At daybreak the enemy was in motion; upon which the women armed the youth with their own hands, and gave them the trench in charge, exhorting them to guard it well, and representing how delightful it would be to conquer in the view of their country, or how glorious to expire in the arms of their mothers and their wives, when they had met their death as became Spartans. And for two days they contrived to aid and encourage them; and by their conduct, saved

the city from pillage and their persons from dishonor.

In that scene in Glover's Leonidas, where the devoted
warrior parts from his wife and children—though the
positive certainty of death makes grief predominate over
every other feeling in her bosom for the time—the
arguments he addresses to her, show what were, to a
Grecian woman under such circumstances, the true
sources of comfort and consolation :—

> " Wherefore swells afresh
> That tide of woe ?   Leonidas must fall.
> Alas ! far heavier misery impends
> O'er thee and these, if, softened by thy tears,
> I shamefully refuse to yield that breath,
> Which Justice, Glory, Liberty and Heaven,
> Claim for my country, for my sons and thee.
> Think on my long unaltered love.   Reflect
> On my paternal fondness.   Hath my heart
> E'er known a pause in love, or pious care ?
> How shall that care, that tenderness be shown,
> Most warm, most faithful ?   When thy husband dies
> For Lacedæmon's safety, thou wilt share,
> Thou and thy children, the diffusive good.
> I am selected by the immortal Gods
> To save a People.   Should my timid heart
> That sacred charge abandon, I should plunge
> Thee too in shame and sorrow. Thou wouldst
>   mourn
> With Lacedæmon, would with her sustain
> Thy painful portion of oppression's weight.

> Behold thy sons, now worthy of their name,
> Their Spartan birth.   Their glowing bloom would
>   pine
> Depress'd, dishonored, and their youthful hearts
> Beat at the sound of Liberty no more.
> On their own merit—on their father's fame,
> When he the Spartan freedom hath confirmed,
> Before the world illustrious will they rise
> Their country's bulwark, and their mother's joy."

The effect of this reasoning is told in the lines that follows :—

> "Here paused the patriot.   In religious awe
> Grief heard the voice of Virtue.   No complaint
> The solemn silence broke."

I might turn your attention to many other passages, illustrative of the influence of the female character, in what Thomson calls—

> "The man-subduing City, which no shape
>   Of pain could conquer, nor of pleasure charm,"

and where

> "The tender mother urged her son to die."

But let us pass on to Rome, where we shall find the same high estimation of valor, military conduct and devotion to the service of the State, under different laws and modifications, but fostered and strengthened in the same manner, by the powerful stimulants of female tuition and influence. How much of the national character is exhibited in the matron Cornelia's reproach to her sons, "that she was still called the mother-in-law of Scipio, and not the mother of the Gracchi;" a reproach, however, which, at a later period, they nobly wiped away. We can see in her presentation of these very sons—whom she was thus privately exciting, but of whose characters she had formed a just idea—to the vain lady of Campania, as her richest jewels, the very pulsations, so to speak, of the whole female heart of ancient Rome.

Indeed, we cease to wonder at the heroic deeds and sentiments of the men, when we contemplate the characters of the women. The account which Plutarch gives of the conduct of Portia, when she distrusted her own courage to preserve the dreadful secret which she saw was preying on the mind of her husband, will help to explain my meaning. She secretly gave herself a deep flesh wound, which occasioned a great effusion of blood, extreme pain, and a consequent fever. Brutus was sincerely afflicted for her; and. as he attended her in the height of her pain, she thus spoke to him :—

"Brutus, when you married the daughter of Cato, you did not, I presume, consider her merely as a female companion, but as the partner of your fortunes. You indeed have given me no reason to repent my marriage ; but what proof, either of affection or fidelity, can you receive from me, if I may neither share in your secret griefs, nor in your secret counsels? I am sensible that secrecy is not the characteristic virtue of my sex; but, surely our natural weakness may be strengthened by a virtuous education, and by honorable connections ; and Portia can boast that she is the daughter of Cato and the wife of Brutus.   Yet even in these distinctions I placed no absolute confidence till I tried and found that I was proof against pain."   She then showed him her wound, and informed him of her motives; upon which Brutus was so struck with her magnanimity, that, with lifted hands, he entreated the Gods "to favor his enterprise, and enable him to approve himself worthy of Portia." The resolute conduct of this noble woman, who swallowed fire rather than survive the death of her husband, on the failure of his enterprise, proves that this was no domestic ruse, but a manifestation of spirit and integrity, characteristic of the country and the age.

It was said of Marcius Coriolanus, that his great actions were not so much performed for the love of his country as "to please his mother."   Shakspeare has caught the true spirit of this lady's character ; and as the sentiments he puts into her mouth are chiefly borrowed from authentic history, embellished of course by poetic language, I may be pardoned for quoting a few lines from him.   It is that passage in the play which precedes the visit of Valeria :—

> " The noble sister of Publicola,
> The moon of Rome ; chaste as the icicle,
> That's curded by the frost from purest snow.
> And hangs on Dian's temple."

"When yet," says Volumnia, speaking of her distinguished offspring, "he was but tender bodied, and the only son of my womb ; when youth, with comeliness, plucked all gaze his way ; when, for a day of King's entreaties, a mother would not sell him an hour from her beholding—I, considering how honor would become such a person; that it was no better than picture-like to hang by the wall, if renown made it not stir, was pleased to let him seek danger where he was like to find fame. To a cruel war I sent him, from whence he returned, his brows bound with oak. I tell thee, daughter, I sprang not more in joy at first hearing he was a man-child, than now, in seeing he had proved himself a man."

" *Virgilia.*—But had he died in the business, Madam, how then?"

" *Volumnia.*—Then his good-report should have been my son; I therein would have found issue. Hear me profess sincerely; had I a dozen sons, each in my love alike, and none less dear than thine and my good Marcius, I had rather had eleven die nobly for their country, than one voluptuously surfeit out of action."

And again, carried away by her own enthusiasm, she exclaims :—

> "Methinks I hear hither your husband's drum;
> See him pluck Aufidius down by the hair;
> As children from a bear, the Volces shunning him:
> Methinks I see him stamp thus, and call thus—
> 'Come on you cowards—you were got in fear,
> Though you were born in Rome.' His bloody
> brows
> With his mailed hand then wiping, forth he goes,
> Like to a harvestman, that's tasked to mow
> Or all, or lose his hire."

Vir.—His bloody brow! Oh Jupiter, no blood!

> *Vol.*—Away, you fool !   It more becomes a man
>   Than gilt his trophy.   The breasts of Hecuba,
>   When she did suckle Hector, looked not lovelier
>   Than Hector's forehead, when it spit forth blood,
>   At Grecian swords contending.
> *Vir.*—Heaven bless my lord from fell Aufidius.
> *Vol.*—He'll beat Aufidius' head below his knee and
> tread upon his neck."

There spoke the true spirit of ancient Rome.   Nor is it a matter of wonder that a people nourished, educated and excited, by such a race of women, became the conquerors and masters of the world.   The wonder would have been, had they belied in the field the admirable training of the domestic hearth.

But the Roman women did not only encourage their husbands and children to fight bravely in war, but to preserve an unblemished reputation for integrity. at home.   They applauded their disregard of the paltry temptations of society, and fixed their attention on the nobler qualities of the understanding and the heart, and on the attainment of the solid honors of the State. "There were not fewer," says Plutarch, "than sixteen of the Ælian family and name, who had only a small house and one farm among them ; and in this house they all lived with their wives and many children. Here dwelt the daughter of Æmilius, who had been twice Consul, and had triumphed twice, not ashamed of her husband's poverty, but admiring that integrity which kept him poor."

I might turn your attention to many other passages,

highly illustrative of the moral influence of the female character in ancient Greece and Rome—to the spirited reply of Gorgo ; the courage of Cœlia, who swam the river at the head of the Roman virgins, under a shower of darts : or the self devotion of Arria, who plunged a dagger into her own breast, to teach her husband how to die ; but we have not time to dwell longer here, and I think the illustrations I have chosen are amply sufficient for my purpose. For they teach us this great lesson, that two of the foremost nations of antiquity were as much indebted to their women, as to their men, for the extended influence, and exalted reputations they achieved. We cannot, perhaps, at this distance of time, say which is entitled to the largest share of praise for originating and strengthening those sentiments of exalted courage and patriotic self devotion, which were the fruitful sources of private honor and public advantage ; but the rational conclusion is, that they were mutually cultivated and inspired ; that where woman's softer nature shrunk from the idea of peril, and the consequences of exposing those she loved, the patriot lord and father, as in the case of Leonidas, inculcated lessons of firmness and public virtue ; and where man himself required a spur to his ambition, it was supplied by Cornelia's taunt, or Volumnia's ardent praise.

We need not dwell on the dark period which succeeded the fall of the Roman Empire. That the influence of woman was felt upon it ; that its horrors were mitigated by her gentle ministrations, by her natural tendernes of heart, we cannot doubt ; for, to believe otherwise, would be to question the known characteristics of the sex in every country and in every age. But let us pass on to that period when the business of conquest having ended, the feudal system arose in every country in Europe, and upon the genius of which it will be seen that women exercised the most admirable and extraordinary influence.

It is the custom to mourn over the fall of the Roman Empire. But when we contemplate the general corruption, the social slavery and degradation of the mass, the depravity and cruelty of the few, to whom birth, wealth, or audacity, had given power, we almost feel thankful for that tide of rude but comparatively virtuous barbarians, by whom its whole boundaries were overflowed, and cease to regret that knowledge and those refinements which were so interwoven with cruelty, imbecility and vice. And it is pleasing to turn from the female character, soiled as it was in the latter days of the Empire by the operation of vile laws and customs, the influence of luxury, and the general corruption of morals and manners, to the simple dignity which it maintained in the fastnesses of the North, and in those remote regions to which the term barbarian was applied. "It was, in truth," says Mills, in his History of Chivalry, "the virtue of the sex, and not any occasional or accidental opinion, that raised them to their high and respectable consideration. The Roman historian marked it as a peculiarity among the Germans, that marriage was considered by them a sacred institution, and that a man confined himself to the society of one wife. The mind of Tacitus was filled with respect for the virtuous though unpolished people of the North; and, reverting his eyes to Rome, the describer of manners becomes the indignant satirist, and he exclaims that "no one in Germany dares to ridicule the Holy Ordinance of Marriage, or call an infringment of its laws a compliance with the manners of the age." It is evident from all the accounts we have that women among these northern nations, while they preserved a virtuous simplicity of manners, stimulated their husbands and lovers to disregard death, and to seek for renown, in those rude contests which, commenced by the encroaching spirit of the ancient Romans, ended but in the downfall of their widely extended power. Plutarch gives an account of a battle between the army of Marius and the Cimbri in which the latter were beaten. When driven back upon their encampments, they found their women standing in mourning by their carriages, who killed those that fled —some their husbands, others their brothers, and some their fathers. They strangled their children with their own hands, and threw them under the wheels and the horses' feet. And Strabo, I think it is, who mentions, that such of them as were taken prisoners wished to be placed among the Vestal Virgins, binding themselves to perpetual chastity; and had recourse to death, as the last refuge of their Virtue, when their request was refused. That hardy tribes, nurtured and encouraged by such women, should subdue a people, however rich in numbers, wealth, and ancient reputation, after discipline had faded, corruption become general, and the female character shorn of its dignity ceased to exercise moral influence, or even to procure respect, cannot be a matter of surprise. But it is curious to mark how, as the feudal system arose out of the turbid waves of northern conquest, women not only preserved her ancient purity and influence, but brightened into a being more elevated and refined than she had ever been in the world's early history, and secure at last, of her own just rights and natural station, shed over hundreds of thousands of mailed warriors an influence the most salutary and benign.

As polygamy was unknown to the manners of the northern tribes, so was it repudiated and contemned in the countries which they conquered ; and when this sentiment became strengthened and confirmed by the spread of Christianity, women began, by their plastic power, to soften and refine the rude men and ruder manners of that barbarous age. War was still, if we except a few Italian and German cities, the great business of life ; and though the sex were neither sufficiently powerful, nor perhaps sufficiently enlightened, to subdue this warlike spirit, with which their very natures were imbued, and with the triumphs and pageantries of which their childish footsteps were surrounded ; still while they urged their husbands and lovers, as the Spartan, the Roman, and Teutonic maids and matrons had done, to fight bravely for their country, and seek glory in the tented field, they inspired them with sentiments in which courage was singularly blended with poetry and religion ; with a repugnance to mere savage warfare ; a love of mercy, a high sense of honor, respect for the plighted word, and veneration for the name of woman ; until the beautiful laws and graceful embellishments of chivalry were introduced, to mitigate the horrors and hide the deformity of never-ending war. If the temple of Janus was rarely shut, its portal was hung with flowers.

"Chivalry," says Mills, "held out the heart-stirring hope that beauty was the reward of bravery. A valiant but landless knight, was often hailed by the whole martial fraternity of his country as worthy the hand of a noble heiress, and the King, could not in every case, bestow her on some minion of his court. Woman was sustained in her proud elevation by the virtues which chivalry required of her; and man paid homage to her mind, as well as to her beauty. She was not the mere object of pleasure, taken up or thrown aside as passion or caprice suggested, but being the formation of honor, her image was always blended with the fairest visions of his fancy, and the respectful consideration which she therefore met with, showed she was not an unworthy awarder of fame. Fixed by the gallant warriors of chivalry in a nobler station than that which had been assigned to her by the polite nations of antiquity, all the graceful qualities of her nature blossomed into beauty; and the chastening influence of feminine gentleness and tenderness was, for the first time in his history, experienced by man."

I might entertain you for hours with the personal achievements and adventures of females, gleaned from the Poets and Chroniclers of the middle ages; for it was no uncommon thing for ladies of peerless beauty and of the highest rank, favored by the quaint disguises and courteous usages of the time, to clothe themselves in armor, break a lance in the lists, draw their swords in the cause of the oppressed, or set an example by their courage and humanity, in the more extended scenes of general warfare, of those qualities, that as a class they encouraged, and which by both sexes were so highly prized.

The victory of the English over the Scotch at Neville Cross is mainly attributed to the spirited demeanor of Phillippa, wife of Edward the Third, who, in a perilous moment, when the King, her husband, was far away, and the fate of England in her hands, rode through the ranks, and by her exhortations and promises, nerved the hearts of her yeomen and chivalry for the struggles of a great occasion, From the History of Scotland I might borrow the details of that memorable siege sustained by Black Agnes, the lady of the Earl of March, in the castle of Dunbar, which she defended against the bravest warriors of England, beating them back from her walls, and mocking them with bitter jests. And the varied adventures of the heroic Countess of Mountford, of whom it was said by Froissart, that, "she had the courage of a man and the heart of a lion," would, had we room for them, afford a striking illustration. Her noble defence of Brittany against the whole power of France ; her pathetic appeal to her soldiers, holding her infant son in her arms, from which the Austrian Queen at a later period may have borrowed, in addressing the Estates of Hungary ; her able dispositions, her gallant sortie, her heroic constancy, and above all, her spirited bearing upon that element so potent in subduing both sexes, when attacked by the Spanish fleet on her passage to England; indeed every incident of her astonishing career, had we leisure to trace them, would show the immense influence which females must have had, in bracing the spirits of men, and prompting to those deeds of almost superhuman valor and address, that distinguished the middle age, and which amidst more tranquil scenes, we often contemplate with a strange mixture of wonder and unbelief. "In the crusades," says the author from whom I have repeatedly borrowed, "parties of fair and noble women accompanied the chivalry of Europe to the Holy Land, charming the seas to give them gentle pass, and binding up the wounds of husbands and brothers after a well foughten field with the bold Mussulman. Sometimes they wielded the flaming brand themselves, and the second crusade in particular was distinguished by a troop of ladies, harnessed in armor of price, and mounted on goodly steeds." Such of my fair hearers as have read Tasso's "Jerusalem delivered," and Scott's "Count Robert of Paris," will readily understand how the influence of these acts and sacrifices would be blazoned and reproduced, by men of genius and imagination—the Troubadors and Novelists of the period—until courage became instinctive, and the man was despised who did not possess those qualities for which woman herself was so distinguished.

I must confess, however, that I admire less those voluntary exhibitions of courage in the field, than the more delightful, because softer, more natural, more feminine influences; which the females of the feudal times exercised, from the privacy of home, on the

manners and spirit of the age. What a splendid light
is thrown upon these by the answer of the French
hero, Du Guesclin, when our Edward demanded how
he could pay the immense ransom which he himself
had fixed. ' " I know a hundred Knights of Brittany,"
said he, " who would sell their possessions for my
liberation ; and there is not a woman sitting at her
distaff in France, who would not labor with her own
hands to redeem me from yours."

But while the women inspired the men with courage,
and prompted the spirit of adventure, courtesy and
humanity were enforced by their noble examples and
gentle ministrations. " In the wars of the Guelphs and
Ghibellines, the Emperor Conrad, as an offended
Sovereign, had refused all terms of capitulation to the
garrison of Winnisburg ; but as a courteous Knight, he
permitted the women to depart with such of their
precious effects as they themselves could transport.
The gates of the town were thrown open, and a long
procession of matrons, each bearing a husband, or a
father, or a brother, on her shoulders, passed in safety
through the applauding camp." The Knight who was
stained with crime ; who was false to his religion, his
country, or his friend ; who took an unchivalric advantage, or broke his plighted faith, won no word of
woman's praise, no favor in her bower.

By such sweet influences, aiding and strengthening
the benign precepts of Christianity, continents that
were once savage and unlettered have become civilized
and refined. The spirit of peace, sustained by the
experience of all history, has spread her wings above

the nations ; war is no longer esteemed as an amusement, and except when waged in defence of some great
principle of civil or religious liberty, scarcely tolerated
as an occupation. The industry, the skill, the genius
of mankind, have been turned into different channels.
Nations seek renown by the cultivation of the arts of
peace, the creation of just laws and noble institutions ;
and those who, under a different dispensation, would
have been first in the lists, and foremost in the tented
field, seek in the higher regions of intellectual achievements, a more useful and durable renown. And it is
delightful to reflect, nay, to feel, that the encouraging
efforts of that Being who formerly sent man forth to
battle with the infidel, now lures him on in his warfare
with ignorance and prejudice ; that the greenest laurel
earned in the paths of peace, won by the triumphs of
the mind, is that which drops from woman's hand,
freshened by her tears, or hallowed by her sweetest
smile.

In the mighty revolutions by which these astonishing
results have been produced, woman has had her part,
and is entitled to her share of praise. If, as I believe,
the diffusion of Christianity be at the root of all these
political and social ameliorations ; that they spring up
as natural consequences, from the divine spirit of justice
and of love, which an almighty mind has breathed ·into
the scriptures, let it not be forgotten that females were
"last at the cross and earliest at the tomb ;" and that,
throughout those long ages of persecution, in which the
humane and devout Christian had to struggle for his
rights and his opinions,—whether with the infidel, or

with those misguided zealots, who, naming the name of Christ, and professing, under various titles, to be his followers, regarded persecution as a duty,—let it, I say, be remembered, that in almost every one of those scenes of religious suffering, some Sophronia or Columba has nerved the hearts of men by her fortitude, and sealed her convictions with her blood.

The cause of civil liberty also, in every quarter of the globe, has been as largely indebted to the operation of female influence. Woman's tenderness of heart makes her the natural enemy of the oppressor, the soother and inspirer of the oppressed. In those exciting epochs of modern history which are emphatically said to have "tried men's souls,"—whether in the British Isles, France, Poland, Switzerland, Italy or Spain, not only have women exercised, well and wisely, through the varied channels of social life, an encouraging and salutary influence, but have often set an example of heroism and self-devotion, which has thrilled through the hearts of a whole people, and challenged the admiration of a world. A Joan of Arc has never been wanting to deliver a Kingdom; a Charlotte Corday to poniard a tyrant; an Augustina to save a City, or a Lady Russel to grace the last hours of a patriot's life, by tenderness and elevation of soul.

Of the blessings secured by these trials and sacrifices, we are admitted to a full participation; while the art, the science, and the literature, every department of which has been enriched by the Mores, the Barbaulds, the Porters, the Montagues, the Martineaus, the Somervilles, the Hemans', and a long line of amiable women of talent, have descended to us with our language, and comprise by no means the least valuable portion of the high privileges and intellectual treasures which we inherit from our Fatherland. And it is for us to consider; it is for you, ladies, especially, to reflect how you can best pay to posterity what you owe to the genius and spirit of the past.

Pardon me if I conclude this paper by reminding you, that to a great extent, you have the destinies of Nova Scotia in your hands. And let me conjure you never to undervalue the character of your own influence or the extent of your moral obligations. Look at the little Province which, small as it is, some of us are proud to call our own; its narrow boundaries, girded by the seas, and surrounded on every side by extensive, populous and powerful states. What resources has such a country to sustain her against the gigantic influences with which she must hourly contend? None, but the character, the intelligence, the energy and self-devotion of her people. Let it be your constant aim, your study, your pride, my countrywomen, to cultivate these qualities, and to inspire your brothers, husbands, lovers, and children with the sentiments from which they spring. Without throwing aside the modest deportment of the sex; without stepping over the bounds of masculine thought and occupation; without neglecting those household cares and feminine accomplishments, for the want of which no public service could atone, let a regard for your country's welfare, its reputation, its prosperity, be ever present to your minds; and let some portion of your time, and the whole weight of your moral influence, bear steadily on the means of its improvemnt.

A Nova Scotian matron needs not as the Spartan or Roman did, urge her husband on to battle and conquest, because " a change has come over the spirit of the world's dreams ; " but she may show him, that, as these states were preserved, enlarged and rendered illustrious, by discipline and valor, so must ours be strengthened and elevated by an assiduous cultivation of the arts of peace. If he complains that our boundaries are contracted, let her tell him, that, with industry and good husbandry, there is land enough to support millions of men ; and that if this were exhausted, the whole world is the freehold of a commercial people—the seas but the high roads which conduct to their domains. Let her remind him that a country possessed of science and enterprise, can multiply physical power as she will ; that, if she be but rich in intellect, in creative genius and steady application she may strengthen herself indefinitely with nerves of iron, and muscles of steam, and condense the energy and productive, power of myriads within the compass of a few miles.

The Nova Scotian mother, too, may do her part, while the graceful forms of childhood glide around her knees, and the ductile elements of the youthful mind are forming beneath her eye ; she may inculcate not only the ordinary principles of morals, but those lessons of public virtue applicable to the situation of the country and the probable duties of life—which, like bread cast upon the waters, will come back to her in pride and admiration, after many days. There is a younger class, whose influence is chiefly felt in that opening dawn of manhood, when the heart is most susceptible to impressions, when the good and evil principles may be said to struggle most fiercely for the mastery over our nature ; and when a word, a glance, a noble sentiment uttered on a summer's eve, may turn the scale in favor of public spirit and honorable ambition ; and if my young friends knew how powerful is their influence at that age, and on such occasions, they would not fail to smile away the sloth, the senseless and besotted pride, the inveterate idleness and inanity of mind, by which too many of our young men are beset ; and which rarely fails to ripen into grovelling vice, and ruinous dissipation. Beauty, leading youth to the shrine of public virtue, is no fable in the world's history ; and there is no reason why in Nova Scotia it may not be amply realized. Let them teach the idlers and triflers of our sex, that our country has neither hands nor mind to spare ; that their favors are to be won by public service, by conquests in the regions of mind ; by trophies won in the ranks of patriotism, literature, science and art ; by what the poet beautifully styles "those glorious labors which embellish life." Nor need my fair friends trust to personal charms alone to sustain this influence ; without any dereliction of domestic duty, without sacrificing one feminine grace, one modest attraction, they may go before their brothers, friends and lovers,—as some of them have already done—into those delightful regions. Science and History will disclose to them rich sources of illustration ; and the pen and the pencil become eloquent, when other fascinations fail.

Be it yours, then, ladies, now that the times have changed, to win with these gentler weapons—as the martial heroines of the middle ages did with lance and sword—a right to stimulate and reproach the other sex, where they fall short of the requirements of patriotism and ambition ; and, as they led the way to rescue the sepulchre of our Lord from the infidel, lead you the way to vindicate those admirable precepts and principles of justice, toleration and truth, which he left for our direction, but which, by the corruption and weakness of our nature, are so frequently sullied and profaned. And believe me, that while you thus wander in the "pleasant ways of wisdom," general admiration and a deathless name are not beyond your reach ; for even the deeds of Jean of Mountfort, as they did less good, shall fade from the world's memory before Mrs. Hemans' moral songs.

I do not ask you to put on an affectation of art, destructive of the freshness of nature. I seek not to entice you from the gentle thoughts and appropriate occupations of home ; but, as the Greek and the Roman caught the spirit which led him on to victory and renown, amidst the relaxations and delights of social intercourse, so would I have my youthful countrymen catch from your enthusiasm, the energy and determination of which Nova Scotia stand so much in need. I would make beauty's flashing eye, and encouraging smile, at once the beacon and reward of public virtue and honorable exertion. I would have woman breathe around her an atmosphere in which idleness, ignorance and selfishness, could not for an hour exist; but in which science and literature, high thoughts and honorable enterprises, would blossom and flourish till they overspread the land ; not choking the domestic affections, or curbing the rational pleasures and enjoyments of life ; but giving to them a dignity, a grace, a charm, in the highest degree attractive ; while they result in an abundant measure of collective reputation and improvement.

Could I but see these sentiments diffused throughout the land, generally appreciated and acted upon by the females of Nova Scotia, I should laugh to scorn every sentiment of despondency and alarm. The present would be viewed with satisfaction ; the future bounded by hope. Though the existing race of men might be ignorant or indifferent, I should know that another was springing up, which, from the cradle to the tomb, would be subjected to a training and an influence, the most admirable and inspiring ; and which must ultimately rival the boast of the Athenian, by converting a small Province into a powerful and illustrious State.

ADDRESS.

[Delivered at the Howe Festival, Framingham, Massachusetts, August 31, 1871.]

Mr. Chairman, Ladies and Gentlemen :—

To be invited to address such an audience as this, in the centre of intellectual New England, I regard as a great distinction.   Yet the position has its drawbacks. The committee have announced an " Oration ; " but a simple and good-humored introduction to the business of the day is all that I shall attempt. If disposed to be more ambitious, and to try a bolder flight, I should be afraid to risk comparisons, that you would not fail to institute, and which I am not vain enough to challenge. You have not forgotten the stately and nervous arguments of Webster, or the polished elocution and silvery voice of Everett ; and though those masters of the art have passed away, you can still sit at the feet of Emerson, listen to the fiery declamation of Phillips, wonder at Lowell's marvellous felicity of phrase and luxuriance of illustration, and fold to your hearts, with a love akin to worship, our good friend Oliver Wendell Holmes. Let us thank God for these great lights, which have diffused or are still shedding their radiance over the industrial and intellectual life of a great nation ; but this is a family party, and as a member of the family, I throw myself upon your indulgence. We are here not to make a parade of our eloquence, if we have any, but to spend a day in holy brotherhood and sweet communion.

Drawn from many States and Provinces, but springing from a common stock, we meet for peaceful and legitimate purposes, to grasp each other's hands, to look into each other's faces, to study each other's forms and to mark how the fine original structure of the race has borne change of aliment, diversity of climate, and the wear and tear of sedentary or active life, amidst the rapid mental and bodily movement of the fast age in which we live.

These family gatherings were, I believe, first suggested in New England, and their success is to be traced to the natural outcrop of feelings that are very rational. A wise nation preserves its records, gathers up its muniments, decorates the tombs of its illustrious dead, repairs its great public structures, and fosters national pride and love of country, by perpetual references to the sacrifices and glories of the past. But, divide the nation by households, and under every roof you will find, let national pride be ever so strong, that family pride, the interest in the narrower circle that bears a common name, is quite as active. Our literature is filled with types of the septs, and clans, and families, into which the wide world is divided, and who cling to their old recollections and traditions with marvellous tenacity.

In the British Islands this family sentiment finds vent, and expands itself with great luxuriance and grace, under the shelter of the law of primogeniture. Emerson, in his delightful book on England, tells us that there are " three hundred palaces," scattered all over the face of that country. A great many of these are comparatively modern structures, reared by the merchant princes and great manufacturers of England, who, in comparatively modern times, have been enriched by the abounding commerce and restless industry of a great and prosperous empire.

But by far the larger number are the growth of centuries ; " the stately homes of England," where her historic families, many of them older than the Conquest, store up and preserve all that can illustrate the brilliant and heroic qualities of the race, and prompt to the highest order of emulation. Many of these old structures, such as Warwick Castle, the stronghold of the king-maker, and Alnwick, the seat of " the stout Earls of Northumberland," though converted into luxurious modern residences, and embellished with all that high art in these recent times can furnish, occupy the commanding sites which made them formidable centuries ago, and wear the outward semblance of strong mediæval fortresses, from which a stone has scarcely been removed. In many other cases the stern front of war has been softened and toned down by the gradual process of decay, the luxuriance of vegetation, or by improvements, which have placed modern structures, of vast proportions, upon the old feudal sites, replete with every convenience for ease and comfort, which, from the thickness of the walls, and the defensive character of the design, could not always be commanded in the old feudal castles.

But whether the style of the structure be ancient or

modern, it is surrounded by an estate, which, from generation to generation, has belonged to one family— been known by one name,—and the honse, whatever the style of architecture may be, is filled with all that can illustrate the manhood and the intellectual vigor of that family, from its rise, amidst the convulsions of some shadowy by-gone age, down to the hour in which, with mingled wonder and admiration, we survey the marvellous results of a system not recognized by the institutions under which we live.

That those families should desire to preserve their estates intact, and gather around them the evidences of their antiquity and achievements, is not at all surprising when we reflect, that a very large proportion of them are inseparably interwoven with the great events which have made the history of their country memorable ; and the valuable services rendered to the nation by many of these families, not only throw around their country seats and personal relics an indescribable charm, but give them a strong hold on the affections of the people.

A Stanley won the field of Flodden. One of the Talbots, who led the English forces in France, and fought against Joan of Arc, was the victor in forty-seven battles and dangerous skirmishes. The Percys have seven times driven back the tide of foreign invasion, and for eight hundred years have stood in the front of resistance to legal tyranny: and, say the writers from whom I quote,* " One Russell has staked his head for the Protestant faith : a second the family

---

* Sandford and Townshend's Governing Families of England.

estates in successful resistance to a despot ; a third has died on the scaffold for the liberties of Englishmen ; a fourth has aided materially in the revolution which substituted law for the will of the sovereigns ; a fifth spent his life in resisting the attempt of the House of Brunswick to rebuild the power of the throne, and gave one of the first examples of just religious government in Ireland ; and a sixth organized and carried through a bloodless but complete transfer of power from his own order to the middle classes."

These are eminent services, and we cannot wonder that the family seats, where such men were bred, are religiously preserved by their descendants, and regarded with deep interest by the nation.

There is no name more familiar to Americans than that of Lord North, who, under George the Third, conducted for many years, the disastrous War which was only closed by the establishment of the Independence of these United States. How few of all the able and distinguished men, who, on your side, led in that great struggle, have left behind them homes that have been preserved, properties still undivided, or common centres where their pictures, books, and family muniments have been treasured up, to keep alive for succeeding generations the memory of their martial or diplomatic achievements ! By the personal exertions of Everett, Mount Vernon has been preserved ; and, to their honor be it spoken, the Adams family, by a rare exhibition of heriditary qualities, have held their property and maintained their positions in the highest circles of political and social elevation. But nearly all the others, though honorably known to history, have passed away, and have left no property to embellish the scenery, no rallying places for their descendants, no familiar evidences of their existence.

In the heart of Oxfordshire stands Wroxton Abbey, the seat of the Norths. It is an old ecclesiastical structure, turned into a modern residence of surpassing beauty, where all that is antique is preserved with religious care, and gracefully interwoven with whatever can administer to refined luxury and convenience. It is surrounded by forty thousand acres of the best land in England. The outlying farms are cultivated by a prosperous tenantry, whose families have occupied the same lands for centuries, many of whom keep hunters worth five hundred guineas, and pay a thousand sovereigns a year annual rent. Ancestral trees older than the Abbey, fling their shadows down upon sinuous walks and carriage drives that appear almost endless; whilst every window in the house looks out upon verdant lawns, well-kept gardens, or clumps of tree roses, interspersed with masses of evergreens, the preservation of which is so much favored by the moist climate of England.

The Baroness North, grand-daughter of Lord North of the Revolutionary War, and her husband, Colonel North, reside on this beautiful estate; and while distinguished for the largeness of heart and great hospitality which become their stations, are not unmindful of the hereditary obligation which devolves upon them to treasure, to enlarge, and to transmit to their descenants, all that can illustrate the daily life, the personal traits, or the distinguished services of the house to which they belong, in all its branches.

You are aware that the family of the Norths was interwoven with the Guildfords and Greys. The hundred rooms and long corridors of Wroxton tell the family story, from its foundation in 1496 to the present hour. Beautiful women, in the costume of the period in which they flourished—children of all ages—eminent Lawyers, Privy Councillors, Soldiers, Ambassadors and Judges, line the walls of every staircase and of every room.

Many of these pictures are valuable as works of art, but their chief value is in the record they supply of forms long past away,—of features that cannot be reproduced, and for the facilities they afford to every rising generation to study and transmit the family story, by the aid of authentic materials, which in our countries, and under our systems, we can very rarely supply.

Two or three rooms in this old house deeply interested me. One was Lord North's Library, in which every book that he had ever owned or handled has been preserved. Though unsuccessful as a War Minister, he was a scholar and a wit, and many of the volumes are rare editions, or presentation copies, enriched by autographs or annotations.

A small room, opening from the library, was Lord North's study. A very remarkable likeness of him overhangs and looks down on the table at which he wrote his despatches. The inkstand, and I might almost add the pens with which they were written have been preserved.

A bedroom in this fine old edifice interested me even more deeply. I slept one night in it without knowing to whom it had belonged. It was a stately chamber, hung with arras, greatly faded, with quaint old andirons in an open fireplace, a low bedstead with high posts; and all the furniture though admirably preserved, bearing the unmistakable impress of antiquity. To my great surprise I was told, on coming down to breakfast the following morning, that I had occupied the apartment of Lady Jane Grey, and slept in her bed, nothing having been changed in the room since her death, but the bed linen, which had worn out. I am not quite sure that I ever slept so soundly in the same apartment a second night as I did the first. Visions of the beatiful martyr to misplaced ambition seemed ever flitting round me, and I sometimes fancied that the grim headsman, with his axe, was lingering in the long shadows flung out by the massive walls.

A volume might be written descriptive of the beauties of Wroxton, and of the treasures of art and of biography which it contains, and yet it is a comparatively modern edifice, nor do the Norths trace back their lineage nearly so far as many of the great Historic families of England.

But I have taken this single house to show you how strong is the family sentiment in our mother country, and to answer, in advance, those who would smile at our humble endeavors to engraft upon our democratic institutions some graceful forms of development for a yearning that is universal, and for the outcrop of feelings as old as history.

Neither in the United States, nor in Canada, is any provision made for this development.　By our old laws two-thirds of the real estate were given to the eldest son, but modern legislation has swept this provision away, and property is now equally divided in all our States and Provinces.　The universal feeling sustains this condition of the law ; entails are discouraged, and fortunes are earned only.to be distributed, often with a rapidity that far outruns the process of accumulation. A spendthrift is too apt to follow a miser, and the thrift-less, bred in luxurious homes, often seem to have come into the world for no other purpose than to scatter what the industrious have earned, and to disperse, with-out a thought of name or race, all that their fathers prized, and in which their descendants, if not below the ordinary scale of humanity, would be sure to take an interest.

The democratic system, which prevails all over this continent, cannot be changed.　It has its advantages, and the evils arising from the law of primogeniture can-not be veiled, even by the graceful surroundings to which I have referred ; and the practical question which we have met here to endeavor to solve is this,—Can we without disturbing the law, or disregarding the common sentiment of the continent, keep alive our family name —trace back our family story, and while dividing our property among our children, divide with them also all that we have been able to learn, to authenticate, and to transmit, of the family from which they have sprung?

May we not do more ?　May we not so pass this day as to make it a festival in the finest sense of the term

—to the repetition of which the thousands who bear our name will look forward with intense delight ?

In England the Howes have lived and flourished for centuries. The Howe banner hangs as high, in Henry VII's chapel, as any other evidence of honorable service, and the battle of the first of June will be remembered so long as the naval annals of England last. In the old French wars, for the possession of this continent, one Howe fell at Ticonderoga, and another was killed on the Nova Scotia frontier. In the Revolutionary War the Howes were not fortunate. I have heard my father describe Sir William, as he saw him leading up the British forces at the battle of Bunker Hill, with the bullets flying like hail around him. But I am apprehensive that in that old war God was not " on the side of the strongest columns," and that the time had arrived, when the peopling and development of a continent could not be postponed by the agencies of fleets and armies .

The Howes, who have been ennobled, trace their family back to the reign of Henry VIII., and seem to have held estates in Somersetshire, Gloucester, Wiltshire, Nottingham, and Fermanagh in Ireland. Jack Howe, as he was familiarly called, who was a member of Parliament in the reigns of William and Anne, was a fluent speaker, and, like a good many other people in those days, had a great dislike to standing armies. His son, who sat for Nottingham in the Convention Parliament, was one of those who established the liberties of England, in 1688.

But many branches of the family are scattered all

about England.   I found three Howes, bearing my own family Christian names, lying side by side in the church yard at Newport, in the Isle of Wight, and I learned that in the western end of the Island a family of honest farmers, who are all Howes, have been living there on the same land, beyond the memory of man.

I found three others, all males, lying just inside the grave-yard at Berwick-on-Tweed.   I could not hear of any Howes in the neighborhood, and I took it for granted that they must have been killed in some old border fight, which is not at all improbable if they came from the south side of the stream.

But, passing over the nobles and the plebeians of England, I must confess that there is one Howe of whom we may all be proud.   This is John Howe, who was Chaplain to Oliver Cromwell, and whose fine form and noble features are preserved in some of the old engravings.   He must have been an eloquent preacher, for he won his place by a sermon which the Protector happened to hear.   That he was a fine scholar, and learned theologian, is proved by the body of divinity, written in classic English, which he has left behind him. That he was a noble man is proved, also, by a single anecdote which is preserved to us.   On one occasion he was soliciting aid or patronage for some person whom he thought deserving, when Cromwell turned sharply round, and, by a single question, let a flood of light in upon the disinterestedness and amiability of his character, which will illuminate it in all time to come. "John," said the Protector, "you are always asking something for some poor fellow ; why do you never ask anything for yourself ?" My father's name was John, and I have often tried to trace him back to this good Christian, whose character, in many points, his own so much resembled. I may hazard one observation, before passing from the English Howes, and it is this: that the present possessor of the peerage had better bestir himself, and do something to add lustre to his coronet, or else we Howes in America will begin to think it has dropped on an inactive brain. He fights no battles—he writes no books—he makes no speeches, and although I believe he is a very amiable person, and was a great friend of the late Queen Dowager, I beg to enter my protest against the apparent want of patriotism, or mental activity, which this very supine recipient of hereditary rank seems to display.

But, passing over the Howes who have figured, or still dwell, on the other side of the Atlantic, I take it for granted that the whole of this vast audience are descended from those who settled in New England between 1630 and 1657. It would appear, by the circular kindly sent to me by your secretary, that there were seven of these, although my father used to tell me that there were but four. Two of them, Joseph of Boston, and Abraham of Watertown, may have been sons of some of the others, if they married early, which is probable: but I take the list as I find it, and to me it is full of interest. What was the Old World about when these men came to America? Why did they come? are questions that naturally occur to us. In 1629, Charles the First dissolved his Parliament, and no other was called in England till the Long Parliament met in 1640.

During the eleven years which intervened, we all know what was going on in England. Laud was Archbishop of Canterbury, Strafford was first Minister, and that hopeful experiment was being tried, of ruling without Parliaments, which ended in the wreck and ruin of the monarchy. Within these eleven years five of the seven Howes were settled in New England, and the reasonable presumption is that they found old England to hot for them.

They had no fancy for paying ship money on compulsion, for having their ears cropped, or for standing in the pillory for the free expression of opinions ; and perhaps foreseeing what was coming, they accomplished what it is said Cromwell, Hampden, and others at one time meditated, and reached America before the Civil War began. The earlier battles of Worcester and Edgehill were fought in 1642, and before this five of the Howes had made good their lodgment in America. If the two who date from 1652 and 1657 were not born in this country, they may have taken the field ; but of the fact we have no authentic record.

It is enough for us to know that these ancestors of ours were God-fearing, worthy men, sprung from the sturdy middle class of English civic and rural life, who left their native country, not because they did not love it, but because they could not stay there without mean compliance and tame submission to usurped authority. We would perhaps have been just as well pleased had they remained behind, and struck a few manful blows for the liberties of England ; but we must accept the record as we find it, with this source of consolation, that no brother's blood was upon their hands when they landed in America.

That they were men of worth and intelligence, there is proof enough. They were freemen, and proprietors, in the townships where they settled ; selectmen, representatives, officers, Indian commissioners, and seem to have brought from the old country, in fair measure, the common sense, industry and thrift, so much needed by the emigrant. That they were men of fine proportions and of sound constitutions, I may infer from the audience before me, and from the fact, which your secretary has recorded, that five of these old worthies left forty-four children behind them.

That those "forefathers of our hamlets" set us a good example, their simple records prove. That the Howe women have been fruitful, and the men vigorous, is consistent with all I know of their descendants on this continent, and this vast audience, where forms of manly beauty and female loveliness abound, shows me that in physical proportions and feminine attraction the race has been well preserved.

But in these sound bodies are there sound minds? What of the intellectual qualities and mental development of the family? Have our women been born "to suckle fools, and chronicle small beer?" Have the men displayed the energy and capacity for affairs demanded of them by the free and rapidly expanding communities in which they lived? It is only by the mutual interchange of fact and thought, at such a gathering as this, that we can answer these questions to our own satisfaction. But if I were challenged by the

trans-atlantic branches of the family to bear testi
mony upon these points, I think, even with my
limited knowledge of your country, I could produce a
group of eloquent senators, eminent soldiers, distinguished philanthropists, and successful business men, to
prove conclusively that, in these United States, the race
has not declined.

In turning to the Provinces it must be borne in mind
that but one of all the Howes in these States took
the British side in the Revolutionary War.   Of my father
I spoke, some years ago, at Faneuil Hall, and my good
friend Lorenzo Sabine (one of the best writers and most
accomplished statesmen produced in the Eastern States)
has kindly embodied what was said in the second edition
of his Lives of the Loyalists, to which I must refer those
who take interest in the British American branch of the
family.   To-day I have leisure to say only this, that if
it be permitted to the saints in Heaven to revisit the
scenes they loved, and to hover over the innocent
reunions of their kindred, my father's spirit will be here,
gratified to see that the family, divided by the Revolution, is again united, and that his son, to use the language
which Burns puts into the mouth of the peasant woman
in his Cottar's Saturday Night, is "respected like the
lave."

Of the past history of the family, on both sides of the
Atlantic, we may be justly proud.   That the present is
full of hope and promise this great festival assures us.
For the future I have no fears.   We meet to gather up
the fragmentary biographies of the family, and to
encourage each other in well-doing, that the family may

not decline. By honest industry and manly exercises we must see to it that the race is well preserved, and by careful cultivation that the brain is well developed. Savage, in his Genealogical Dictionary, tells us that seven of the Howes, prior to 1834, had graduated at Harvard University, and twenty-three at other colleges in New England. Nearly all the Howes, that I have ever known, were dear lovers of books, and reasonably intelligent. To keep abreast with the active intellect of the age we must be students still. We inherit a rich and noble language. We are the "heirs," says Professor Greenwood, "of all the ages in the foremost files of time." "Knowledge," Disraeli tells us, "is like the mystic ladder in the Patriarch's dream. Its base rests on the primeval earth—its crest is lost in the shadowy splendor of the empyrean ; while the great authors, who for traditionary ages, have held the chain of science and philosophy, of poesy and erudition, are the angels ascending and descending the sacred scale, and maintaining, as it were, the communication between man and Heaven."

But we must not be mere students. This is not an age wherein people should be content to see visions and dream dreams. The work of the world is before us, and on this continent there is work enough and to spare for centuries to come. We must do our share of it, and the family will be judged by the style and manner in which it is done. The Scotch have a familiar phrase, " Put a stout heart to a stiff brae:" and Goethe tells us, " All I had to do I have done in kingly fashion. I let tongues wag. What I saw to be the right thing that I did."

May your hearts be "stout" when the "braes" are "stiff." Let the world take note of you that you are good husbands, good fathers, good citizens, and true and honorable men ; that your descendants may come up here to Framingham, looking back at this festival as though from its fruits it were worth a repetition ; and come, not to glorify a mere name, that has no significance, but to see that an honorable name, which they inherit, is kept untarnished, and transmitted with new lustre to their children.

But let us hope that these family meetings may be made to subserve a higher purpose than the mere renewal of broken ties of relationship in limited circles. May they not embrace a wider range, ascend to a higher elevation, and have a tendency to draw together, not only single families, but that great family that the unhappy events which led to the Revolutionary War divided into three branches?

Germany had its Seven Years' War, and its Thirty Years' War, to say nothing of centuries of rivalries and divisions, and yet a common sentiment, "the Fatherland," is rapidly uniting all who speak its language, love its literature, and are proud of its martial achievements. The Civil Wars of France have been endless, and yet the common ties of literature and language, however rudely those of brotherhood are broken at times, draw the whole people together ; and, though Kings and Emperors, Republics and Communes, pass away, under them all the common sentiment is, "Vive la France!" and this is the cry of a united people, when each system in its turn has been overthrown.

Great Britain and the United States have had eleven years of war, eight at the Revolution and three in the foolish struggle which lasted from 1812 to 1815. What are eleven years in history? Your own Civil war lasted nearly four, and more men were killed in it than Great Britain and the United States could ever put into the field in those old contests which sensible men everywhere remember only to regret. You hope to be, and I trust the hope may be realized, a united people. Why should not the the three great branches of the British family unite, our old wars and divisions to the contrary notwithstanding? This is "a consummation devoutly to be wished." Ocean steamers, railroads, cheap postage and telegraphs, make a union possible ; and gatherings such as this may hasten on the time, when, living under different forms of government, and each loyal to the institutions it prefers, the three great branches of the British family may not only live in perpetual amity, but combine to develop free institutions everywhere and to keep the peace of the world.

Such a union, to be permanent, must be based on mutual respect, and on a just appreciation of the position and resources of each branch of the Great Family. The marvellous growth and vast resources of these United States are frankly acknowledged by every rational English and British American man that I know. That your country contains nearly forty millions of people, as intelligent, industrious, inventive, and martial, as any other equal number on the face of the earth, we frankly admit ; but I am often amused at the style of exaggeration adopted in this country, and at the mode in which we Britishers are talked of on platforms, and in circles not over well-informed. Four millions of freemen on the other side of the line, who govern themselves, and who can change their rulers when Parliament sits, any night of the year, by a simple resolution ; who could declare their independence to-morrow, or join the United States, if so inclined, are often spoken of as serfs and bondmen, because they do not care to rupture old relations, and go in search of political guarantees, which, by their own firmness and practical sagacity, they have already secured. That we are not laggards and idlers over the border may be gathered from the growth of our cities, and from the rapid development of our industry in all its branches. Though but a handful of people commenced to clear up our country at the close of the Revolutionary War; we have already a population more numerous than Scotland, and have peacefully organized into provinces a territory more extensive than the United States, larger than the whole Empire of Brazil ; the volume of our trade has increased to $120,000,000 ; and the mercantile marine of the Northern Provinces places them in the rank of the fourth maritime country in the world. My own native Province, I am proud to say, takes the lead in this honorable form of enterprise. Nova Scotia owns more than a ton of shipping for every man, woman, and child on her soil. The babe that was born yesterday is represented by a ton of shipping that was built before it was born.

But are the British Islands so decrepit and effete as we sometimes hear in this country? Is the empire which is sustained by the two other branches of the family, unworthy of the friendship of these United States ? Would it not bring its share of everything that constitutes national greatness into the union of which I have spoken? Republican America, impoverished by the war of Independence, loaded with debt, having a great country to explore, finances to reorganize, institutions to consolidate, and a navy to create, has done her work in the face of the world in a manner that challenges its respect and admiration. Her contributions to literature, her able judges, sagacious statesmen, eloquent orators, acute diplomatists, and eminent soldiers and sailors, have won for her a place in civilization and history which all British Americans and Englishmen proudly acknowledge. You are " bone of our bone," and as one of your Commodores exclaimed, when lending a helping hand to Englishmen in the Chinese rivers, " blood is thicker than water," and the laurels you win, and the triumphs you achieve, even at our expense, but illustrate the versatility and vigor of the life-currents which we share.

Now let us see what the elder branch of the family has been about for the last eighty years, and whether, as we approach the fountain-head, the stream shows less animation. At the beginning of the seventeenth century, all London was built of wood, and thirty years after the Howes settled in New England, four hundred streets and thirteen thousand houses were consumed in the great fire. In 1783, the population did not exceed six hundred thousand, and the docks were not yet constructed. By the time I saw London first, in 1839, the population had increased to a million-and-a-half : but within the last third of a century the numbers have swelled to about four millions, so that the metropolis of our empire is nearly as large as the cities of New York, Brooklyn, Philadelphia, St. Louis, Chicago, Baltimore, Boston, Cincinnati, New Orleans, San Francisco, and Buffalo, all put together.

. At the close of the Revolutionary War, the British Empire was assumed to be on the decline. Thirteen noble provinces had just been lost. She had been humiliated by land and sea. Her power on the American Continent had been shaken to its foundation. Her great rival had defeated and triumphed over her; and, with her capital imperilled by mobs, and her treasury loaded down with debt, she had but a grim outlook for the future, at that disastrous period. But the people around the old homestead were not discouraged. The brain power was not exhausted, nor the physical forces spent. They went on thinking, working, and fighting, as though, like Antæus, they gathered strength from their fall; and now at the end of four-fifths of a century, let us see what they have accomplished. On this continent, profiting by the lessons of the past, and learning the science of colonial government, they have planted and fostered great provinces as populous as those they lost. They have explored and planted Australia and New Zealand, conquered an empire in the East, taken Singapore, the Mauritius, British Guiana, and Hong Kong, and now, instead of the few feeble colonies left to them, in 1783, when this country broke away, they have nearly seventy great provinces and dependencies, scattered all over the world, to whom Webster's "drum-beat" is familiar; which contain a population of hundreds of millions, and secure to the Mother Islands an abounding commerce, independent of all the rest of the world; but which they threw open to free competition, with a somewhat chivalrous confidence in their own resources.

Of the men produced in these modern days, why should I weary you with a bead-roll? Nelson and Wellington, Clive and Napier, stand in the front of a noble army of warriors, who have carried the Red Cross Flag by land and sea; and under its ample folds great statesmen have remodelled their institutions, reformed their laws, enlarged the franchise, limited the prerogative, and laid the foundations of civil and religious liberty broad and deep. Nor have the Mother Islands hung their harps upon the willows; while their engineers have covered the ocean with lines of steamships, and their architects have embellished the scenery with noble structures, their great writers have remodelled history, and the melodious strains of Scott and Byron, of Hemans and Campbell, have been heard above the din of workshops that never tire, the ebb and flow of capital enlarging with each pulsation, and the gradual unfolding of that marvellous web and woof of finance, whose meshes envelop the world,

I have but little more to say. If it be wise to gather the Howes together, and renew old family ties, how much more important will it be to bring together the three great branches of the British family, and unite them in a common policy, as indestructible as their language, as enduring as the literature they cannot divide !

Out of such a union would flow the blessing of perpetual peace, for no foreign power would venture to assail us, and we would be sufficiently strong to be magnanimous when international difficulties arose. Ships enough to keep the peace of the seas would be all we should require. With a landwehr of millions in reserve, our standing armies might be reduced to the minimum of cost. Capital would ebb and flow freely over the whole confederacy : our transports, instead of carrying war material, might carry the surplus population to the regions where labor was wanting and land was cheap ; ocean telegrams would come down to a penny rate ; and our national debts would disappear, by the gradual increase of the population, and the growth of the general prosperity. May the great Father of Mercies hear our prayers, and so overrule our national counsels, that we may come to be one people, living under different forms of government it may be, but knit together by a common policy, based upon an enlightened appreciation of each other's strength, and on a sentiment of mutual esteem.

THE LOCKSMITH OF PHILADELPHIA.

(A Tale.)

In the sober looking city of Philadelphia, there dwelt, some years ago, an ingenious and clever mechanic named Amos Sparks, by trade a locksmith. Nature had blest him with a peculiar turn for the branch of business to which he had been bred. Not only was he skilled in the manufacture and repair of the various articles that in America are usually regarded as "in the locksmith line," but, prompted by a desire to master the more abstruse intricacies of the business, he had studied it so attentively, and with such distinguished success that his proficiency was the theme of admiration, not only with his customers and the neighborhood, but all who took an interest in mechanical contrivances in the adjoining towns. His counter was generally strewed with all kinds of fastenings for doors, trunks, and desks, which nobody but himself could open ; and no lock was ever presented to Amos that he could not pick in a very short time. Like many men of talent in other departments Amos Sparks was poor. Though a very industrious and prudent man, with a small and frugal family, he merely eked out a comfortable existence but never seemed to accumulate property. Whether it was that he was not of the race of money-grubs, whose instinctive desire of accumulation forces them to earn and hoard without a thought beyond the mere means of acquisition, or whether the time occupied by the prosecution of new inquiries into still undiscovered regions of his favorite pursuit, and in conversation with those who came to inspect and admire the fruits of his ingenuity, were the cause of his poverty, we cannot undertake to determine; but perhaps various causes combined to keep his finances low, and it was quite as notorious in the city that Amos Sparks was a poor man, as that he was an ingenious and decent mechanic. But his business was sufficient for the supply of his wants and those of his family, so he studied and worked on and was content.

It happened that in the Autumn of 18— a merchant in the city, whose business was rather extensive, and who had been bustling about the Quay, and on board his vessels all the morning, returned to his counting-house to lodge several thousand dollars in the Philadelphia Bank, to retire some paper falling due that day, when to his surprise he found that he had either lost or mislaid the key of his iron chest. After diligent search with no success he was led to conclude that, in drawing out his handkerchief he had dropped the key in the street or perhaps into the dock. What was to be done? It was one o'clock, the Bank closed at three, and there was no time to advertise the key, or to muster so large a sum as that required. In his perplexity the merchant thought of the poor locksmith; he had often heard of Amos Sparks; the case seemed one peculiarly adapted to a trial of his powers, and being a desperate one, if he could not furnish a remedy, where else was there a reasonable expectation of succor? A clerk was hurried off for Amos, and, having explained the difficulty, speedily reappeared, followed by the locksmith with his implements in his hand. A few minutes sufficed to open the chest, and the astonished merchant glanced from the rolls of bank notes and piles of coin strewed along the bottom, to the clock in the corner of his office, which told him that he had still three quarters of an hour; with a feeling of delight and exultation, like one who had escaped from an unexpected dilemma by a lucky thought, and who felt that his credit was secure even from a momentary breath of suspicion. He fancied he felt generous as well as glad, and determined that it should be a cash transaction.

"How much is to pay, Amos?" said he, thrusting his hand into his pocket.

"Five Dollars, Sir," said Sparks.

"Five Dollars? why, you are mad, man; you have not been five minutes doing the job. Come" (the genuine spirit of traffic, overcoming the better feelings which had momentary possession of his bosom,) "I'll give you five shillings."

"It is true," replied the locksmith, "that much time has not been employed; but remember how many long years I have been learning to do such a job in five minutes or even to do it at all. A doctor's visit may last but one minute; the service he renders may be but doubtful when all is done, and yet his fee would be as great, if not greater than mine. You should be willing to purchase my skill, humble as it may be, as you would purchase any other commodity in the market, by what it is worth to you."

"Worth to me," said the merchant with a sneer, "well, I think it was worth five shillings, I could have got a new key made for that, or perhaps, might have found the old one."

"But could you have got the one made or found the other, in time to retire your notes at the Bank! Had I been disposed to wrong you, taking advantage of your haste and perplexity I might have bargained for a much larger sum, and as there is not another man in the city who could have opened the chest, you would gladly have given me double the amount I now claim."

"Double the amount! why the man's a fool, here are five shillings," said the merchant, holding them in his hand with the air of a rich man taking advantage of a poor one who could not help himself; "and if you do not choose to take them, why, you may sue as soon as you please, for my time is too precious just now to spend in a matter so trifling."

"I never sued a man in my life," said Sparks, "and I have lost much by my forbearance." "But," added he, the trodden worm of a meek spirit beginning to recoil, "you are rich—are able to pay, and although I will not sue you, pay you shall."

The words were scarcely spoken when he dashed down the lid of the chest, and in a moment the strong staples were firmly clasped by the bolts below, and the gold and bank notes were hidden as effectually as though they had vanished like the ill-gotten hoards in the fairy tale.

The merchant stood aghast. He looked at Amos, and then darted a glance at the clock, the hand was within twenty minutes of three, and seemed posting over the figures with the speed of light. What was to be done. At first he tried to bully, but it would not do. Amos told him if he had sustained any injury, " he might sue as soon as he pleased, for his time was too precious just now to be wasted in trifling affairs," and, with a face of unruffled composure, he turned on his heel and was leaving the office.

The merchant called him back, he had no alternative, his credit was at stake, half the city would swear he had lost the key to gain time, and because there was no money in the chest ; he was humbled by the necessity of the case, and handing forth the five dollars, " There Sparks," said he, " take your money and let us have no more words."

" I must have ten dollars now," replied the locksmith ; " you would have taken advantage of a poor man ; and besides opening your strong box there I have a lesson to give you which is well worth a trifling sum. You would not only have deprived me of what had been fairly earned, but have tempted me into a lawsuit which would have ruined my family. You will never in future presume upon your wealth in your dealings with the poor without thinking of the locksmith, and these five dollars may save you much sin and much repentance."

This homily, besides being preached in a tone of calm deliberation, which left no room to hope for any abatement, had exhausted another minute or two of the time already so precious ; for the minutes, like the Sibyl's books, increased in value as they diminished in number.   The merchant hurriedly counted out the ten dollars, which Amos deliberately inspected to see that they belonged to no broken Bank, and then deposited in his breeches pocket.

"For Heaven's sake, be quick, man, I would not have the Bank close before this money is paid for fifty dollars," exclaimed the merchant.

" I thought so, " was the locksmith's grave reply ; but not being a malicious or vindictive man, and satisfied with the punishment already inflicted, he delayed no longer, but opened the chest, giving its owner time to seize the cash and reach the Bank, after a rapid flight, a few minutes before it closed.

About a month after this affair the Philadelphia Bank was robbed of coin and notes to the amount of fifty thousand dollars.   The bars of a window had been cut, and the vault entered so ingeniously, that it was evident that the burglar had possessed, besides daring courage, a good deal of mechanical skill.   The police scoured the City and country round about, but no clue to the discovery of the robber could be traced.   Everybody who had anything to lose, felt that daring and ingenious felons were abroad who might probably pay them a visit ; all were therefore interested in their discovery and conviction.   Suspicions at length began to settle upon Sparks.   But yet his poverty and known integrity seemed to give them the lie.   The story of the iron chest, which the merchant had hitherto been ashamed, and Amos too forgiving to tell, for the latter did not care to set the town laughing, even at the man who had wronged him, now began to be noised abroad.

The merchant, influenced by a vindictive spirit, had whispered it to the Directors of the Bank, with sundry shrugs and inuendoes, and, of course, it soon spread far and wide, with all sorts of extravagant variations and additions. Amos thought for several days that some of his neighbors looked and acted rather oddly, and he missed one or two who used to drop in and chat almost every afternoon; but, not suspecting for a moment that there was any cause for altered behaviour, these matters made but a slight impression on his mind. In all such cases the person most interested is the last to hear disagreeable news; and the first hint that the locksmith got of the universal suspicion, was from the officer of police, who came with a party of constables to search his premises. Astonishment and grief were of course the portion of Amos and his family for that day. The first shock to a household who had derived, even amidst their humble poverty, much satisfaction from the possession of a good name—a property that they had been taught to value above all earthly treasures—may be easily conceived. To have defrauded a neighbor of sixpence would have been a meanness no one of them would have been guilty of, but fifty thousand dollars, the immensity of the sum seemed to clothe the suspicion with a weight of terror that nearly pressed them to the earth. They clung to each other with bruised and fluttered spirits while the search was proceeding, and it was not until it was completed and the officer declared himself satisfied that there was none of the missing property on the premises, that they began to rally and look calmly at the circumstances which seemed, for the moment, to menace the peace and security they had previously enjoyed.

"Cheer up, my darlings," said Amos, who was the first to recover the sobriety of thought that usually characterized him,—"cheer up, all will yet be well; it is impossible that this unjust suspicion can long hover about us. A life of honesty and fair dealing will not be without its reward: there was perhaps something in my trade, and the skill which long practice had given me in it, that naturally enough led the credulous, the thoughtless, and perhaps the mischievous, if any such there be connected with this inquiry, to look towards us. But the real authors of this outrage will probably be discovered soon; for a fraud so extensive will make all parties vigilant, and if not, why then, when our neighbors see us toiling, at our usual occupations, with no evidence of increased wealth or lavish expenditure on our persons or at our board, and remember how many years we were so occupied and so attired, without a suspicion of wrong doing, even in small matters, attaching to us, there will be good sense, and good feeling enough in the City to do us justice."

There were sound sense and much consolation in this reasoning: the obvious probabilities of the case were in favor of the fulfilment of the locksmith's expectations. But a scene of trial and excitement, of prolonged agony and hope deferred, lay before him, the extent of which it would have been difficult if not impossible for him then to have foreseen. Foiled in the search, the Directors of the Bank sent one of their number to negotiate with Amos; to offer him a large sum of money, and a guarantee from further molestation, if he would confess, restore the property, and give up his accomplices, if any there were. It was in vain that he protested his innocence, and avowed his abhorrence of the crime; the Banker rallied him on his assumed composure, and threatened him with consequences, until the locksmith, who had been unaccustomed to dialogues founded on the presumption that he was a villain, ordered his tormentor out of his shop, with the spirit of a man who, though poor, was resolved to preserve his self-respect, and protect the sanctity of his dwelling from impertinent and insulting intrusion.

The Banker retired, baffled and threatening vengeance. A consultation was held, and it was finally decided to arrest Sparks, and commit him to prison, in the hope that by shutting him up, and separating him from his family and accomplices, he would be less upon his guard against the collection of evidence necessary to a conviction, and perhaps be frightened into terms, or induced to make a full confession. This was a severe blow to the family. They could have borne much together, for mutual counsel and sympathy can soothe many of the ills of life : but to be divided—to have the strongest mind, around which the feebler ones had been accustomed to cling, carried away captive to brood, in solitary confinement, on an unjust accusation, was almost too much when coupled with the cloud of suspicion that seemed to gather about their home and infect the very air they breathed. The privations forced upon them by the want of the locksmith's earnings were borne without a murmur, and out of the little that could be mustered, a portion was always reserved to buy some trifling but unexpected comfort or luxury to carry to the prison.

Some months having passed without Sparks having made any confession, or the discovery of any new fact whereby his guilt might be established, his persecutors found themselves reluctantly compelled to bring him to trial. They had not a tittle of evidence, except some strange locks and implements found in the shop, and which proved the talent but not the guilt of the mechanic. Yet these were so various, and executed with such elaborate art, and such an evident expenditure of labor that but few, either of the judges, jury, or spectators, could be persuaded that a man so poor would have devoted himself so sedulously to such an employment, unless he had some other object in view than mere instruction or amusement. His friends and neighbors gave him an excellent character; but on their cross-examination all admitted his entire devotion to his favorite pursuit. The counsel for the Bank exerted himself with consummate ability; calculating in some degree on the state of the public mind, and the influence which vague rumours, coupled with the evidence of the mechanic's handicraft exhibited in Court, might have on the mind of the jury, he dwelt upon every ward and winding, on the story of the iron chest, on the evident poverty of the locksmith, and yet his apparent waste of time, if all this work were not intended to ensure success in some vast design. He believed that a verdict would be immediately followed by a confession, for he thought Amos guilty, and he succeeded in making the belief pretty general among his audience. Some of the jury were half inclined to speculate on the probabilities of a confession, and, swept away by a current of suspicion, were not indisposed to convict without evidence, in order that the result might do credit to their penetration. But this was impossible, even in an American Court in the good old times of which we write. Hanging persons on suspicion, and acquitting felons because the mob think murder no crime, are modern inventions. The charge of the Judge was clear and decisive : he admitted that there were grounds of suspicion—that there were circumstances connected with the prisoner's peculiar mode of life that were not reconcilable with the lowness of his finances ; but yet, of direct testimony there was not a vestige, and of circumstantial evidence there were not only links wanting in the chain, but in fact there was not a single link extending beyond the locksmith's dwelling. Sparks was accordingly acquitted ; but as no other clue was found to direct suspicion, it still lay upon him like a cloud. The vindictive merchant and the dissatisfied bankers did not hesitate to declare, that, although the charge could not be legally brought home, they had no doubt whatever of his guilt. This opinion was taken up and reiterated, until thousands who were too careless to investigate the story, were satisfied that Amos was a rogue. How could the character of a poor man hold out against the deliberate slanders of so many rich ones?

Amos rejoiced in his acquittal as one who felt that the jury had performed a solemn duty faithfully, and who was glad to find that his personal experience had strengthened, rather than impaired, his reliance on the tribunals of his country. He embraced his family, as one snatched from great responsibility and peril, and his heart overflowed with thankfulness, when at night they were all once more assembled round the fireside, the scene of so much happiness and unity in other days. But yet Amos felt that though acquitted by the jury he was not by the town. He saw that, in the faces of some of the jury and most of the audience, which he was too shrewd an observer to misunderstand. He wished it were otherwise ; but he was contented to take his chance of some subsequent revelation, and if it came not, of living down the foul suspicion which Providence had permitted, for some wise purpose, to hover for a while around his name.

But Amos had never thought of how he was to live. The cold looks, averted faces, and rude scandal of the neighborhood, could be borne, because really there was some excuse to be found in the circumstances, and because he hoped that there would be a joyful ending of it all at some future day. But the loss of custom first opened his eyes to his real situation. No work came to his shop. He made articles but could not sell them ; and, as the little money he had saved was necessarily exhausted in the unavoidable expenses of the trial, the family found it impossible, with the utmost exertion and economy to meet their current outlay ; one article of furniture after another was reluctantly sacrificed, or some ittle comfort abridged, until, at the end of months of degradation and absolute distress, their bare board was spread within bare walls, and it became necessary to beg, to starve, or to remove. The latter expedient had often been suggested in family consultations, and it is one that in America is the common remedy for all great calamities. If a man fails in a city on the seaboard, he removes to Ohio ; if a clergyman offers violence to a fair parishioner, he removes to Albany, where he soon becomes " very much respected ; " if a man in Michigan whips a bowie knife between a neighbor's ribs, he removes to Missouri. So that in fact a removal is "the sovereign'st thing on earth " for all great and otherwise overwhelming evils. The Sparks' would have removed, but they clung to the hope that the real perpetrator would be discovered, and the mystery cleared up : and besides, they thought it would be an acknowledgment of the justice of the general suspicion, if they turned their backs and fled. They lived upon the expectation of the renewed confidence and companionship of old friends and neighbors, when Providence should deem it right to draw the veil aside. But to live longer in Philadelphia was impossible, and the whole family prepared to depart ; their effects were easily transported, and, as they had had no credit since the arrest, there was nobody to prevent them from seeking a livelihood elsewhere.

Embarking in one of the river boats they passed up the Schuylkill and settled at Norristown. The whole family being industrious and obliging, they soon began to gather comforts around them ; and as these were not imbittered by the cold looks and insulting sneers of the vicinage, they were comparatively happy for a time. But even here there was for them no permanent place of rest.   A merchant passing through Norristown on his way from the capital to the Blue Mountains, recognized Sparks and told somebody he knew that he wished the community joy of having added to the number of its inhabitants the notorious locksmith of Philadelphia.   The news soon spread, the family found that they were shunned, as they had formerly been by those who had known them longer than the good people of Norristown, and had a fair prospect of starvation opening before them.   They removed again. This time there was no inducement to linger, for they had no local attachment to detain them. They crossed the mountains, and descending into the vale of the Susquehanna, pitched their tent at Sunbury. Here the same temporary success excited the same hopes, only to be blighted in the bud, by the breath of slander, which seemed so widely circulated as to leave them hardly any asylum within the limits of the State. We need not enumerate the different towns and villages in which they essayed to gain a livelihood, were suspected, shunned and foiled.   They had nearly crossed the State in its whole length, been driven from Pittsburgh, were slowly wending their way further west, and were standing on the high ground overlooking Middleton, as though doubtful if there was to be rest for the soles of their feet even there; they hesitated to try a new experiment.   Sparks seated himself on a stone beneath a spreading sycamore—his family clustered round him on the grass—they had travelled far and were weary; and without speaking a word, as their eyes met and they thought of their prolonged sufferings and slender hopes, they burst into a flood of tears, in which Sparks, burying his face in the golden locks of the sweet girl who bowed her head upon his knee, joined audibly.

At length, wiping away his tears, and checking the rising sobs that shook his manly bosom, " God's will be done, my children," said the locksmith, "we cannot help weeping, but let us not murmur ; our Heavenly Father has tried and is trying us, doubtless for some wise purpose, and if we are still to be wanderers and outcasts on the earth let us never lose sight of his promise, which assures us of an eternal refuge in a place where the wicked cease from troubling and the weary are at rest. I was, perhaps, too· proud of that skill of mine ; too apt to plume myself upon it above others whose gifts had been less abundant ; to take all the credit and give none to Him by whom the human brain is wrought into mysterious adaptation to particular sciences and pursuits. My error has been that of wiser and greater men, who have been made to feel that what we cherish as the richest of earthly blessings sometimes turns out a curse."

To dissipate the gloom which hung over the whole party, and beguile the half hour that they intended to rest in that sweet spot, Mrs. Sparks drew out a Philadelphia newspaper, which somebody had given her upon the road, and called their attention to the Deaths and Marriages, that they might see what changes were taking place in a city that still interested them though they were banished for ever from its borders. She had hardly opened the paper when her eye glanced at an article which she was too much excited to read. Amos, wondering at the emotion displayed, gently disengaged the paper and read " BANK ROBBERY—SPARKS NOT THE MAN." His own feelings were as powerfully affected as his wife's, but his nerves were stronger, and he read out, to an audience whose ears devoured every-syllable of the glad tidings, an account of the conviction and execution of a wretch in Albany, who had confessed among other daring and heinous crimes, the robbery of the Philadelphia Bank, accounting for the dissipation of the property, and entirely exonerating Sparks, whose face he had never seen. These were " glad tidings of great joy " to the weary wayfarers beneath the sycamore, whose hearts overflowed with thankfulness to the Father of Mercies, who had given them strength to bear the burden of affliction, and had lifted it from their spirits ere they had been crushed beneath the weight. Their resolution to return to their native city was formed at once, and before a week had passed they were slowly journeying to the capital of the State.

Meanwhile an extraordinary revulsion of feeling had taken place at Philadelphia. Newspapers and other periodicals, which had formerly been loud in condemnation of the locksmith, now blazoned abroad the robber's confession, wondered how any man could ever have been for a moment suspected upon such evidence as was adduced at the trial; drew pictures of the domestic felicity once enjoyed by the Sparks', and then painted, partly from what was known of the reality and partly from imagination, their sufferings, privations, and wrongs, in the pilgrimage they had performed in fleeing from an unjust but damnatory accusation. The whole

city rang with the story; old friends and neighbors who
had been the first to cut them, now became the loud and
vehement partisans of the family. Everybody was
anxious to know where they were. Some reported that
they had' perished in the woods; others that they
had been burnt on a prairie; while not a few believed
that the locksmith, driven to desperation had first destroyed the family and then himself. All these stories of
course created as much excitement as the robbery of the
Bank had done before, only that this time the tide set
the other way; and by the time the poor locksmith and
his family, who had been driven like vagabonds from
the city, approached its suburbs, they were met, congra-
tulated and followed by thousands, to whom, from the
strange vicissitudes of their lot, they had become objects
of interest. In fact, their's was almost a triumphal
entry, and as the public always like to have a victim,
they were advised on all hands to bring an action
against the Directors of the Bank; large damages would,
it was affirmed, be given, and the Bank deserved to
suffer for the causeless ruin brought on a poor but
industrious family.

Sparks was reluctant to engage in any such proceed-
ings; his character was vindicated, his business restored;
he occupied his own shop, and his family were comfortable and content. But the current of public opinion
was too strong for him. All Philadelphia had determined that the bankers should pay. An eminent
lawyer volunteered to conduct the suit and make no
charge if a liberal verdict were not obtained. The locksmith pondered the matter well: his own wrongs he

freely forgave ; but he thought that there had been a readiness to secure the interests of a wealthy corporation by blasting the prospects of a humble mechanic, which, for the good of society, ought not to pass unrebuked ; he felt that the moral effect of such a prosecution would be salutary, teaching the rich not to presume too far upon their affluence, and cheering the hearts of the poor while suffering unmerited persecution. The suit was commenced and urged to trial, notwithstanding several attempts at compromise on behalf of the Bank. The pleadings on both sides were able and ingenious ; but the counsel for the plaintiff had a theme worthy of the fine powers he possessed ; and at the close of a pathetic and eloquent declamation, the audience, which had formerly condemned Amos in their hearts without evidence, were melted to tears by a recital of his sufferings ; and when the jury returned with a verdict of Ten Thousand Dollars damages against the Bank, the locksmith was honored by a ride home on their shoulders, amidst a hurricane of cheers.

ADDRESS.

Delivered before the Young Men's Christian Association, Ottawa,
February 27, 1872.

Mr. Chairman, Ladies, and Gentlemen,—

When a Veteran, in the decline of life, undertakes to
address a body of young men just entering upon its
active duties, his heart is apt to be too full for utterance. The past comes rushing by, as the impetuous
tides of Fundy roll round the base of Blomidon, and
the mind's eye vainly endeavors to "look through the
blanket of the dark," and estimate, for others, the
nature and extent of those perils which youths are
sure to encounter, and which, by the goodness of God,
rather than by any skill or wisdom of his own, he may
have happily escaped. But how rare the instances
where experience has been gained without hazard—
where the helping hand of Providence has always been
stretched out—where the battle of life has been fought
without a wound ; and it is this conviction that makes
me tremble at the task I have assumed to-night, however gladly I would make it a labor of love. To me
the battle of life has been no boy's play, and I address
you with a vivid impression of the work that lies before
you, and of the dangers which beset the paths you are
to tread, however they may be fenced by a mother's
prayers or a father's watchful forethought.

But let us brush aside these depressing feelings, in

which memories of the past and apprehensions for the future are strangely interwoven, and face the duties of the hour, that it may not be wasted. By you the battle of life must be fought. Why should I discourage you? Believe me, I would not. Nay, if permitted, I would fight it all over again. There is no strength where there is no strain: seamanship is not learned in calm weather: and, born of the vicissitudes and struggles of life, are the wisdom, the dignity, and the consolations, which in all your cases, I trust, may distinguish its decline.

In addressing such a Society as this I am relieved from many apprehensions. Your organization protects you from much evil and many dangers. I take it for granted that the Young Men's Christian Association of Ottawa is a worthy and fruitful branch of that wide spread and invaluable Association, which is to be found in full activity, not only in all the large cities of this continent, but within the mother isles, and almost all the provinces of the British Empire.

This Association, if I comprehend aright its history and its objects, is neither sectarian nor political. It excludes no man on account of his creed, his origin, or his party leanings. It is neither Monarchical, Republican, nor Aristocratic. It will live and flourish though Dynasties decay and Cabinets be overthrown. Its limits are not defined by geographical lines, nor its resources affected by financial convulsions. It has no secrets like masonry. Its aims and its objects are distinct and above board. Its regalia are the ornaments of a meek and quiet spirit. It recognizes the Creator and the Saviour, and seeks to throw around young men, as they grow up, the restraints and the protection of mutual encouragement and watchfulness, that the snares of life may be avoided, and that reverence and respect for the higher principles of morality may be interwoven with its daily duties.

These Societies live and flourish on the voluntary principle. Their taxes are self-imposed. There is no jobbery or corruption. No sacerdotal or ministerial distinctions to aspire to—no high salaries to enjoy—no patronage to divide—no uniform by which its members can be distinguished from the rest of the communities, in whose midst they live and labor for the common good. Looking into your young faces, I am disarmed of half my fears for the future, by the strength and vitality of those relations to each other which you have already formed, and by the high standards of moral obligation and christian duty everywhere recognized by the wide spread Association to which you belong.

To make its Members moral and respectable are the chief objects of this organization. But pardon me if I venture to suggest, that without weakening these main springs of action, you should aim at even a wider range of thought, and cherish aspirations that may fit you for the noblest fields of action. I would have the young men of Ottawa not only dutiful and good, but refined, accomplished, and intellectual—ambitious to make the political Capital of the country the home of the Arts, the literary centre of the Confederacy, the fountain head of elevated thought and laudable ambition. She can only attain this rank by the combined and persistent efforts of the men who come here to claim citizenship, or who have been been bred within her limits.

Nature has been very bountiful to Ottawa. Built upon a dry limestone formation the site is elevated and healthy. At the head of navigation on the River from which it takes its name, the City commands free water communication with the St. Lawrence ; and, by the aid of its Canals, with the great Lakes above, and with the Gulf below. The Rideau Canal gives it easy access to the country through which that work has been constructed, with Kingston and with Lake Ontario; and the main River, with its twenty tributaries, draining a country of vast extent, brings into the City's bosom not only the boundless wealth of those great plantations which God has given her as an inheritance, but the agricultural products, won from a fertile soil, to which the tide of immigration is being annually attracted as the forest recedes before the axe of the lumberman. The Canada Central Railway, and the Ottawa Navigation Company, give you easy access to this region for 150 miles, and the time is rapidly approaching when the whole Country around Lake Nipissing will be enlivened by population, whose business must ebb and flow through this city, following the line of the great water communication which nature has already provided, or of that national highway, which, before long, will connect the Atlantic with the Pacific.

Though Ottawa, in point of natural scenery, cannot compare with Quebec, which has no rival on this continent, and although I prefer my native City of Halifax, with its varied aspects, and fine sea views, still, for an inland town, it is richly endowed and not unattractive to the eye. The Laurentian range gives it a fine bold background, a little too far removed; but the two rivers, winding round and through the city, afford glimpses of water in endless variety, that relieve the eye where the land is most level and monotonous. The looks-out from Kingston, over the harbour and sur-rounding forts, and from the table land behind Hamil-ton, over Burlington Bay, are fine, but are scarcely sur-passed by those up and down the river, from the cliffs behind the Parliament house; or the view, which one catches of a summer evening, from the Sapper's bridge, with the spires of the Cathedral on one side, and the Public Buildings on the other, the canal at your feet, and the river and the mountains beyond.

With waterfalls Ottawa is richly endowed. The twin falls of the Rideau give us those of the Genesée and of the Minnehaha in our very midst; and the Chau-diere, where the main River tumbles over the rocks to a lower level, would perhaps impress us more if it were not so near and familiar; and if the skill and enterprise of our great manufacturers had not transformed a scene of natural beauty into one of such varied industry, that what man has supplemented to nature's handiwork appears to be the most wonderful part of the turbulent combination. Here is the centre of that great industry which maintains an army of men in the woods all win-ter, and in the mills and on the watercourses all sum-mer, which has already built a city where there was but a scattered hamlet within the memory of the present generation, and which is destined, with the aid of the government expenditure, to ensure the growth and prosperity of Ottawa for many years to come.

When I first saw this city, ten years ago, the weather was bad, the public buildings were in course of construction, unsightly and unfinished. The materials required for their completion, were being dragged through the streets, cut up into ruts and mud-holes, or were lying about the banks in the most admired disorder. The impression left was unfavorable, and was often frankly expressed, during the animated political discussions which followed that visit. Since then the public buildings have been finished, and are certainly not inferior to any to be found on this continent. The streets are improved, and the city doubled in size ; and a three years' residence has enabled me to make myself familiar with its scenery, its climate, and resources, and it gives me pleasure now to correct any hasty prejudices or prepossessions that I may have formed in a single afternoon.

But apart from the attractions of its scenery, or the extent of its industrial resources, Ottawa presents to young men advantages that are rarely found in any other city of its size on this continent, or anywhere else. The administration of the government requires the presence in your midst, of some three hundred persons who are, or ought to be, gentlemen. I will not venture to assert that they all are. The Civil Service of the Dominion, like all other services, has perhaps its black sheep, men who have found their way into it with but slight appreciation of the high spirit, gentle manners, and prudent conduct, so eminently required of public officers in all the Departments ; but, taken as a whole, it constitutes a valuable addition to the society of a growing city like Ottawa. I speak not now of the ministers, who come and go, but of the permanent officers who reside here, who must live and die among you, be your exemplars, companions, and guides, and I am gratified to know that the Civil Service includes men of wide experience, of varied accomplishments, of profound erudition, and stern integrity—men whom it is a privilege to live with, and whose examples I advise you to imitate.

But you have other advantages. Once a year, at least for eight or ten weeks, Parliament assembles here, and the young men of Ottawa can see, hear and associate with the picked and prominent men of all the Provinces, gathered from the highest ranks of social and political life in the wide expanse of territory that lies between the Islands of Cape Breton and Vancouver. The sayings and doings of these men, filtered through the newspapers, in telegraphic or condensed Parliamentary reports, convey, even to their own constituents, but faint and shadowy outlines of the scenes in which they wrestle and debate. But to you, who can sit above their heads, mark every gesture, vibrate with every tone, to whom the sarcasm comes with a flash as vivid as lightning, and the bursts of eloquence are as voluble as thunder—to you the nightly debate brings reality and distinctness, intensely to be enjoyed and never to be forgotten.

Even where debates are fully and correctly reported, they are read at a distance with a calm pulse and are rarely long remembered. You or I would find Henry the VIII, played at the Princess's Theatre, with all the advantages of brilliant elocution and fine scenery, a very different affair from the same play read in the closet. Rebecca, looking out from the casement at Torqulstone, hearing every battle cry, and seeing every blow struck, would never forget the siege, that you or I, charmed for the moment by Scott's marvellous word painting, throw aside when the last page of Ivanhoe has been read. You have the political arena before you night after night—the combatants, who are myths and shadows to people at a distance, are realities to you. Men who are moulding the future, and perhaps are to figure in history, are there, at your feet, making sport for you, as Sampson did for the Philistines, often as blind perhaps, but fortunately, with no power to pull the structure about your ears.

The Houses of Parliament, then, are great Schools of Oratory for the young men of Ottawa. They are something more. They are halls where the great interests of the Country, its resources, wants, and development, are talked over and explained by the most capable and intelligent men that the six Provinces can produce ; and, if you are wise, my young friends, you will, as often as you can, without neglecting other indispensable duties, avail yourselves of the privileges, which youths at a distance may envy you, but can very rarely enjoy.

To be a fluent and easy speaker is a great accomplishment. The man who can think upon his legs, and express his thoughts with energy and ease, doubles his power for good or evil in the community in which he lives, and carries with him abroad a passport to cultivated and intellectual society of the utmost value. Almost every winter night the young men of Ottawa can take lessons in oratory, in the Commons or in the Senate. Their own good sense will teach them to distinguish what is grotesque and absurd, from what is impressive and worthy of imitation ; and my advice to you is, not to neglect opportunities which circumstances so favorably present, and even if politics never attract you into the National arenas, you will find that the graceful elocution which gives animation and wins deference at the festive board or at the fireside, gives power and influence at those gatherings where men must congregate to transact the business of life.

But Ottawa has, for its crowning glory and advantage, the custody of the Parliamentary Library which the liberality of the Nation has provided, and which has been selected and arranged by Alpheus Todd, one of the most amiable and accomplished men to be found on either Continent. The great Libraries of London and Paris are of course more extensive and complete than our own. The City Library at Boston, and the Astor Library at New York, admirably selected and most spiritedly sustained, are creditable to those great cities. I need not weary you with comparisons, but when I say that our Parliamentary Library includes 70,000 volumes, that it exhausts the classics and current literature of France and England—that every book worth reading, ever published in America, is to be found upon its shelves—that the best works of Continental Europe, and of the East are there, either in the original, or in the most approved translations—that all the periodicals, from the first number to the last, invite us to sharpen our critical taste and store our minds with information ; and when I add, that, so soon.as the new wing of the Parliament Buildings is complèted, this great collection will be housed with a magnificence, and displayed with facilities for reference, worthy of all praise, I shall but convey to intelligent strangers abroad a feeble idea of the intellectual aids and advantages which the youth of Ottawa enjoy, superior as they are to those within the reach of the studious within hundreds of other cities of larger population.

To the Giver of all Good the young men of Ottawa should daily offer up thanks and praise for the mercies and advantages by which they are surrounded. They have a healthy climate, and occupy the centre of a wide tract of country, drained by great rivers, and filled with natural resources. They have a body of trained' and accomplished men, and their families, to associate with— they have the two branches of the Legislature for schools of instruction, and they have the Parliamentary Library in their midst, a great store house from whence to draw intellectual life without effort or expense.

Now my young friends, let me say that the worst return you could make for these blessings, would be to show a callous indifference to the bounties of Providence, and not to acknowledge and illustrate them in your daily lives and conversation.

When Ottawa was selected for the seat of Government, other cities, of older growth, and of larger population, Montreal, Quebec, Kingston and Toronto, were compelled to make sacrifices for her benefit ; and now that Confederation has been established, Halifax, Fredericton and Victoria have been somewhat shorn of influence and advantages which they formerly enjoyed. The population of those cities may reasonably demand, not only that the youth of Ottawa shall not be unmindful of those sacrifices, but that they shall rise to the level of intellectual life, and varied accomplishment, which ought to distinguish the Federal Capital of the Union. They may be reasonably patient while the elements of society, thrown in here by new political combinations, fuse, assimilate and assume new forms of development, but they will not be patient, if, ten years hence, it should be discovered that their contributions have been thrown away—that Ottawa is, after all, but an outside Bœtian region, where lumber is manufactured, where books are not read or written, which produces no princely merchants, no orators or artists, no learned professors or divines ; which draws pecuniary resources and intellectual life from all the other cities of the Confederacy, and gives nothing in return.

Now my young friends, you must see to it, and others like you, that Ottawa does not incur the great misfortune of losing the crown that she has won. Trust me her glories will pass away if they are proved to be undeserved. If, when the Confederacy comes to take stock, as it will every eight or ten years, it discovers, that not only is Ottawa far behind, in material growth and business activity, but in the culture, refinement, broad views and cosmopolitan spirit, which ought to distinguish the Capital of a great nation.

The Jew went up to Jerusalem, and the Mahomedan turned his face towards Mecca, because those cities were the fountain heads of the spiritual life and soul-stirring theology upon which they ` relied for their salvation. It remains to be seen whether Ottawa can take rank as the foremost city of the Dominion, worthily advancing its banner and upholding its reputation, where good work is to be done, a good example is to be set, or sound principles require advocacy and illustration. The beautiful piles of masonry on the cliffs above will not save her from abandonment if her sons fail to make her what she ought to be—the fountain head of intellectual life for half a continent—the model city, to which men's eyes will turn' for inspiration and guidance ; where elegance of manners and simplicity of attire shall be woman's highest distinctions ; and where a man, in the lowest grade of the Civil Service, or in the humblest walk of life, can challenge respect by the culture which marks the gentleman—the broad views which include the great interest of the whole Confederacy, and by that hearty sympathy with the feelings, and even the prejudices of all the Provinces, which can alone reconcile them to the sacrifices they have made, and unite them round a common centre by ties more enduring than the clauses of an Act of Parliment.

Before passing to other topics, I may be permitted to say that if Ottawa is to take the rank that it ought to hold, its ratepayers and municipality must evince more enterprise and circumspection. The debates in their City Council and in their School Boards should be redeemed from puerility and bad language. The City should be drained and cleansed, or cholera will scourge it; flanked as it is on both sides by square miles of piled lumber, the fate of Chicago is in store for it, if an efficient supply of water is not speedily introduced ; and the streets should be planted without delay, that the present generation may enjoy the luxury of shade in the hot summer months, and of shelter from the biting blasts of winter when they come.

In almost all our northern cities we are far behind our Republican neighbors in arbori-culture. For the first fifty years, in the settlement of a new country, trees are regarded as man's natural enemies. They shelter the savage and they cumber the land, and, as in the "forest primeval" they protect each other, and grow spindling and tall, they are of little use when the groves are broken, and are rarely preserved. To cut them down and burn them up seems a labor of love. The old States and Provinces passed through this iconoclastic period a century in advance of us. They commenced to replant trees about the time when we seriously began to cut them down, and, now, nearly all their cities and towns are planted. "A thing of beauty is a joy forever," and what more beautiful than a fine shade-tree? An old gentleman, three parts of a century ago, planted three or four elms on the front street of Windsor, the shire town of the county I represent. They have shaded and embellished it for fifty years, and I never pass under them without blessing the old man's memory.

How prettily are all the towns and villages around

Boston shaded. What debts of gratitude do the people of New Haven, Salem, Richmond, Portland and Cleveland owe to the liberality and forethought of the wise old men who embellished their streets, disarmed the winter winds, and have endowed, with a luxuriance of umbrageous beauty, the retreats of erudition and the busy marts of trade.

Ottawa must be planted. Colonel By, who laid it out, evidently meant that it should be. The streets are straight and wide. There is room enough everywhere for trees, and for an abounding commerce and a busy population. Ottawa must be planted, drained, protected from fire, and then, when the Dominion Government has enclosed and ornamented the public grounds, as it must do without delay, the city will, in outward semblance at least, begin to wear the aspect which strangers expect to see when they come to visit the Capital of a great Confederacy.

In the promotion of these objects, of proved utility and municipal concern, the members of this Society can greatly aid, as they bring their cultivated minds to bear upon the masses around them ; but they must not stop short at city limits, nor allow their mental horizon to be circumscribed by the boundaries even of the Capital of their country. They must think in wider circles, and, rising to the height of the main arguments upon which the Confederation Act was based, they must regard British America as a whole, and demand that, equitably and honorably, its population shall be dealt with as brethren having common rights and one nationality. The miserable sneer about " Parish Politics," applied to the smaller provinces by a Canadian some time ago, was inspired by a spirit the very opposite of that which the young men of Canada should cultivate, if this Confederacy is to be kept together. It was forgotten, let us hope, as soon as uttered, and ought never to be repeated. A province should not be judged by size, but by the mental calibre of the men who represent her. Ontario should get credit for an idiot, if she prefers to send him to Parliament instead of to a lunatic asylum ; and British Columbia, if she has got an able man, should not have his value estimated by the extent of her population.

I have said, that to meet the requirements of your position you must endeavour to grasp the whole Dominion ; and, let me add, that in no country that I have ever heard or read of, in ancient or modern times, was the strain on the mental and bodily powers of the whole population greater than it is in this Dominion. We cannot afford to have a laggard, an idler, or a coward. There are not four millions of us, all told, and we have undertaken to govern half a continent, with forty million of ambitious and aggressive people on the other side of a frontier three thousand miles long. If each British American could multiply himself fivefold, we should not have more than half the brain power and physical force necessary to keep our rivals in check, and to make our position secure.

To enable us correctly to estimate our true position, it will be only necessary to enquire into the reasons why France, with a warlike population of thirty millions, studded with fortresses, and with its Capital elaborately protected by the highest engineering skill, was, during the last summer, overrun, beaten down, and amerced in hundreds of millions of pounds by the victorious Prussians. What is the secret, the explanation, of the extraordinary military phenomena which have startled the whole world in the year 1871? Why, simply that the Prussians contrived to have one man and a half, and sometimes two to one, on almost every battlefield where they met their enemies. Whether they were better prepared, whether their combinations were more scientific, or their strategy was more perfect, may be matter of controversy; but, as far as I have been enabled to study the aspects of the war, the French were simply overpowered because they were outnumbered.

Now, in any contest with our neighbors assuming that we are united to a man, if the enemy knows his business, and the Republicans have had more experience than we have had in the art and practice of war, we must expect to have ten men to one against us— ten needle-guns, or Snider's, or Enfield's, whatever the weapons may be, so that you will perceive that we must face at least five or six times the odds by which the French were overpowered. But this is not the worst of it. Ten children are born on the other side of the line for one that is born on this; and, however, we may change the proportions by increased energy, five emigrants go to the United States for one that comes to Canada, so that at the end of every decade, the disproportions with which we have to wrestle now, will be multiplied to our disadvantage.

We may disregard this state of things, overlook these

inequalities, and live in a fool's paradise of imaginary security; but, if we are wise, we will face our dangers, and prepare for them, with a clear appreciation of their magnitude.

But, it may be said, are we not part and parcel of a great Empire upon which the sun never sets, which contains three hundred millions of people, whose wealth defies estimate, whose army is perfect in discipline; whose great navy dominates the sea. What have we to fear when this great Empire protects us? This was our ancient faith, and proud boast under every trial. In the full belief that they were British subjects, that the allegiance which they freely paid to the Crown of England entitled them to protection, our forefathers helped to conquer, overrun and organize these Provinces. Every settler who broke into the forest, every mariner who launched his bark upon the ocean, every fisherman who dropped his lead upon the banks, toiled with a sense of security that never wavered. For more than a century our people having sung their national anthem, and turned their faces to the sea "with that assured look faith wears," and have never doubted of their destiny, or faltered in their allegiance to the British Empire.

But of late new doctrines have been propounded in the Mother Country. The disorganization of the Empire has been openly promulgated in leading and influential organs of public sentiment and opinion. Our brethren within the narrow seas have been counselled to adopt a narrow policy,—to call home their legions, and leave the outlying provinces without a

show of sympathy or protection ; and under the influence of panic, and imaginary battles of Dorking, troops
are to be massed in the British Islands, and their shores
are to be surrounded by ironclads. One Cabinet
Minister tells us that British America cannot be
defended, and another, that he hopes to see the day
when the whole continent of America will peacefully
repose and prosper under Republican institutions. And
a third, on the eve of negotiations which are to involve
our dearest interests, strips Canada of every soldier,
and gathers up every old sentry box and gun carriage
he can find, aud ships them off to England.

I do not desire to anticipate the full and ample
discussion which Parliament will give to England's
recent diplomatic efforts to buy her own peace at the
sacrifice of our interests, or of that Comedy of Errors
into which she has blundered ; but this I may say, that
the time is rapidly approaching when Canadians and
Englishmen must have a clear and distinct understanding as to the hopes and obligations of the future. If
Imperial policy is to cover the whole ground, upon the
faith of which our forefathers settled and improved,
then let that be understood, and we know what to do.
But if "shadows, clouds, and darkness" are to rest
upon the future — if thirty millions of Britons are to
hoard their " rascal counters " within two small islands,
gather round them the troops and war ships of the
Empire, and leave four millions of Britons to face
forty millions, and to defend a frontier of three thous-
and miles, then let us know what they are at, and our
future policy will be governed by that knowledge. No

Cabinet has yet dared to shape this thought and give it utterance. ˙Leading newspapers have told us that our presence within the Empire is a source of danger, and that the time for separation is approaching, if it has not already come. Noble lords and erudite commoners have sneeringly told us that we may go when we are inclined. As yet, neither the Crown, the Parliament, or the people of England have deliberately avowed this policy of dismemberment, although ˙the tendency of English thought and legislation daily deepens the conviction that the drift is all that way. We must wait, my young friends, for further developments, not without anxiety for the future, but with a firm reliance on the goodness of Providence, and on our own ability to so shape the policy of our country as to protect her by our wit, should Englishmen, unmindful of the past, repudiate their national obligations.

In the meantime, let us pray that our women may be fruitful, that our numbers may increase, and let every young Canadian feel that his country has not a man to spare for the follies that enervate, and the vices that degrade. See to it that the hardy exercises of the country do not decline. Work is the universal strengthener of ·those who live by manual labor ; and those whose occupations are sedentary, should counteract the tendency of such pursuits by the habitual resort to those pastimes which give vivacity to the spirit and energy to the frame. To ride well, to row, to swim, to shoot, are essential parts of a gentleman's education in every country ; and to skate, to fence, to spar, and to handle the racket and the cricket bat with skill and dexterity, are not only accomplishments which young men should cultivate for the pleasure they yield, but for the health and vigor they infuse, when our muscles are relaxed and our minds enfeebled by the indoor employments which sap the springs of life.

But brains are not less required for the development and elevation of this great country than physical force. Canada cannot afford to have one drone in the intellectual hive. There never was a country with so many natural resources flung broadcast before so limited a population. Forests of boundless extent—a virgin soil to be measured by millions of square miles—the richest fisheries in the world—mines the value of which no man can estimate—and water power running to waste everywhere, but in a few favored spots where the vagrant streams have been harnessed to machinery and turned to profitable account. The Inland Provinces are enlivened by great Lakes and Rivers, and the Maritime are surrounded by the sea, where the carrying trade of the world invites to enterprise and adventure, and where, as the argosies multiply in numbers and value, a hardy population are nurtured, that, if England knew how to train and handle them, would not only defend their headlands but man her Ironclads, and help her to maintain the dominion of the seas upon which her insular security depends.

That the most may be made of these great natural resources, British America requires the active intellects of all her children, aided by the highest mental culture. The idler and the vagrant are simply traitors to the Country of their birth. I do not linger to indicate the directions in which any of you should think and labor. Kind parents and guardians have already placed the Members of this Society on the paths of duty, and on the roads to knowledge. I may be permitted to say this, however, that whatever may be the chosen pursuit, work will be found the secret of success, and that he will be most successful who takes the highest style of minds that have elevated and adorned his particular walk of life for examples to guide and cheer him on his way. Young men who devote their energies to trade should study the biographies of those Merchant Princes, who, in all ages have wedded commerce to literature and the arts, founded or embellished Cities, and have become benefactors to the race.

Young men intended for the professions should, in like manner, aspire to be something more than Quacks and Drones and Pettifoggers. The highest names in medicine, the great sages of the law, the pulpit orators who have rivalled the prophets of old, by their elevation of thought and luxuriance of illustration, should be hung around their chambers and be ever present to their minds. With respect to manners and deportment but little need be said. I assume that you will conduct yourselves like gentlemen, and in conclusion, have only to say, in the language which Shakspeare puts into the mouth of Wolsey.

> "Let all the ends you aim at
> "Be your country's, your God's and Truth's,"

that the parents who dearly love you may be honored by your behavior, and that the rising generations who come after you may be inspired by your example.

INDEX.